Room Number Ten

I was feeling more tired than tongue can tell, as the month of August trailed its suffocating days along—tired of my work, tired of people and things, especially tired, I think of the neighbourhood in which I lived—a village so rapidly becoming a suburb of a large manufacturing city, that it was neither true country nor true town, the inhabitants also gave one the impression of being neither one thing nor the other—they certainly were not "country" people, nor were they what they struggled hard to appear, "town"—for people who truly live near nature, have big, broad outlooks, and busy town dwellers are too much occupied to attend to much save their own affairs.

While here, in this growing village, the concerns of one, were the concerns of all, from Mrs. So-and-So's new hat, and how much she paid for it, down to the domestic and marital affairs of all and sundry; it was a soul-killing spot to live in, and I was very weary of it and its perpetual creed of "Thou shalt not—or if thou dost, I shall repeat and add to it, until thou no longer knoweth thine own act or words!"

And so, on this blazing August day, I hailed with delight a pressing invitation to visit some friends at their house in Scotland. The invitation was oddly worded, but they were odd people—I mean uncommon—therefore interesting; they were workers, for a greater part of the year, but as much time as all could spare, was spent in this somewhat isolated spot in Ayrshire; sometimes all of them managed to get there together, at times, only one or other of them could get away, and although I had often been asked

7

to form one of their party, I had never been able to do so, and now just when I was hungering for quietness, and freedom, and could get away, their invitation reached me—it ran—

Dear Old Man,
Ella and I both needed a rest, so have collected a few kindred spirits and fled to our refuge. Alec will be with us, and probably some of our chums also. We shall fill the house, but if you don't mind where you sleep! come along.
Your old Chum,
Norman Stuart.

I read the note over more than once, it was so curious to say "if I didn't mind where I slept," of course I didn't mind, I'd sleep in the bath or on the billiard table if need be, so that I could pack and shake the dust of this trying village from my feet as quickly as possible.

I answered the note by return, in the same spirit, merely saying I was delighted and would be with them soon after this letter, adding that it would cheerfully sleep in a pigsty.

As soon as my letter was despatched I shook myself figuratively, and felt all my woes and irritations slipping away into nothingness, even the village with its talking and gossip seemed to recede into its proper state of no importance, as I gaily began—what to me is ever a joy—the collecting of the little odds and ends, which go to make a holiday a real holiday and not a thing of rushing and racing from one excitement to another, so to this end I wandered round my small domain, picking up a favourite book, tucking it under my arm, while I collected writing materials, favourite pencils, fishing tackle, oldest boots, and shoes, with fine disregard of the orthodox method of packing.

Some people make packing a fine art, to me it only means throwing into a large box all that tends to my comfort or happiness, and then dropping in a few clothes, and sitting on the lid. All this I accomplished before the clock struck eleven p.m., and then with a sigh of relief I lit my final pipe, and turned in.

The following morning I was up betimes, waking with that

happy feeling of exhilaration, which foretells pleasure to come, my breakfast was a hurried affair, and I was in the train and off, feeling like a schoolboy, and not by any means the staid literary man of forty-eight, that in very truth I was.

A journey is always a delight to me, and, once in my corner seat, with pipe and book, sure in the knowledge of happy days ahead, I gave myself up to the real enjoyment of this first part of my holiday. Changes at various stations only added zest and interest, for I was one of those people somewhat giving to weaving romances about the most everyday looking people.

My station was about 10 miles from my friend's house, and not the least enjoyable part of my trip was the long drive in an old-fashioned open wagonette, the only vehicle kept by my friends—they would not hear the word "motor" in their rest corner, so the 10 miles was only accomplished in a little over an hour, but the scenery was splendid, and I believe after all, there is something which appeals tremendously to everyone in the steady trotting sound of a good pair of horses—far above the buzz of a motor engine! At any rate, it fitted much more appropriately with both the scenery and my mood, than the hum of the best 60 h.p. Daimler could have done.

It was growing dusk, when we drew up at an old-fashioned white wooden gate, with the name of the house written upon it in black letters—"High Crags"—Here my worthy coachman descended stiffly to open the gate, with a pat for each steaming gee as he passed them. He had not been a very talkative companion during my long drive, and I had called him grumpy in my own mind, but now as he once again clambered into his seat, he seemed to unbend.

"Staying long, Sir?" he asked. I said I was not sure.

"House a bit full," he volunteered next.

"Is it?" I said indifferently, feeling aggrieved that after silence for 10 miles, he should now feel it incumbent upon him to talk.

"Aye," he replied, "'ppears like as if they'll have to use it this time."

"Use what?" I asked.

" It," he answered, lowering his voice, and bending towards me. "It, Sir, Room Number 10, but I pity the one who sleeps in it, I do so."

"Why?" I asked, with a faint feeling of interest. "Best not ask, Sir, best not ask, but there we are, whoa—whoa—my beauties," he went on, all in one breath, as he rattled up to a big wide open door from which a welcome blaze of light streamed out lighting up glimpses of thick shrubberies.

"There you are at last!" sang out a cheery voice as my friend, big, strong, rugged looking, Norman Stuart, stretched out a welcoming hand and led me into the hall, where a big wood fire blazed, before which stood two figures—girls—both of whom eyed me curiously, as, without waiting for an introduction, they said simultaneously "Come and get warm, it's nearly dinner-time, so we must run," and run they did, with a flash of pretty frills and high-heeled shoes.

"And now, old man, let me have a look at you." And with this remark my friend wheeled up a big chair in front of the blazing fire. "Come and get a warm first," he added, "and then I'll trot you upstairs to your room."

He stopped speaking somewhat abruptly, busying himself with his pipe, while I revelled in the warmth and comfort.

After a few minutes I asked him who the pretty girls were, and he laughed.

"Two of Ella's pals," he said—"Miriam Langdale and Joyce Wood, great sports they are, full of nonsense."

"Who else have you here?" I went on.

"Let me see, he replied, "How many are we? There are Ella and I, those two girls, Alec and two young fellows from the same Hospital—Medical Students both of them; Professor Sturges, though he doesn't bother with any of us, being fathoms deep in his scientific studies, is an interesting old chap, when he cares to talk; and Miss Brown."

"Oh!" I said, "and who may Miss Brown be?"

"She's just Miss Brown," he said with a laugh—"rather an oddity, but a clever woman, one of those rather silent women with curious ideas on many things, a woman who never appears to hear or see half the time, but who never misses anything really—a woman apparently hard, cold and reserved, but, to those who know her, one of the most loyal, true, tender-hearted beings in the world, and always ready with a helping hand for any trouble."

"A nice mixture," I said, "do they all agree?"

"Um," he muttered, "more or less, though the professor and Miss Brown spar a bit, and those two saucy girls lead them both a bit of a dance, but anyway," he added, "form your own judgment, you will see them all in half an hour—you have just that time before dinner, so I will take you to your room. We have done our best for you, so I hope you will be—er—comfortable—and—er—sleep—and all that," and pulling himself together, he started off, up the dark oak staircase, I following, admiring as I went, the whole scheme, if one could call it so, of the decorations, the dark oak stairs, vivid crimson stair carpets, walls of duller red, bare of the orthodox pictures, which people put on their stairs and landings, when they won't fit anywhere else!

The old beaten copper lamps at the corners of the banisters and on the landing above, each dark oak door with its own specially designed knocker and number of the room in copper figures—an old oak chest, an oak table with an orange-coloured azalea in a quaint pewter jar, and one or two old engravings, gave a tone of comfort, and the whole atmosphere was one of soft restfulness.

"Sorry, old chap, we are crammed to overflowing on this landing—you are down here," said my host, as he led me down two steps and along a passage somewhat narrow and feeling slightly chillier than the other part of the house, to a room at the far end. "You are rather far away from the rest of us," he said, as if apologising, "but you said you did not mind," and he put his hand on the handle of a door, at the same instant my eye fell on the copper number. *Room No.* 10, stared me in the face, and the words of my worthy driver beat in my brain, as I entered.

My friend having opened the door and ushered me in, did

not come in with me, but turned, muttering—

"Hope you've all you want, come right down when you are ready," and bolted from the door, shutting it after him.

Probably if I had never heard the words "Room No. 10" spoken as they were by my driver, I should have been wholly, as I was in part, entranced by the room in which I found myself, and as I gazed around me, I determined to wipe from my memory any previous thought of the room, and put the driver's words in their proper category, as the silly vapourings of a stupid servant, and to give myself up to the enjoyment of my surroundings.

The room was spacious, but with a somewhat low ceiling, the floor of black oak had a square of peacock blue carpet in the centre, the ceiling was painted with gold stars, representing the Northern Hemisphere, there was an enormous oak four-poster bedstead, piled high with snowy pillows, and covered by a thick eider-down of satin in shades of blue and gold, the fireplace was roomy and old-fashioned, with steel fittings which shone like silver in the dancing firelight, a big basket chair, with a blue and white cover, was drawn near to the fire, and a log box of beaten copper stood near at hand, piled up with logs of wood.

The only thing that struck me as out of keeping was a small modern brass and black bedstead, in a corner of the room, and this also was made ready for occupation. Was I to have a companion? or stay, possibly it was for choice, as many people do not care for a four-poster—to me, however, it appealed, and I straightway ignored the modern bed.

My dressing-table was a fine old piece of furniture, only thinly covered by a muslin cover, on it stood a quaint jar, full of late dahlias—the only really vivid note of colour in the room. It was in my opinion an ideal room, my eye fell on the fitted-up writing table in the window with joy, as I foresaw many quiet hours of happy scribbling.

No one came to help me to unpack, so I concluded the staff was limited, but I managed to unearth my dinner garments, and clothe myself unaided, just as the dinner-gong boomed in the distance. With a last glance of admiration round my quarters, I blew out the candles, and prepared to make my way down to the hall.

All the company were assembled round the fire, as I came down the stairs, and my hostess, Mrs. Stuart, came quickly to meet me.

"So sorry, Peter, I was not here to receive you, but you know us of old, also our unconventional ways, so I knew you would understand. Now let me introduce you, children," she went on addressing them all—

"This is Mr. Peter Maxton of literary fame, some of you may have read his books, and if not, you will find them in the library. Peter, these are two naughty girls, Miriam Langdale and Joyce Wood, of no use, except as ornaments; Professor Sturges with whom you will quarrel; and, Miss Brown, whom you will hate tonight, dislike tomorrow, endure the day after, and finally adore, as we all do. The boys are late, so we will not wait for them, but go in like Indians, single file, and eat."

Miss Joyce Wood promptly attached herself to me, with the remark—

"Sit by me, Mr. Maxton, and I'll give you all the wrinkles about our motley crew, and their fads. I haven't read your books, so don't talk about them, all my time as given to other things."
"Bridge, I suppose," I answered, "and golf, and buying clothes, and such things."

"If you care to consider you have read and summed me up, very well, we will leave it at that," she answered demurely. "How do you like your room?" she went on, "Miriam and I arranged it; it's nice, isn't it?"

"It is delightful," I answered, "No one could fail to be happy in it."

She glanced at me quickly, but did not pursue the subject of my room, chattering through the remainder of dinner on all sorts of subjects.

The evening passed all too quickly, without any attempt at entertaining in its best known sense, but, in what *I* consider the truest form of it—the leaving each and all to follow their own bent. If anyone wanted to sing or play, they wandered to the piano, and did so, without any of that wearisome "Will you play?—Oh, I really can't—I only play to myself."

The professor I did not see again, so concluded he had gone to the library, where I afterwards learnt he spent most of his time.

Miss Wood played and sang, my host and Miss Brown were lost to all in a game of chess; the young men had 'phoned they were dining with friends, and we were not to wait up for them, so my pretty hostess and I drew up our chairs for a gossip of old times and friends.

It was a quiet, restful evening, but my long cold drive had made me sleepy, and I was glad when about 11 o'clock a move was made, bedroom candles were lit, and we made our way upstairs.

Laughing 'Goodnights' were exchanged on the main landing, as one after another vanished through their numbered doors. My hostess lingered a moment and then said—

"Do you remember your way, Peter, or shall I show you?"

"Not a bit," I answered, "I know, quite well," and I fancied a distinct look of relief passed over her face.

"Very well," she said, "sleep well, oh!—and—er—sleep in whichever bed you prefer, both are ready—"

"Right-o!" I answered, "but give me the big one for preference; I've always longed to sleep in four-poster."

She smiled—"Please yourself, and change if you don't like it," and with a little wave, she followed the girls and I wended my solitary way down the other corridor to Room No. 10. The room was in darkness as I entered, save for the red embers of a departing fire which apparently no one had made up for the night; still, it looked very cosy, even if a trifle sombre. I soon had a more cheery blaze and sat down before it, for a short read, as was ever my habit, before turning in. I was soon deep in my book, deeper than I had intended to get, and as my wood-fire subsided with a little rush of sparks, I realized it was close upon midnight, so, hurriedly prepared for bed; for a brief instant I surveyed my two beds, both looked the acme of comfort, and though, for some unaccountable reason my inclination now turned to the modern one, I nevertheless decided in favour of my four-poster, and was quickly in a comfortable nest of pillows and beginning to feel very sleepy, so, blowing out my last candle, I closed my eyes and gave myself up to sleep.

Possibly I had been asleep an hour, maybe less, when I awakened suddenly and completely, in full possession of my senses—I could not account for it, and yet was possessed by the feeling that something or some person had awakened me. The room was in complete darkness, and I groped for my matches on the table by my side where I had placed them. I could not find them, though the table was small, and my hand swept the whole of it from side to side, and end to end—"Odd," I thought, "for I certainly remember putting them there." However, they were not to be found, so I settled down once more. Hardly had my head touched the pillow, when I heard a faint, soft sigh—there was no mistaking it—I could not call it the wind moaning in the chimney, or anything else, but just what it was, a soft, faint sigh!

I had always thought I was a hard-headed materialist, a stolid matter of fact John Bull, but to my last day, I shall never be able to say what my feelings were at that moment—either my heart stopped and my blood froze, or my heart beat trebly as fast, and my blood boiled, I was either in a dead funk, or else I was annoyed beyond words at something quite inexplicable—I shall never know which state of mind was mine, all I was really conscious of was that I lay inert, incapable of moving, dreading I knew not what, until by sheer will power I forced myself to think.

Should I endeavour to reach the door?—the door, by which I had entered this room but twice, and left once, could I then locate it in the inky darkness in which my room was now plunged? I doubted it. Should I yell—for what—to what end? I could not very well yell "help" or "murder" for I was in no need of help, and no one was being murdered, moreover, no mere yell would be heard from this backwater of a passage where my room was.

What then was I to do? I lay trembling, trying to keep steady; all was still now, and I cautiously raised myself on my elbow, straining my eyes to peer into the darkness. As I did so, my pillow was gently shaken, so gently, that it seemed as if the idea of shaking it was merely to add to my comfort—it did not, for it reduced me to a state of terror. Suddenly the thought shot through my brain—the other bed! and my hostess's words—

"Change if you are not comfortable."

Dare I? The bed I knew was almost beside the four-posters for I had noticed that the little table for my candle, matches and books, stood just between the two beds, thereby being of the same use, whichever bed I chose to occupy. To think was to act now, so I slid out of bed, felt the table by knocking my shins on it, and fell headlong on to the other bed, grabbing the table wildly, to pull it closer, feeling at least it could be hurled at intruders. The first thing my hand came in contact with was—my matches! I seized them wildly, and with trembling hands struck one and lit my candle; holding it aloft I surveyed as much of the room as I could.

Nothing of the slightest account seemed altered, everything looked perfectly normal, beyond one simple item, which I might be wrong in—I had rather hurriedly shed my garments, when I felt sleepy, and man-like had left them in a heap—I am prepared to swear to this, but, now, I saw them distinctly folded neatly and laid ready for me in the morning. Fool that I am, I thought, someone must have entered my room and tidied it, and it was that someone who sighed. That it was a fantastic and highly unlikely thing to have happened, did not seem to occur to my overwrought brain, and nature, now asserting herself, helped me to slip off into restful slumber, from which I awakened, to see the sun pouring into my room, and all as I had left it—even to my garments, in an untidy heap, on the hearth-rug!

"Then I dreamt it," I said aloud, and feeling foolish and half-ashamed, I carefully remade the little brass bed, and got into the four-poster, where I lay contentedly smoking my pipe, until a trim maid brought my early tea, and announced—"Bath ready, sir, and breakfast in an hour."

I dawdled over my dressing, happy in the knowledge at the back of my mind, that there were many hours before me ere I again went to bed, a weak form of reasoning surely, for a man with any brains at all, to indulge in.

An hour later as I joined the rest of the house-party in front of the jolly fire in the hall, my misgivings were fading quickly, and I was inclined to vote myself a silly ass, for being disturbed by what I was now convinced was a bad dream, resulting from too late a meal, following overfatigue. It might have been my fancy that one and all of the party round the fire, eyed me rather curiously, but I flattered myself that I looked fit and fresh, and showed no signs of my troubled night. My hostess asked me in a voice she endeavoured to make natural, " If I slept well."

"Quite," I answered, smiling, for I had made up my mind to say nothing of what I thought had taken place. Then the old professor ambled in, glaring at me from under his shaggy brows as he barked out—

"Comfortable night?"

"Why, yes," I answered, "perfect."

"Umph," he grunted, "no accounting for tastes."

Then we settled ourselves at a well-spread breakfast table, and began to discuss plans for the day.

Mrs. Stuart merely said—

"Entertain yourselves and be happy, luncheon will be ready here at 1.30, but those who wish to take it out are at liberty to do so. I am driving into Drayton—there are a few things I need, though the shops there are not much to see—anyone come?" she asked.

Now was my chance. I would go with her, and procure, if possible, an electric torch, or failing that, would wire home for mine, which I had left behind me. Joyce Wood looked at me with a bright quick glance, as I accepted my hostess's invitation, and said—

"I'll come too, if I may, I want some silk."

"Come along," said Mrs. Stuart, "there is just room for three

17

of us, and you can show Peter round while I shop. We will lunch at the 'Bear Inn,' and get tea here, on our return."

" Is it far?" I asked.

"No," she replied, "only fifteen miles, but slow with horses, though I love them; we will start in an hour," she went on, "so mind you are ready." And she went gaily away to attend, I suppose, to all those little duties, which make a house like this run as if with oiled machinery.

One by one the party dispersed, until the only people left before the fire were Miss Brown and myself. I really had not noticed her much the previous evening, but now, as she sat in a deep chair, her white hands busy with some knitting, I was rather struck by the restful feeling she seemed to have about her. She was not a tall woman, but proportionate, and her face, though pale, was not an unhealthy pallor, her head bent down over some intricate part of her work, was a glossy brown—very neatly dressed and with an absence of combs and big pins, such as most women love. I could not see her eyes, but I was watching her white firm hands, with their beautifully-kept nails, when my eye caught sight of the only ring she wore, a curious ring, an ancient emerald in a dull silver setting; it was more like a man's ring than a woman's, and something made me say, in spite of appearing rude—

"I am admiring your ring, Miss Brown."

She looked up with a quick start, meeting my eyes, with a pair nearly as green as her emerald stone. I was startled. She laughed a low amused laugh.

"And now you are comparing my ring with my eyes. Everybody does," she said, "though that is not why I wear it."

"May I look at it?" I asked.

"From a distance," she replied. "It has a curious history and does not bring luck to most people, so I never let it leave me."

"You are not superstitious, surely?" I asked, for her answer amazed me. She looked so little like a person of that kind.

"What do you mean by superstitious?" she asked. "If you mean will I walk beneath a ladder, most certainly I will, and

18

spill salt and sit down thirteen, quite cheerfully, but if you mean do I believe that certain gems have evil, attached to them, I do, as I also believe that certain impressions are retained by things worn by people at tragic moments, and, given sensitive people to handle them, I believe they can and do bring about curious happenings."

"You amaze me," I answered, "Will you talk to me again on this subject?"

"Yes," she answered, "tomorrow, not any more today." And with this I had to be content, and as she seemed to have relapsed into silence and her knitting, I wandered away in search of boots and coat, to be ready for my hostess and pretty companion for our jaunt to the market town. It was a gay little drive, the country was looking superb, and it was one of those days when bushes and banks were veiled in shimmery gossamer, when shadows seemed deep and long, as the sun lit up vivid patches of red leaves here and there, making a wonderful scheme of colour and beauty.

Mrs. Stuart drove, and was too much occupied with her team to bother much with her passengers, so Miss Wood amused me by running comments on most things, though once or twice she seemed on the point of saying something, then seemed to suddenly pull herself up, relapsing into silence. Our drive took almost two hours, for the roads were hilly, but about one o'clock we rattled up the main street of Drayton, and pulled up at the "Bear Inn." Here Mrs. Stuart gave the gees into the care of an aged ostler, and we entered in search of a meal, after which, she left us to do her shopping, leaving me wondering greatly how I was to get rid of my companion to transact my own little bit of business.

"I am going to buy some sweets," Miss Wood announced presently, "so come along."

I was a little surprised to find the girl in a rather quiet mood, and more than a little surprised, when she suddenly said—

"Mr. Maxton, tell me the truth, did you *really* sleep well last night?"

I answered her in my most off-hand manner—

"Of course, Miss Wood, but why do you ask?"

She turned and glanced at me, but without answering my question, merely said—

"Oh! very well, either you are well able to hide your feelings, or else you passed a night—not usual—for those who sleep in No. 10."

"Is there anything to prevent my sleeping peacefully there?" I asked.

"Oh! never mind," she said, in rather annoyed tones—"Mrs. Stuart may be vexed if I say anything, so don't ask me, only try to endure it, it would be a pity if you cannot, I think we are a jolly little party too," adding—"I shall be a quarter of an hour in this shop, will you meet me again then?"

Rather with too much alacrity, I said I would, and turning away, I left her to her own devices, while I hunted for a torch. I was afraid I was to be doomed to disappointment, so visited the post office to send the wire requesting my own torch should be instantly despatched. I was relying upon a dependable light perhaps more than I was fully conscious of.

The old postmaster, on reading my wire, raised my spirits tremendously by saying—

"If it will save you, sir, I have one of them new-fangled lighting things—it was give to me a week or two past by a visitor, and I've no sort of use for such things, for when I'm home, I likes my lamp, and when I'm out, the stars is good enough light for me. I'll sell it you, sir, and glad to be rid of it."

I was thankful, gladly paying him the three shillings he asked for a twelve-and-sixpenny torch. Having tried it and found it sound, I slipped it in my pocket, and went on my way rejoicing, to meet Miss Wood.

"You are punctual," she said, "now come and buy sweets," so with my spirits higher, because of my torch, and with its possession, my dread of the night much less, we behaved like two children let loose in a sweet shop, laughing, fooling, tasting, and buying.

"The others will welcome us home," she said, "but, oh! do stow some of these parcels in your pockets, we look so greedy!

Without a thought, I took the torch from my pocket to make more room, but I realised instantly that I had given myself away as her eyes fell on it, and a quick "Oh!" fell from her lips. "Then you did tell me untruths," she said, "and I believed you. I suppose you think buying sweets is all I am capable of understanding, very well, so be it," and she drew herself up in offended dignity.

I made no attempt to explain, but followed her from the shop as if in disgrace.

Our drive home a little later, was dull and strained, fortunately Mrs. Stuart was too busy to notice us, and as we reached our own door, we were hailed with shouts from three young men, who all rushed to be first to assist pretty Joyce, so our somewhat forced remarks to each other passed unnoticed.

Tea was a merry meal, though Miss Wood did not appear, she was tired she said, and would rest in her own room.

It seemed to me that there was a constant effort on the part of everyone to keep the tone of conversation as light as possible, and, as evening approached, there was an outcry for lamps, instead of firelight. The two young medicals promptly hauled me from my cosy chair, and marched me off for a game of billiards.

'Won't you come, too, Miss Brown?" I asked, seeing the little lady sitting a little apart as usual, absorbed in her knitting.

"No, thank you, Mr. Maxton, I must finish this sock," she said. "But, later, perhaps after dinner, I will play you a game."

'That is a promise," I said, laughing, as I followed the two young fellows.

We played on until one of them said—

"By Jove! we've only twenty minutes before dinner, come on you chaps," and fled.

The other man, a tall, slim youth of about twenty-nine or so, with a pale face, sleek black hair and rather piercing dark eyes, linked his arm in mine and escorted me up the stairs and along to my room, which he entered with me, and he poked up the fire, while I was lighting my candles.

"Which bed did you sleep in?" he asked, abruptly.

"Why?" I asked.

"I was only wondering," he answered, "personally, I loathe four-posters."

" I like them," I said, "I slept in that one."

"What! all night?" he gasped.

"My dear chap," I replied, "would you get out of a warm bed into a cold one in the middle of the night?"

"I might," he answered, "one never knows, but I must dash off now, my room is the first you come to at the end of this passage, if—er—if you should want anything," and he went off hurriedly. Once again I surveyed my room, and once again I thought it a perfect room. I carefully locked the torch up in my bag, hurried my dressing, and went down to dinner. I was still conscious of odd glances at me, and was faintly aware that for some reason I was of interest to the little company, even the glum old professor cast a questioning eye upon me from time to time, but I showed nothing, gave no hint of any unusual happenings, so dinner and a merry evening passed pleasantly, although Miss Brown failed to keep her promise, saying she had some letters to write for the early post, and had promised to go and see Miss Wood who had a headache.

We were all off to bed early tonight—at least we all separated early—my friend Norman accompanied me upstairs after a last glass of whisky, but as before, he did not linger chatting to me, but merely saying—

"Pleasant night, old chap," he went off, leaving me, for my second night in Room No. 10.

I proceeded to make my arrangements for the night, in a most thorough manner. I heaped up the fire first until the leaping flames lit up even the dimmest corners of the room, making the polished floor between the rugs shine like glass. I calmly surveyed my two beds, quickly making up my mind to occupy the four-poster, so drew the little table well between the two, but in such a position that I could, if needs be, easily reach the little brass bed. I had decided *not* to sit up in the orthodox way and await the arrival of my visitors, ghostly or otherwise. No! I determined, I would go to bed, and to sleep if possible. I whistled cheerily to myself as I undressed, tucking my torch into the pocket of my pyjamas. I turned in, and settled myself comfortably. After about an hour's reading, I blew out my candles, and prepared for sleep. I did sleep, and was awakened as suddenly as before, but this time by hearing the fire being gently stirred. I looked, expecting to see a bright blaze as the result, but black darkness greeted me, yet I could hear the coal being moved. I strained my eyes and ears, listening intently, and trying not to light up my torch, now ready in my hand. I heard the poker laid down. I heard the soft shuffle of felt slippers crossing the polished floor, nearer and nearer to the bed they came.

I heard what sounded like a tinkle of a spoon against a glass, and a soft hand was laid on my wrist, rendering me powerless to light my torch, and turning me cold with terror. With a frantic plunge, I got to the other side of the bed, hoping and praying I should have strength to hurl myself across the little space into the brass bed, but to my unspeakable and everlasting horror, the other side of my four-poster was not empty! Someone was there—some form! With frenzied strength I sat up, flashing my torch as I did so, I suppose I *was* awake—I suppose I *was* sane though I would prefer to think I was asleep, or mad.

In my four-poster lay an old man—a man with a drawn livid face, closed eyes, and snow-white hair, one of whose hands lay outside the covers—claw-like, livid—on one finger of it shone a ring—an uncut emerald in a dull silver setting! winked in the light of my torch, as I held it tremblingly, for the light to shine as far as could be. Beside him stood a woman dressed as a nurse, holding a medicine glass in her right hand, while the other hand held his wrist; an evil smile hovered on her thin lips, and her hair, lit by my torch, was dull iron grey, flattened into a hard line above thin straight eyebrows; I glanced hurriedly round, my whole room seemed changed—a large screen stood round the bed, shielding the window, the writing table seemed full of

23

bottles, in place of my books, garments, which were not mine, lay scattered about.

I was so paralysed with terror, I could neither speak nor move, but clung to my torch as the cold sweat poured from me. I saw her raise the old man's head. I saw him drink the contents of the glass held to his lips, and then, with a frenzied leap, I made one dash for the little bed, and fell on it, fainting.

It must have been some time after when I regained consciousness, for the dim light of early morning was struggling through my drawn curtains. I got up, flung back the curtains, letting in the light; it was Just five o'clock, so the horror had occupied possibly some hours, and I was still alive, though badly shaken. My room was as I had left it; I, wearied beyond telling, now, in the blessed light of day, dropped off to sleep, heavily, dreamlessly, and did not awaken until, as before, my little maid entered with my tea, she gave a little start of surprise on seeing me in the little bed, but made no remark, beyond—

"Your bath is ready, sir, and breakfast in an hour."

I took my tea and my bath, though I felt unhinged, and worn out. Later when I met the party at breakfast, I did not attempt, as before, to conceal the fact that I had *not* slept, and was not feeling very fit.

No one made any remark, except the old professor, who curtly said—

"Better come and have a talk with me in the library, I will give you a pick-me-up." Norman, my friend, was ill at ease, and his wife seemed troubled, Miss Brown calmly eating buttered toast, eyed me, and I noticed her curious ring was not on her hand; she saw I missed it, smiled, saying, as if answering my unspoken thought.

"You need not let that trouble you, Mr. Maxton, its absence is for a purpose."

After breakfast during which meal a sort of cloud seemed to hover over us, I wandered away alone, feeling that solitude and fresh air best suited my need. No one made any move to accompany me, so with my pipe alight, I tramped round the garden, scarcely noticing the autumn flowers, reddening leaves, or ripening fruit. The garden, like the house, was old and picturesque, flowers grew as they liked—set borders, and that most inartistic thing carpet bedding were things unknown. Late roses hobnobbed with gaudy sunflowers, and flaunting hollyhocks, a riot of many coloured phlox, seemed herded together, guarded by a hedge of sweetbriar, and here and there a fading clump of night-scented stock drooped pensively; until evening, when it opened its eyes, and scented all the garden with its strange arresting perfume, a quaint sundial, moss covered, and cracked, stood in a clearing and its motto—"I only count the sunny hours," gave one thought as one passed, of other hours, hours that were *not* sunny.

At one end of a long path, was a white wood seat, flanked on one side by a laburnum tree, and half hidden from sight by a lilac bush—my steps took me towards it, as I came upon it, I saw, too late to go back, that it was occupied, occupied by Miss Brown and her everlasting knitting. Courtesy demanded that I should stop to speak, though the lady did not raise her head.

"Busy as usual, Miss Brown," I said, in tones I tried to make cheery.

"Come and sit down," was her reply, "I want to ask you a question.

"Am I bound to answer it?" I said.

"No," she replied, "not bound, but I hope you will.

"How many people did you see in your room last night?"

"Two," I replied, unhesitatingly, as if the words were pulled out of me.

"Ah," she breathed, "did you—er—have you—ever seen anyone like them before?"

I gazed at her amazed.

"Seen anyone like them?" I said. "Why of course not, they were not real—I mean they could not have been alive!"

"No," she said, "of course not, but oh! never mind, I only asked from idle curiosity. Are you leaving us today?"

"Certainly not," I replied, "at least, I had not thought of doing so, do you wish me to leave?"

"It might be better for you if you did," she answered, "but if you stay, you are a plucky man. I must go now. Miss Wood is not well, and I am looking after her."

"You would be a good nurse," I said politely, and for something to say, but I was unprepared for the change which came over placid Miss Brown, her face went paler than its usual pallor, her lips compressed themselves into a tight line, and a gleam shot into her usually quiet eyes, as she sprang to her feet, and holding the back of her seat, flashed out at me—

"I *can't nurse,* I loathe the very word, but these things seem against our will to pass down from generation to generation, and who knows what other instincts pass down with it," and with that she was gone, and I was alone.

I felt a little taken aback at Miss Brown's quick change of manner, also her abrupt departure, but I had desired solitude so must make the best of it. The white seat appealed to me, and my pipe was always a good companion. It was odd, I thought, as I tried to go over in my mind the strange things that had befallen me, I had been here three days, at least this was my third day, and already I had unwittingly offended two of the house party—Miss Wood first, then Miss Brown—the former because I preferred to keep my own counsel, the latter, by the mild remark, that she would make a good nurse. What strange creatures women are! I should have thought any woman would have liked to have been called a good nurse, there are so few who know the meaning of the word "Nurse," and to my mind they, the modern nurses, are the dullest of women, to judge by those I have known.

Well I've certainly made a mess of things, how to extricate myself I couldn't think. An hour passed quickly in my musing frame of mind, the horrors of the night were fading or had faded here in the sunlit garden, among the perfumes of a hundred flowers. Dare I be unsociable any longer, I wondered, or was it my duty as a guest, to go and seek the other members of our party? My question was answered by the approaching sound of footsteps, followed by the hurried appearance of my hostess, Mrs. Stuart, who breathlessly flopped on to the seat saying—

"Oh, Peter, you idiot! you've gone and upset Miss Brown. Wasn't Joyce enough for you, you big clumsy manbody?"

"Dear lady," I managed to say, "I am quite at a loss to understand you, I merely intimated to Miss Wood that a still tongue suited a certain happening, and to Miss Brown I paid the highest compliment of saying she would make a good nurse!"

Speechless for an instant, Mrs. Stuart looked at me, and then—

"Peter, you didn't? Not really? Oh, for heaven's sake, tell me you didn't say *that!*"

"Most surely, I did," I answered, "and why not, good nurses are extinct, or so it has seemed to me—tell me where I have stumbled please, that I may go on bended knee humbly apologizing!"

"Stop fooling," she ordered, "and listen, though I am under a promise not to tell you anything really, I can explain your *faux pas*, I care nothing for Joyce Wood's touchiness, *that can be* explained later, but Miss Brown! that is another story!"

"We only got to know her through taking this house, it had belonged for generations to her people, and. although she didn't live here herself, she would only consent to let it to people who would allow her to retain some link with the place, allowing her to stay in it in their absence or some arrangement of that kind. We were so taken with the place, its quaintness, its beauty, but above all its remoteness, that we rather hurriedly agreed to anything, so that we got possession of it."

"The first time we came, we did not see Miss Brown, the second time, she was here when we arrived, quite at home looking as if the place belonged to her, I was, I confess, not too cordial, but she speedily disarmed me, telling me she was not filling up our space, because her quarters were in a part of the house little used, in fact, rather shunned by most people, but she preferred it, and had not any nerves, moreover at this time of the year (that was just this time last year) she really must be in her old home, there was nothing I could say, and she very soon won us all, so much so, that now, whenever we are here, so is Miss Brown—she is invaluable to me, she attends to so much in the house for me, leaving me free to rest or enjoy myself. I couldn't do without her," she added—"and there! you've ruffled the dear, like, oh like anything,"

"I'm still in a fog," I murmured.

"I know you are," she answered, "and am I not doing my best to get you to see through it."

"Proceed," I said, "I may see daylight before luncheon."

"Peter, you're impossible." This with a stamp to emphasize it.

"The point is this," she went on.

"So that there is a point!" I ventured.

"Don't interrupt please, as I said the point is this—all of Miss Brown's relations for ages have been nurses!—one after another, great grands, grands, and so on, have all developed nursing tendencies; they don't seem able to help it, and years ago, one of the grands or great grands—I forget which—murdered a patient by poisoning him in this very house; it was never quite known for what reason other than spite, or carelessness, the jury said 'carelessness' but her family didn't, and one or two of the family who subsequently became nurses, were obliged to give it up, because the stain had somehow stuck, and people feared them. Nothing was ever missed, belonging to the old man the woman murdered, except a ring he always wore, but, as there was never any proof to show he had not given it to her, as she said at the trial, it remained in her possession, and has been handed down."

"The emerald jewel, I suppose," I asked.

"Yes, the emerald jewel," answered Mrs. Stuart, "but it has an uncanny reputation, and no one has ever worn it as long as Miss Brown has, and she says she will wear it in spite of the curse it seems to have attached to it."

"What's the curse?" I asked sceptically.

"You needn't sneer," she replied, "you know something of it by now, if I am not very much mistaken. I may not tell you more, Peter, but, to tell Miss Brown she would make a good nurse, was simply awful! The poor soul loathes the very word, yet the tragedy is, she can no more help nursing than she can keep from walking, it's in her blood, and she's *always* nursing someone. A headache!—there's Miss Brown,—a sick animal!—there's Miss Brown, she simply can't keep off it, but, the horrible thing is, that just as he died, the old man cursed his nurse, and all her descendants, swearing that others should also be denounced as murderesses, whether they deserved it or not, and several of them got into trouble of sorts, one gave wrong medicine in the dark, and all but killed her patient, and so on, there are still one or two Nurse Browns about, but they have not an enviable reputation. Our Miss Brown swears she will never be a nurse, and feels most acutely the disgrace of it all, and the very name 'Nurse' is like a red rag to a bull."

"How on earth, Ella, was I to know?" I queried.

"Oh!" she answered me, "didn't last night show you."

"Lord, no," I said, "how could it?"

"Well you are blinder than I thought," she snapped, and then, as swiftly changing, she went on—in honey-sweet tones—"Tell me, Peter, are you too scared to go through tonight?"

"Not a bit," I answered valiantly, "but you seem pretty sure I've got to go through it."

" Miss Brown says so," she answered demurely.

"Oh! d—— Miss Brown," I said, losing patience at last, "it's some got-up tale, I don't believe a word of it, and anyway what has Miss Brown got to do with me?"

"She gave up *her* room, that you might come—Room No. 10 you know—and she is doing all she knows, that you may not be disturbed, that is all," she answered—"the professor is helping her and we shall be thankful if you will go through it, and stay on, it will be over tonight, and you will have peace."

"Try not to think about it, I may not tell you more, I should go to bed early, *in the little bed,* if I were you, and tomorrow, *not* today, you can apologise to Miss Brown, she may perhaps believe then that you did *not* make an intentionally cruel insinuation, but now, she believes you did, she can't see how it could be otherwise."

"Dear Lady," I said, "the fog is thicker than at the beginning."

"I know," she answered, "and it will just *have to be* until to-morrow, then we shall see and all be free to talk, but until then the professor insists on your being left in the fog, as you choose to call it. I must go now, Joyce and Miss Brown are spending the day together in my morning-room you will not see either of them, so get a good tramp with the other men, tire yourself out and keep as cheery as you can. See you at lunch," and with airy wave she had gone, leaving me to my solitude and a good deal to occupy my thoughts.

Thinking things out, I speedily found, was but to land my-self deeper in the maze of perplexity. I had grasped the main idea, that a murder had been committed in the room I slept in, presumably by a long-since departed relative of Miss Brown, who, feeling the disgrace still clinging to her name and family, comes to sojourn here, where it all took place, to keep it ever fresh in her memory! How like a woman! A man would have shunned the spot, unless he could do any good. I wonder if our Miss Brown has some idea of laying the restless spirits, which— let me whisper to myself—most certainly do take possession of Room No. 10! Why does the silly woman wear the emerald ring? Where is it, that she is not wearing it today, and not least, what is the programme for tonight?

Ah! tonight—let me confess, in spite of fooling, my sarcasm, my bluffing with Mrs. Stuart, I am sick when I think of tonight, I am in a dead funk, and dread it unspeakably, but I'm going through with it, with my teeth clenched, it can't surely be worse than last night. Well, I can but wait for what transpires. The day was not happy, nor could I shake off entirely the feeling of fear, any more than I could feel content, knowing I was in disgrace with two women of the party. Luncheon was soon over, the usual standing about with cigarettes after it, seemed by mutual consent to be abandoned, Mrs. Stuart and I alone remaining. A happy thought occurred to me.

"Mrs. Stuart," I began, "do you think the two fair ladies with whom I am in disgrace, would permit me to visit them in their seclusion?"

"No, Peter," she replied quickly, "no, they are both determined not to see you until tomorrow, I think they are right, you must do something else to pass your time."

"May I see the professor then?"

"Better not," she answered, "I'm real sorry, Peter, but they all know and understand the position, and do not wish to speak of it. If you really funk the thing, I'll make up a bed on a sofa for you."

One instant I thought, feeling myself wavering, then—

"No thanks," I said, "I will see the thing through, don't bother about me. I was going to ask one of the men to share my vigil and have a talk by my fire, instead of going to bed, but I find they will be away until late, so there is nothing for it but just my lonesome. As a matter of fact, dear lady, I utterly disbelieve a third of the yarn, and the rest doesn't matter."

"That's a good view to take," she said, with a smile, "but now I must go. See you later." And once more I was left to my own devices. I would shelve the whole wretched affair, and go for a good tramp alone, I decided, so, without waiting for company I set off, and tramped steadily over moor and hills until nearly five, the country was at its best, or rather as I loved it best, except for a feeling of sadness the autumn always brings, I prefer the bracken, golden and bronze, rather than in spring when its tender green fronds run the risk of being cut and blackened by icy wind; I love the trees turning to crimson glories, the berries scarlet or purple banging from every hedge, best of all I love the vivid red of the mountain ash berries, those glorious clusters, which the wandering gipsies say bring luck to the wearer.

There are not any tints even in the freshest of spring green and yellow, to compare in my mind with the glory and colour of waning summer. A thought of tea, however, hastened my footsteps, but no matter how belated one was, fresh tea at once appeared, nor were the toasted cakes all cold and sodden for late comers. It was as I expected, tea was almost over, but I was not by any means neglected.

"Now we'll be cosy," said our hostess, when the last scone had vanished, "Miriam, dear, play and sing to us; you come and sit by me, Peter, and you, professor, you will stay for some music, won't you?"

"If Miss Miriam sings, madam, I could not go," the old fellow answered, as I wondered what manner of voice was this I was to hear, for the first time—I had been too absorbed in other things to have paid much attention hitherto—to the slim fair haired girl—who now moved quietly to the piano, in a dim corner of the Hall—

"Shall I light the candles, Miss Langdale?" I asked.

"Not unless you wish, Mr. Maxton," she answered in a soft low voice, "I like best to sing or play in the firelight."

Silence fell upon our chatter, as the first soft notes of her choice reached us. I do not know the name of anything she played; I am a mere man, whose busy life had neither time for music nor romance in it, but there was both in this girl's music, her soul was in her playing, and memories long called dead were awakened, sad memories, sweet ones, all came, as if at the call of a Pied Piper, memories I had relegated to the dust-heap of forgotten things, now stood before me, as if to say, "you may relegate us to the dust-heap, but memories that have once lived, never die, sooner or later something recalls us, maybe a perfume of a flower, or perhaps music—sooner or later something brings us back."

Presently, but without a pause the music altered, a few soft chords floated softly through the fire-lit hall, and a soft deep voice, clear, resonant, full, yet without a trace of strain, or effort, took up the air, every word, every syllable reached us—old as the song was, often as I had heard it, its beauty and charm as sung by Miriam Langdale that evening, in the silence and warmth in that old hall, I shall never forget.

The hours I spent with thee, dear heart,
Are as a string of pearls to me,
I count them over, every one apart,
My Rosary, my Rosary.

Softly, thrilling, the words came—

Each hour, a pearl, each pearl, a prayer,
To still a heart in absence wrung,
I tell each bead unto the end,
And there, a cross is hung.

Fuller, deeper, rang the lovely voice, there were tears in it now—

Oh, memories that bless and burn,
Oh! barren gain and bitter loss,
I kiss each bead, and strive at last to learn
To kiss the cross, Sweetheart,
To kiss the cross.

The last line rang out—*To kiss the cross, Sweetheart,* and died away in a sob of anguish—

To kiss the cross.

Unmoving, silent, we sat, each one wrapt deeply in their own memories, and surely those hours spent with one beloved, were truly likened to a string of pearls, as surely as there are very very few who have not known the "bitter loss" or who do not, agonised by sorrow, strive to "*kiss the cross.*"

The professor was the first to move, but he only went to the piano, laying his hand for an instant on the bright hair of the singer—he attempted no thanks. Miss Langdale rose from the piano, and kneeling by Mrs. Stuart said—

"I have saddened you, but I wanted to sing your favourite."

"I am not sad, dear, I loved it," answered Mrs. Stuart, "but those words always arrest me, however the tune has been maltreated, but let us light up now," she added, "it is time we dressed—matches please, somebody, not all of you," She went on smiling, "only one box," turning as she spoke to light up the three standard lamps, dispelling in a few seconds the mystery of firelight and music, landing us suddenly in a matter-of-fact world, in place of our separate dream-worlds.

"By jove, we haven't much time," I remarked, glancing at my

watch as I turned to make my way upstairs.

The room, as I entered it, looked cheery, candles had been lit, fire newly made up—I noticed there were more candles than before—I suppose with the idea of banishing all idea of gloom or creepiness, yet, in spite of it the room did not feel normal, I couldn't explain it, but the feeling was there, a feeling I could not give a name to, possibly the music had made me unduly sensitive, at any rate it had not soothed me, and I did not care to linger over my dressing, feeling glad that some slight hustle on my part was really necessary, if I was to be ready when the dinner-gong sounded.

With an idea of keeping my illumination until later, I blew out all the candles but one, as soon as I was ready, but that one I left on the extreme corner of the mantelpiece nearest to the door, as I reached the door, I remembered I had left my handkerchief on the dressing-table, I knew I was foolish, but I had not any desire to walk back to that now dim part of the room where the dressing-table stood, I mentally pulled myself together as I moved towards it. As I did so, a light as from a candle seemed to suddenly light it up, and I turned quickly—the candle was where I had left it, but was *not* alight—the *only* light was seemingly poised in the air, close to the bed, about the exact height it would be if held in a person's hand who was standing beside the bed.

I made no further attempt to find my handkerchief, but, trembling in every limb, staggered to the door, nor did I turn then to see where the candle was. The rest of that evening was neither more nor less than a ghastly nightmare to me—I believe I sat through a dinner, I know I drank a good deal of champagne, I know I talked and laughed, and later smoked, and played billiards, but like a wound-up toy not like a living being. Towards eleven it was no use anyone playing the game, the game was up, we all knew it, everyone present shared to some extent the feeling of foreboding that had me in its clutches.

"I am going to bed," I announced, when I had come to the end of my grip on things—"Goodnight, everybody, wish me luck, or at least, sleep."

All answered me in a sort of chorus, all that is except the professor, who had apparently slipped away in his usual manner.

I arrived at my room feeling that one straw more would send me flying from the house. As I opened the door the pungent aroma of a cigar met me, and my eyes fell on the figure of the old professor, enveloped in a weird dressing gown of green and yellow, in which he had the appearance of a large caterpillar, his grey head was adorned by a scarlet skull cap, his feet encased in large red worsted slippers, and his whole attitude was one of benign, complacent restfulness. I felt my fears slip away, he looked so comfortable, so at home, so composed, as if quite unruffled by aught that could happen.

"You are surprised, dear lad," he said, in his mellow tones, "I thought you would be, I admired your grit, in sticking to it, so thought, if you would permit me, I would keep you company."

"I am overjoyed, sir," I said, beaming on him, "I—I was rather dreading it, it is jolly good of you, I shall be glad of your company."

We settled ourselves cosily beside the fire, first lighting up all candles, and chatted on every subject, until nearly 1 a.m., neither of us feeling like sleep, indeed it seemed to me the old man grew more alert as time passed.

"Are you cold, sir?" I asked suddenly.

"Yes, I am," he replied, and together we heaped on more fuel.

"There isn't much warmth in these sir, is there?" I asked.

No," he replied, "one could almost think the fire was dying down."

"It is," I gasped, "look at it." And surely but slowly it dwindled, until its last remaining flicker died away, and sank as dead fires do, back into the grate in cold blankness.

I looked at the professor, he was staring intently at the fourposter, which in the now cold gloomy room had taken on a new aspect. It appeared hung with white, a white sheet lay stiffly spread upon it, a rigid form was beneath it, and the unforgettable scent of funeral flowers filled the air.

I cowered down beside the professor's knees, trembling, speechless, he held my hand in a tense grip and we waited, watching.

The door softly opened to admit the nurse, whom I had seen the night before—softly she seemed to slip-shod over the floor in her felt slippers, taking up her position beside the bed—she uncovered the face of the old man, to whom I had seen her administer a dose, and raising the candle she had picked up from the table as she passed, she peered intently at the old man's face for an instant, turning away finally, with a slow, evil smile on her features—"*Her*" features! I called them, my heavens! in spite of the lank iron grey hair, tight lips, and death-like face, her features—nay, her very movements and expression were those *not* of a stranger, but—of— Miss Brown!

"Is it Miss Brown?" I gasped, in a hoarse whisper.

"Hush! no, it is *not*," whispered the professor, "keep quiet."

Before our eyes men entered that ghastly room, placed that rigid figure in a coffin, raised it, and slowly shuffled out of the room. I shivered as the icy coldness of a wind swept by me, when they passed through the door. We heard them shuffling along the passage, their steps growing fainter and fainter, then silence— only the nurse remained, standing immovable, pale, shadowy, the dim light of the now flickering candles dimly lighting her, as she stood with a grim smile twisting her face, one hand outstretched towards us, as if triumphantly, and on her finger a single ring— an uncut emerald in a dull silver setting!

Slowly before our eyes she faded, and we were alone, but to my last hour, I shall smell the sickly perfume of funeral flowers, and feel the icy wind sweep by me whenever I see the white cap and apron of a nurse.

"Dare you follow?" whispered the professor.

I nodded, unable to speak, as he rose leading me by the arm to the door. A sound as of faint music came wafting towards us, and everywhere there seemed the penetrating scent of funeral flowers.

As we reached the top of the stairs, there, just ahead of us, stood the figure of the nurse, as if watching with malignant eyes the slowly moving procession, as it went down the stairs; beside the nurse, almost touching her, stood—Miss Brown—gowned in a long trailing black robe, her head held defiantly, as if commanding this scene to cease. There was not any mistake now in the relationship of the two women, as they stood facing each other, for even I, in my terror-stricken state, was well aware, that, feature for feature, the nurse's face was identical with the face of Miss Brown, though older.

The professor spoke to her, but she gazed at him, as if with unseeing eyes of a somnambulist. Suddenly the nurse turned, and, with a swift movement, flashed the emerald ring before Miss Brown's face, then, smiling her evil smile, she, too, descended the stairs, fading away into nothingness, ere she reached the foot, in the same way as both coffin and bearers had faded. The quiet of a house at 2 a.m. enveloped us, Miss Brown, without word or sign, went slowly back to her room. The professor drew my arm quickly through his own, as he led me, half fainting as I was, to his own room. I think I must have fainted, for the next thing I remember was the smell of hot coffee! and opened my eyes to see Mrs. Stuart pouring it out, as if a coffee party at 2 a.m. in a guest's room was the most usual thing!

I finished the night on the professor's sofa, though sleep was denied me; he nevertheless would not allow me to talk.

"Wait until daylight," was all he would say, as I obediently swallowed a dose he gave me. Morning came at last, but I felt ill and shaken, though refusing to rest, I joined the breakfast party; after that, we gathered round the fire, and talked over the whole thing. I was allowed to tell my story of the three nights I had passed in No. 10, only to learn that I had witnessed every detail of the gruesome tale.

"Why didn't you warn me?" I naturally enquired.

"Peter," said Mrs. Stuart, "we one and all ought to ask pardon for that, but we all thought you would go right through it alone. There is a sort of tag to the curse, to the effect that someone seeing it all though *alone* will, in part, remove the curse. *No one* has so far done so. Miss Brown has tried and failed, the professor would not attempt it alone, but seeing the state of tension you were in, last night, said he would not be responsible if you were allowed to go to your room alone."

"Now you know how you upset Miss Brown. She naturally thought you saw the likeness to herself in the gruesome nurse, and thought you were twitting her with it."

"But Miss Wood?" I questioned.

"Oh!" said Mrs. Stuart, with a smile, "she was nervy and wanted to warn you, only you treated her like an infant, she said, so she kept out of your way."

"One question more," I asked. "The emerald ring, why does Miss Brown wear it?"

"That is the horrible part of it all," said Mrs. Stuart, "the Brown family always felt that the ring ought to be put back in the old man's coffin, so, many years ago, the body of the nurse was exhumed, and the ring taken from her hand; but, as ill-luck would have it, the records, or whatever they are called, showing where the old man was buried, could not be found, so the Brown family have kept the ring. Miss Brown thought she would leave it outside the house last night, to see if it made any difference to the sequence of events, apparently it did not, and the professor says it is not by any means the first time a curse has followed the stealing of a man's jewel, and he is doing his utmost, so far without success, to find the grave, and restore the ring, it may or may not cause the haunting of this house to cease, but meantime no one *can* see the thing through and keep sane, alone, and Miss Brown wears the stolen jewel until it can be restored to its dead owner. It is a horrible story, and one apparently impossible to clear up. You've been jolly plucky, Peter, but you shall not again sleep in Room No. 10."

Nor did I, but I spent some very happy weeks wandering about the country. No! not with Miss Wood, but with Miss Brown. I fulfilled Mrs. Stuart's prophecy, spoken in jest—and ended by adoring her.

We talked over the haunting of her house until it was threadbare, but knowing, as we both do, the ghastly three nights which takes place in that room every autumn, we have decided, or rather *I* have decided, that if she will tolerate a somewhat dry, old book-worm, we might make "High Crags" a very cheery abode together; but we both say emphatically, we must find that grave, restore that jewel, or entirely pull down Room No. 10.

Until that day comes, I confess to rather enjoying comparing Miss Brown's green eyes with the emerald stone stolen by her ancestress who first nursed, then murdered, her hapless patient, in the room she seems yet to consider her own, at a certain time of the year, so much her own, that such trifles as the stirring of a dead fire, the shaking the pillow of an unsuspecting guest, are usual happenings, though only in autumn does one see the final act of the tragedy; but I, who saw it, shall never in my life forget, nor do I care who sneers, who laughs at what they are pleased to call my imagination, I saw—I know—as others will—until the emerald stone is restored—the horrible ghastly murder that took place in Room No. 10.

Two Little Red Shoes

All my life, or at least as far back as I can remember, empty houses have always had an irresistible attraction for me, though uninhabited gardens are almost as attractive. I cannot call the gardens empty, though people may be absent, for a garden is never really empty—spring, summer or winter—there is always life in a garden! Spring! and the singing of mating birds. Summer! hot, drowsy summer days, with the ceaseless hum of millions of insects; just to lie listening, in what most people call silence, though it is a silence fraught with countless sounds. Winter! the most still, has its sounds and life.

A notice board inevitably draws my footsteps nearer to an empty house, the more weatherworn the "To Let" the greater the attraction.

My infatuation for empty houses has led me into curious situations at times, and has often been the source of very real pleasure and interest. Occasionally I have had unpleasant episodes; but, on the whole, happy hours predominated. Long years ago my prying tendencies had about them the elements of a game of "Let's pretend," for in imagination dwelt in one or other of those silent, houses, always with a tender lover by my side: I used to choose my drawing-rooms, and furnish them—I chose my nurseries, and peopled them with little people; my colour schemes were many and very varied, and in this way I passed many happy hours— so happy indeed, that those hours spent in empty houses were more my real life, than the other.

Years have passed, and part of my game has come true—only

part of it—for my colour schemes were somehow never attainable in a work-a-day, practical world, and there were other parts of my daydreams, and they, too, remained "daydreams." In spite of passing years, in spite of work, in spite of all, I have never outgrown my fondness for empty houses and uninhabited gardens, and to this day I am known to visit a tenantless house, light a fire, from a hidden store of coal and wood, seat myself in an old broken-down chair, and there, in the silence—a silence unbroken by the ring of telephone or any other bells—I dream my dreams and revel in unbroken solitude—with every nerve at rest, sure in the knowledge that none can disturb my peace, since none know my whereabouts—I have said strange episodes have befallen me at times—one so strange as to be almost unbelievable—yet let those explain who can!

A long hot summer was drawing to an end—a summer of almost tropical heat, which had left the earth parched and brown, green lawns looked like brown felt, and people had at last given up in despair the sprinkling of water in their thirsty gardens—it seemed waste of energy and water, the flowers were too thirsty—so were left to droop and fade away almost before they were fully out; leaves tumbled off trees while yet green, simply because they were sun-baked and dry. Even the birds waited about expecting some thoughtful human creature to give them a dish of water to drink and play in.

Most people had gone either to the sea or hills, certainly all who could afford it had fled, and those unfortunate ones whom work or duties chained to the towns, were deserving of pity, as they toiled through the hours of day, returning, in what they tried to call the cool of the evening, to their dried-up bits of garden, or suffocating rooms. I was one of those unlucky ones—doomed to stay in town until the end of August, after which I was free—Free! with a little sum of money at my disposal to squander as and where I pleased. For some reason it pleased me to save that bit of money and *not* spend it in train travelling other than one short journey, for I had long ago made up my mind that when next the Fates were sufficiently kind as to leave me in undisputed possession of our happy home, and granted me a few days' freedom from the daily round—the common task, I would spend that time in pursuance of my favourite pastime—the hunting out and getting into uninhabited houses and gardens—I already knew of one such house, and had long made up my mind to inspect it—so, on this first day of my freedom, I made a parcel of some food, a book, some paper and pencils, and donning old garments, I set forth.

A short train journey and a long walk landed me at a pair of massive old iron gates—they were shut, and, to my intense disappointment, padlocked! I peered through them up a long grassy drive, with high banks of rhododendrons on each side—the drive was not newly grass-grown, it had always been a grass drive—and straight ahead at the far end of it, stood the house—I meant to reach it, I intended to get inside, and I was not going to be daunted by a merely padlocked gate—even though the said gate was too high to climb, and, moreover, had spikes at the top. I wandered on past the gates and spotted a thin part of the close thorn hedge, where the paling behind had rotted and given way.

Through this thinned hedge I scrambled, and over the broken paling, but didn't intend to spoil my approach that way, so crept back inside the fence until I reached the gates. "So much for your padlock," I thought, as I started triumphantly to march up the length of that old grassy drive—odd little paths branched off it from time to time, leading I knew not whither, and all of them were grass; gravel or paving of any kind was unknown. As I neared the house, I found myself thinking what a silent place it must have been to dwell in, with all the approaches of soft turf, no sound of feet or wheels would be heard, such silence would have pleased me well.

Probably most people would have gone straight to the house and peered in at the windows. I did not. I sat down on the short turf, under the shadow of a giant copper beech tree, and stared at those many blank windows, looking down on me, as if they were so many eyes. It has always been my way to approach those things which please me in a lingering kind of manner, as if, like the children do, I tried to make them last longer. I felt like this as I sat gazing at the house I had long waited to inspect, but having attained my desire, I lingered, even though longing to get inside.

It was a dull, red brick house, with many windows, but all flat—not a "bay" window or jutting corner anywhere—only the front door broke the monotony, it having a curious porch—two sides glass, with a heavy oak door in the-centre. The bell-pull attracted my eye next, it was a heavy copper chain, and green with age in many places—the handle, a horse-shoe—of rusty iron. I wondered if that had been the original, or whether some inmate, with a tendency to superstition, had hung it there.

From my comfortable seat, I let my gaze wander to and fro from window to window, trying to picture the rooms within, yet still putting off my attempt to enter—no thought of being unable to do so entered my mind, for by some means or other I intended to accomplish what to me was a definite purpose. I would eat my lunch first, I decided, then find a way indoors, and later, as it grew cooler, wander in the garden. It was gloriously still there under the beech tree, so still, that I grew drowsy, and all but fell asleep (that would waste time, I thought), so roused myself with an effort, and drew nearer to the house. I believe in my heart I feared being foiled in my desire, and that was one reason why I delayed, but time, relentless always, was passing along, and I must really make a start.

I peered through the windows to the right of the door.

"Oh! Lovely!" I exclaimed, and hurriedly peeped in those on the other side of the door. "What a contrast," I thought, I *must* get in; so almost ran round the back of the house in my eagerness. Window after window I tried in vain, but at last caught sight of one with a broken hasp. This, by using a penknife, and sharp-edged stone, I raised sufficiently to get my fingers in and lift it up, then, jumping on to the sill, I crept through, closing the window softly behind me. I found myself in a big lofty kitchen—minus furniture of any kind, though oddly enough two little dish covers still hung on the walls. From there I wandered along a stone passage, which had many doors—I don't mean doors opening on to them, but heavy doors across them—every few yards—as if the dwellers in the house had intended cutting off all sound from the kitchen premises being heard in other parts of the house—the end door was cedar wood, and as I closed it, I realised that the living rooms seemed quite in another world. I entered the room to the right of the front door, the room which had caused me to exclaim "lovely!" when I peered through its windows.

It certainly was a beautiful room—long and low—with walls of white and gold, with a frieze of laughing cupids driving each other with chains of pink roses. This room was likewise devoid of furniture, except for two very small chairs-one upholstered in faded blue, the other in tatters of pink. I smiled, and supposed they were too small to bother to remove, probably the little folks to whom they had once belonged had long since out-grown them. I loved the laughing cupids, and pictured the gay revels they must have looked down upon before the pink of their roses faded. There was another door leading from this room—it was slightly ajar—so I peeped in before continuing my wandering on the other side of the front door. I say at once, emphatically and decidedly, I did not like it. It was a small, round room—with three windows, none of which one could see through without getting on to a chair; the walls were slate coloured, the floor was stone, there wasn't a fireplace, but pushed against the wall were two little high wooden stools, and to each stool was attached a long, thin steel chain. I didn't like it.

The stools looked as if two small dogs might have been fastened there, and made to sit still. I left it hurriedly and entered the room on the other side of the front door. This had quite a lot of furniture in it, and, to my amazement, many toys—there was a dappled, well-worn rocking-horse—not one of the modern apologies for a rocking-horse, the thing on patent springs which only wobbles to and fro in perfect safety—oh! no, *this* was a real old-fashioned gee, which *really* rocked, until you were rather in danger of slipping over its scanty tail, or sliding forward to grasp its cocked-up ears; there was a broken doll, too, with what had once been a pretty face, not a monstrosity, or fat policeman with a red nose or hideous golliwog; there was a battered engine, some bricks, and on the hearth a little pair of scarlet shoes. I picked these up and fell to wondering what little atom had worn them—someone had once had happy times in this room of toys I thought. I had spent a long time in the few rooms I had prowled through, and already long shadows were dimming the bright glare of the sun.

I glanced at my watch, and decided I would move to the garden, the house was beginning to feel chilly—that odd chilliness of a house long tenantless and fireless. I would come again tomorrow, and then explore upstairs, but now would just have one peep at the garden, then trot homewards. The room of toys held me somehow, and I was loth to leave it and the little red shoes! I had a wild desire to put those in my pocket, surely no one would miss them, and I—oh! well—I liked to handle them and imagine the wee soft pink feet that they had covered. It couldn't be stealing, I argued, for by the dust on them they must have been long lying unthought of, besides, I would bring them back tomorrow—but just for tonight I wanted them—so I took them in my hand as I strolled from the room, to commence retracing my steps along the corridor of many doors.

Just as I closed the door behind me I heard a sound—a sound that always had the power to arrest my steps—I heard a long-drawn whimpering cry of a little child!

"Then there *is* a caretaker, and family," I said, aloud. "How stupid of me not to have thought of it, and looked more carefully before I made the house so very much my own."

I went on through another door, and I heard the cry again. I was closer to the sound, or was it nearer to me? I hurried a little, slipping the little red shoes into my pocket for safety. I did not want to be called a thief—beside, I would bring them back tomorrow. I passed through the last door before the kitchen, and again a long, whimpering cry broke the silence, so close to me, so close, I felt as if I had but to stretch out my band to touch that troubled, little child. I quickened my steps, raised the window, and slipped through, fully intending to explore the back premises to discover the whereabouts of the worthy caretaker and her fractious child. I stood for an instant when safely through the window, and as I stood there, I heard, distinctly, unmistakably, the whimpering cry and the soft tapping of tiny baby fingers on the window pane, tapping as if they could scarcely reach, but tapping insistently and clearly, and always, always, the same little, wailing cry.

I turned away, satisfied that either in rooms above or below, I should next day stumble upon the caretaker, but, though unafraid, I was not by any means sure that I could so easily explain away those persistent, tapping baby fingers.

I travelled home in a thoughtful mood, for though I had enjoyed my day, the memory of those deserted toys lingered in my mind.

Of my home life I need not speak, it was just the usual routine of most women, the everlasting ordering of meals, and the doing of the hundred and one small duties which go to make up the everyday life of the everyday woman, therefore my return home and usual humdrum evening was got through as countless others are—perhaps mine were, at least in the opinion of some folks, duller than the evenings of others, because some of my ideas happened to be different—for instance, I much preferred the silence of my own sanctum with my books and odds and ends to spending an evening in the company of a few other people, with our noses buried in packs of cards, oblivious of all other interests save to win. Cards never attracted me, there is always so much that is more worthwhile.

An evening of music does appeal to me, but people are forgetting how to play and sing, and so I stay at home, dreaming my dreams in my leisure hours of peace. Tonight, as I sat by my open window, watching the stars peep out, I pondered much on the old empty house. The little scarlet shoes lay on the table at my side, and often I picked them up, trying to picture their wee owner—how old was "she?" for it must have been a girl I was sure—was she fair or dark? where had she gone? and why had her little shoes been left behind? I looked at them carefully; they were not much worn although the tiny soles showed that they had done some running about. She must have been the owner of the broken doll, but who then was the owner of the engine? All my questioning left me no wiser, so I resolved to go early to bed, bent on an early start in the morning, to visit my "House of Mystery," as I called it.

True to my resolve, I was up and away betimes, reaching my house while the dew was still on the grass, part of the house was still in the shadow, the birds were still busy over their morning toilets, otherwise the place looked as silent and deserted as before.

I sat down for a few moments under the copper beech to rest and make up my mind whether to make straight for my window, and go on with my prowl from where I left off, or to try if I could unearth the caretaker. I had a wish to interview the crying baby, who rather spoiled my departure on the previous evening. A sudden thought decided me. I would first hunt up the caretaker, with a view to gaining some sort of permission to prowl as I liked, when and where I liked, it would be worrying if I were turned out, as I might very well be, unless armed with a permit of some kind, and knowing the rules of the game, I ventured to think a promised pound of tea or toy for the baby would in all likelihood grant me a free pass. To this end I would inspect all the back premises first, make my, peace with the good lady, and then spend the whole long day in the garden, reserving the house for a wet day or a day too cold for the garden.

Having made up my mind, I proceeded towards the back of the house. There were three or four doors, one labelled "Tradesmen." A useless label I always found, for they inevitably used any other door save the one so marked—our own side door bore a similar inscription, but it never prevented a long line of errand boys tramping past the front of the house, bearing their milk cars, butcher's baskets, or loaves of bread in full view of all and sundry.

I peeped into many outhouses, coal-shed, boot room—I

even found the stable yard, but most of the doors there were broken or off the hinges, as if these places had long been known as domiciles for tramps. I was able to see through every window, at the back of the house, every room was empty, dusty and tenantless, not a sound or sign of life was to be heard, so I arrived at the conclusion that the worthy caretaker lived at a distance, only paying occasional visits, and must just have come upon the scene as I was leaving last evening. Then the chances were I should be left in peace today.

The house attracted me, and for a moment I wavered, but the garden called, so I would adhere to my plan, leaving the house for another visit. I would just pop in, replace the little "stolen"— or, as I preferred—"borrowed" red shoes, and then return to the garden.

"Oh, how stupid!" I suddenly exclaimed, aloud, "I have come without the little shoes, I have left them on my dressing table. Well, they are safe, and no one will miss them, and I can bring them tomorrow. I need not enter my window, I can go straight to the garden and explore, but would go to the front door, and start from there." This I did, wandering away to the right, down a winding grassy path, with high bushes on each side interspersed with overhanging laburnums, the golden glory of them had long since departed, but their waving graceful foliage mingling with the darker glossiness of the rhodies, was cool and refreshing.

Quite suddenly the grassy path widened and led me down three rough, stone steps on to a little lawn, closed in with a riotous wilderness of late roses—climbing roses chiefly, but of the old-fashioned kind—I saw a friend of my childhood, a little, squashed-looking white rose, I never knew its name, nor do I now, but it grows in profusion, the buds are just tinged with pale coral, and when open, the little rose is white; with a faint, soft scent—pale pink, monthly roses mingled with them, also crimson peonies and tall, blue larkspurs, while old-fashioned sweet-williams and pansies formed a border, or what once had been a border.

At one side of the lawn was a grassy bank, and opposite to it a huge cedar tree, with a rough, wooden seat below it, or rather the remains of a seat. The shut-in-ness of it, the silence of it, together with the riot of colour and indescribable sweetness of the many flower scents, made me pause enraptured, yet sad to think so much loveliness should be wasting unseen, unknown. I sat down at the foot of the bank, leaning against it, facing the path I had just come down, and closed my eyes with a sense of complete restfulness and peace.

I may have dozed there in the heavily-scented air, or perhaps I was tired, without realising it, but I had probably been lying there an hour, or more, when I suddenly sat up, with the distinct feeling of being no longer alone. I was right, though for the moment I could not see anyone, and yet I heard soft movements. I can't describe them, it was like the passing and repassing of soft footsteps, *little footsteps,* near me. I found myself staring, and then—ah! me—it seems both impossible and useless to describe—yet perchance, some day, someone may read this and believe—I saw two little children, hand in hand, trotting along in the busy little way children have when on affairs entirely their own.

Past me they trotted—a tiny boy in a sailor suit, bareheaded, with clustering curls round a pale, resolute little face—and by his side, a dainty wee girl in white, bare headed, as he was, but with a golden, silky down covering her tiny head. He wore sturdy little brown shoes—she was barefooted—and at times, as I watched them, she pointed with tiny, dimpled fingers to her little bare toes, and seemed half inclined to cry.

No other thought occurred to me in those first few moments except that they had somehow strayed in from somewhere, and—watched them, fascinated, *though I never heard them speak!* Presently they sat down still intent on each other, and for the first time it struck me how utterly oblivious they were to me.

They were so sweet and lovely, I wanted to run to them, catch them in my arms, and cover them with kisses. Should I try and catch their attention, I wondered—perhaps they would play with me, but I would watch them a little longer first.

Slowly the little lad got up as if listening, and then a change came over the little faces, a dreadful heart-breaking change—and a look of awful fear was in each face—the wee girl stumbled to her feet, and began to cry—I could see, but I could hear no sound—and then, with pale cheeks and trembling little limbs, they started to cross the lawn.

I could not endure it. What had frightened them? I must help them, I sprang to my feet; they reached the tree of white roses by the beginning of the path, just as I came up to them, and as I reached them, putting out my hand to hold them—*they were not there!*

Then, and then only, did I realise that my dream children were dream children indeed. Children from another world, still visiting this one—if, indeed, they had ever really left it!

I sank down, half-faint, and wholly bewildered, and for a long time I lay with my eyes hidden, and feeling unable to stir; I managed to pull myself together after a while, and glanced at my watch. It was four o'clock, the same hour at which I left yesterday when those tapping baby fingers on the window beat themselves into my brain.

I would go, I felt I could not, dare not, venture to the house, but I was determined, though a little shaken, that I would come back. I must, some power compelled me, and I knew I should return.

I reached home again and went at once to my room. There were the wee scarlet shoes just as I had left them, but I handled them in a different spirit, for, vividly before my eyes, I saw those tiny, bare feet, and the odd little pucker of the baby lips as the small girl pointed down to them. "Very well, baby, you shall have them back, never fear!" For now I felt brave again, and intended to see more of my dream children.

I went to bed wondering what the next day would bring forth.

I suppose I was a bit unnerved, for I passed a restless night, only falling asleep as the dawn came, so sleeping later than my wont, and I woke to find a dull, grey morning, a sobbing wind, and threatening-looking clouds overhead, no trace of sun or blue sky—such is our dear English climate! But, such as it is, I love it in all or most of its moods. Today it suited me. I would journey to my "House of Mystery" and spend the hours indoors. I am not braver than other women, indeed, am a veritable coward over many things, but I am *not* greatly alarmed by the supernatural.

I suppose because of my unchanging belief in a life hereafter, and a very firm faith that those we love, who have passed over, are very, very near us, and not as some would have it, out of our ken for all time, and so, though I have a natural dread of things not understandable, I still was not afraid, certainly not sufficiently afraid to prevent my visiting my dream children at least once more.

I reached the house on this my third visit shortly after one o'clock, and went straight to the window, raised it, and crept through. I had a kind of feeling that if I saw my babies it would not be until four o'clock. Little did I guess what was in store for me, or even I, good as my nerves were, would have gone gladly a hundred miles in another direction.

The house was very still, very silent, as I moved about, my footsteps seemed to make the sounds of a giant at least.

Slowly I wended my way upstairs, through room after room— all had been beautiful, artistic, and varied in colour and design. At last I reached a large, airy room, done in shades of blue, and this room had brass rods before the large window.

"Night nursery," I murmured, and I noticed two small hard-looking beds. Strange, I thought, in all this vast place, just two little things left in various rooms—two little beds, two little dish covers, two little wooden stools, in that horrid room downstairs, what did it mean?

What can have been the story of this house, for story there had been, of that I felt sure. Maybe some little children had died here, or, was it that they had lived, and then gone elsewhere, leaving their little belongings behind them? No! that could not be right, for, almost unwillingly, I was forced to admit that those little beings I had seen and heard were not of this world, nor were they the children of my imagination; so that hidden story was apparently to remain hidden unless—unless—I had the courage and will power to unearth it. Will power I had, I knew that, but courage? Ah! that was a different story, and I felt that a certain amount might be needed in the face of what I had already seen. Resolutely I had made up my mind I would continue to visit the house, trying to take things calmly, trusting nothing would happen to try my powers of endurance too severely.

The garden did not look so attractive today, rain had fallen off and on all morning, beating down the few late flowers, making muddy puddles on the grassy paths, and I did not feel as if I dared to venture as far as the shut-in lawn. I would prowl about indoors, I decided, though to tell the truth, the place was eerie in the chill gloom of this wet day, now and then a moaning wind howled through keyholes and chinks. Sometimes a far-off door slammed to, making me jump, or the sound of a rattling window echoed through the empty rooms, the trees made the house dark, too, lacking the brilliant sunshine of previous days, when I revelled in exploring both house and grounds.

However, here I was, and here I intended to remain, at least for another hour or two. This night nursery, as I called it, was anything but an attractive room, so I decided to leave it and pursue my investigations elsewhere, so merely glanced round it as I wandered towards the door, pausing, as I did so, to look at the two little beds. I felt one of them, and was shocked to feel the hardness of it; for though fully made, even to pillows and blankets, all was of the poorest description, the bedding itself almost like wood, so hard was it.

"Poor babies!" I murmured, "if their sweet, little bodies had been obliged to rest on them." I found it difficult to picture those lovely little people as I saw them in the sunny garden, sleeping uneasily on such hard beds. The room chilled me, and I was glad to leave it, though I paused uncertainly at the door, wondering whether to go further amongst the upstairs-rooms or go down again. It was curious the attraction the toy-room held for me. I liked to look at the toys, picturing the games and frolics of the little ones amongst them; moreover, I had the wee scarlet shoes in my pocket, ready to replace, but first I intended to watch if they were still missed. So, I only gave a passing glance into one or two other rooms on my way to the staircase.

All were empty, dusty, cold and faded, though once, as in the rooms below, the decorations must have been beautiful, one large, airy room particularly charmed me, especially the ceiling—hand-painted, apparently—a dull, cream ground with tiny, naked babies flying about, holding up pale blue ribbons, all of them gathered, so to speak, by one baby of a larger size in the centre, who held in his wee hands the ends of the ribbons almost as if driving a team of other babies. What held my attention was the exquisite beauty of the child faces; truly, this house had held one lover of children at any rate. I stayed a little while in that room, sitting on the broad window sill, happy with my fancies amongst those pretty babies. The room, I imagined, was just over the "toy-room," judging from the view from the window, so perhaps this was the room of their mother.

Perhaps she rested here where her quick ear could catch the sound of little voices in the room beneath. Happy mother! and happy babies. Was she a mother in the old, real meaning of the word—someone to whom the children could go always sure of sympathy for woes and joy in their joy. Mothers like that are rare today, they have not time. Children weary them, pet dogs are so much less trouble.

This room, with its painted babies, was filling my eyes with useless tears; I felt I was losing time, sitting brooding here of things, which, after all, were probably "Direction that I could not see," so, with a lingering look at the lovely, laughing faces, I quietly stepped away, wending my way back along the long corridor, to the head of the staircase, where there was a quaintly-carved white gate. The babies again, I thought, as I paused beside the gate, noticing that on the top of it was fixed a little silver bell which gave out a sweet deep-toned ring, as the gate was touched, evidently once inside the gate, the bell was a signal if it was opened again; probably for mischief, sometimes a tiny hand would shake the gate, calling instantly some person, maybe nurse, or mother, quickly to gather in the straying baby. I sighed again as I went down the stairs. So far today the house had been singularly quiet. I was glad in a way, yet somehow disappointed. I wanted my babies. Very well, then—the toy-room should be my next room.

Softly I opened the door, almost feeling as if I should catch them at their play, but all was silent. I would wait, so went quietly to where an old, much-used rocking-chair stood. No fancy affair this, but a solid yellow, wood chair, with big cane seat and back, and large rockers, the right sort of chair in which to rock tired kiddies. I sat down in it and silently waited. I knew I *was* waiting—it is one thing to merely sit down to rest—it is quite another to sit down to wait—wait—for something— or someone, not knowing what or for whom. I tried to read a little book I had put in my pocket, but my eyes refused to keep on the page, and my ears seemed awaiting sounds. They came at last—the sounds—not the babies, sounds that made me spring from my chair and listen, listen! with thumping heart and cold terror gripping me!

Scream after scream, rang through the silence—piercing shrill, the screams of a little child— no, of little children—not the screams one hears in a nursery, when squabbles occur; not the screams of rage or vexation of thwarted wishes, or bedtime orders, but the awful heart-rending screams of children in dire pain and terror. I could have screamed also, merely hearing them, and yet I felt powerless to move or stir, my limbs refused their office. I could only stand shuddering. Two more piteous cries reached my ears, and then silence, but only for a brief space, as suddenly the door was flung violently open and two small, naked figures fell rather than walked into the room—fell, as if pushed in, and the door swiftly banged to—the bang brought me more or less to my senses, and I stared horror-stricken, aghast—the two little figures were my sunny smiling children of the garden; but oh! the pity of it, their little faces smiled no longer, tears coursed down each baby face, as they stood clinging together, tremblingly; their lovely, little bodies covered with marks as of a lash or stick, weals and cuts which showed like blood; even across their wee legs were hideous marks.

Even now, as I look back after many years, I find it difficult to believe those little figures were not "real," so real did they appear to me. I wanted to go to them, to kneel beside them, soothing, comforting, but something—was it their absolute unconsciousness of my presence, I wonder— kept me still, and watching, slowly their sobbing ceased, as still trembling they moved together to where an old-fashioned sofa stood. I saw them, with difficulty, drag their little, sore and battered bodies up on to it, and cower down under the old, worn blanket, flung on it; I saw them, arms round each other, fair head and dark, close, close together; I saw the quivering limbs grow still, as I heard little moans die away on their lips, and then I saw a soft, unearthly light hover for one instant over the old couch, and then—I was alone, the sofa empty— the room silent!

For a long time I stood staring, and then I knew my first feeling was one of intense relief, that those little, ill-used babies were *not* real—though my heart was aching, sickeningly, at what must once have been; my second feeling was one of stern resolve to know and fathom, to punish, if not too late, the author of such misery. Poor little babies! What had been their fate, and why?

Slowly my wits resumed their balance, and my nerves lost some of the strain. I ventured near the sofa, half-expecting to see the little faces, but only the worn, old blanket lay on the sofa; so, stepping swiftly to the fireside. I knelt down, and taking the little shoes from my pocket, I laid them gently in the spot from whence I had taken them, and, for the first time, glanced at my watch. Five minutes past four! "The usual time," I murmured. "How strange it all is, yet there are those whose fixed and unalterable belief is that *if* there ever are "ghosts" seen, it can only be at midnight!" How little such people know!

Evidently, then, I had been the witness of varied visions of these little ones—the story of their little lives was rapidly un-folding before me. I had *heard* them on the first afternoon, when I took the little shoes; I had *seen* them happy in the garden on my second visit, and today, my third visit, I had *seen* them tor-tured, torn. Should I see them again, I wondered, or was this last awful scene the final one! At any rate, I felt I should not see them again today, so prepared to take my leave.

I had just reached the hall, when the sound of a heavy groan fell on my ears—a groan and a sound of a moving chair. Noth-ing unearthly about that, I thought, though why I was so sure of it I could not tell. The moving chair brought the caretaker to my mind, probably groaning at having to come at all, I thought, but, anyway, I will track her for once. Again something moved. "The other front room," I murmured, as I bravely went towards it, and opened the door. It was empty, but the door leading from it into the little, horrible room, where the two little stools were, was slightly ajar. I hated the thought of entering it, but felt com-pelled to do so; as I neared it, moving as softly as I could, I heard strange words and mutterings. I had just reached the door when the words—

"My God! is there no peace?" uttered in a man's voice, ar-rested my steps, and then, in louder tones—

"Help, oh, help!"

Instantly I pushed the door open.

"Well," I said.

A gaunt, misshapen figure rose suddenly—a man with long, white beard and hair, eyes sunken and burning, fixed themselves upon me, as with a shriek, he yelled—

"Yes, yes, the well! That is it, the well, it is there they are. Who are you? How did you find out? Oh, God! my sin is found out, my punishment is upon me—I confess—I confess. There, take it, take it, it is all there; too late, too late for reparation, make proper use of it, take it," and he flung a heavily-sealed packet almost in my face, and then—swiftly pulling out a small phial from his coat pocket, he raised it to his mouth, and ere I could stay his hand, had drunk the contents, and, raising his hand upwards, said—

"God forgive me—pardon—I have atoned," and fell forward, face downwards, on the stone floor.

I need not dwell upon the horror I went through, when, in my headlong flight from the house, I stumbled blindly to the nearest police officer, and there, with hurried breath, I told of my visits to the empty house, by way of passing idle hours, and of my suddenly coming upon this man, with my exclamation— "Well?" which apparently startled him into giving up his guilty secret. I did *not* deem it necessary to tell of the little children, at least not to police, because they would, if not openly grin and deride me, most certainly have suggested to the nearest medical man that a young woman who moons about empty houses and sees ghosts was not a fit person to be unattended, so I kept my "dream babies" to myself, and one other.

To my unspeakable annoyance, I was dragged into the affair, and forced to give evidence as to the finding of the man and of his subsequent act—the taking his own life.

The sealed packet, being addressed to "The person who found him out," was, therefore, proved to belong to me, and to my unfortunate self fell the task of reading and making it known, and later, carrying out the instructions contained therein.

The confession of a man apparently driven to it by awful fear was a terrible thing to read, and for this story need only be put briefly. He wrote—

I write this my confession as the one atonement I can make for a sin which has rendered my life and the life of my son a living torture. I have travelled by land and sea, I have visited many strange lands, I have done all that mind could plan or money achieve, in a vain attempt to deaden the relentless voice of conscience or dull the sound of children weeping, which rings in my ears daylight or dark. Sleep is a friend unknown to me, save only drugged sleep. Joy or happiness I have never known.

If the sun shines, I remember the sunny garden and the children at play, ready to tremble if they heard my voice or that of my son.

If it rains, I remember the punishment room, where we tortured those innocent little ones. Nowhere can I rest, Oh, God! save in my grave, and only then, if I atone—

He relates how he was left by his brother, then in India, as guardian to these children of his, and how he and his son Roger made up their minds from the first to get the vast sum of money, left to the children, into their own hands; and, as later evidence proved, they treated the children with systematic cruelty, though no one suspected it—their torturing of them always taking place during late afternoon or evening hours, but during the day, when people were about, money was lavished upon the children, and a certain amount of care taken of them.

In his confession, he relates how he and his wretched son used to fasten the children to two high stools in the dismal room, and whip them until the blood ran from their little bodies. There was no one to shield them; his son and their nurse, as evil as himself, aided him in his cruelty, having been promised a large sum as soon as the children were safely disposed of.

The father of the children was killed in some Frontier trouble, soon after his return to his regiment, and the shock of his death reduced their mother to a helpless invalid who seldom left her own rooms, believing her little ones were in good hands.

They were always taken to see her at noon—their nurse watching them evilly, having threatened them with punishment if they "told tales."

Systematic cruelty was dealt out to these hapless babes, day by day, until one day, they were beaten so vilely, that both died from shock, and were found on the old couch in the toy-room clasped in each other's arms—dead.

Here his confession reaches frenzy, as he adds—

Together my son and I took the bodies we had so ill-used and flung them, into the old disused well in the sunk garden, where, I am certain, their spirits will haunt us all our days.

We told their mother that gipsies seen in the neighbourhood must have stolen them, and pretended to try and
find them, and use every available means, unavailingly. This
added grief killed the poor lady, leaving us to enjoy—if we
could—our ill-gotten gains.

My miserable son was killed in a motor accident, soon
after, and I—God knows!—a miserable haunted creature,
roam the earth seeking peace and finding none.

And finally, the hand of fate drew him back to the scene of
his crime, and he endeavoured to make reparation by leaving the
vast fortune he now possessed—

To benefit some children in whatsoever manner the finder
of this confession shall decide.

Many years have gone by, and a beautiful "Home for Convalescent Children" has taken the place of my "House of Mystery."
Upstairs, in gay, cheery rooms, are long rows of little, white beds.
Downstairs, in the "Room of Toys," are still more toys, and little
tots in dainty, blue overalls play, and grow strong and well.

In the "Punishment Room," now called "Matron's Room,"
sits a sunny-faced, gentle lady, ever ready to help her little ones,
and adored by her nurses.

In the sunk garden are swings and couches, and many games.
One corner of the garden has been opened out, and a high, grass
mound made there; on it is an exquisite white marble Angel,
holding in her arms two tiny children—that is all. No names or
dates are given—simply "In memory of two children."

Only once has the old story been brought vividly to my
memory. I was visiting the Home, and the night nurse, a sweet
motherly woman, asked me—

"Was there ever a story about this house, ma'am?"

"Why, nurse?" I asked.

"Oh, it may be fancy, ma'am," she replied, "but once or twice
I thought I heard a little child crying, but all my little ones were
asleep, and at times I've heard tiny pattering feet when none of
my babies were out of their beds; and once, ma'am, a woman

brought a tiny girl here, and the little thing had on a pair of wee scarlet shoes. That night, I heard soft, baby laughter and little chuckles of glee, and though I, myself, put those little shoes in a safe place, they had been moved by the morning, but this was before the beautiful white angel was put in the garden ma'am, just about the time the gardeners filled in that unsafe old well. I have not heard anything since then."

I gave no explanation, I could not, I only said—

"If all the babies sleep in peace nurse, all is well."

Outside the House

If I say I was just engaged to be married, you will forgive my thus intruding my own affairs for a moment because, through being engaged, I was led into the most curious happening of my life. I had been in France some two and a half years before the bit of shell met me, which landed me back in Blighty, with a leg that was not going to be of much more service to me. I had had many and varied experiences in France—horrors, of course—but of these we do not often speak, much of deep interest, and much which goes to the furthering of knowledge of many kinds— knowledge which has led thousands of men to get down to realities—and to shun for evermore the superficial shams which made up their existences before 1914—but this is not a war story, except in so far that it transformed me, an officer in a well-known regiment, into a very ordinary civilian, with a game leg, and fathoms deep in love with the sweet child who nursed me—Elsie Falconer was my nurse—in the stately Home of England in which I and my mangled leg found ourselves after a long, troublesome journey.

It was a home—there are many such, especially in the south of England—given up by their owners to needs of "wounded." Homes, where, in many cases gallant young heirs have laid down their lives for king and country, leaving none to inherit the stately borne which for so many generations had belonged to their honoured name— so it comes to pass, that the old house is metamorphosed into a well-equipped hospital, strict routine taking the place of former hunting, shooting, and careless living.

It was a wonderfully beautiful old grey stone house, with an old-world garden; no money was spared, no labour was withheld to make it what it was now, a well-worked comfortable happy hospital.

I had been there some six weeks in the hands of an austere but clever elderly nurse, before Elsie was given charge of me. She was a joy to look at, to talk to, to joke with—but, she was *not* a nurse—Some women are born nurses—some have nursing thrust upon them—and some achieve nursing— Elsie was none of these, but she was very sweet, very sympathetic, and it was a delight to watch her little fingers bandage my poor leg, though I would not for worlds have let her guess the agonies I endured until, in her time off, I could capture the sister, and beg a little relief, saying my bandages were not quite tight enough. Sister would smile, and being a sport, keep her own counsel.

It was an easy matter to step from sympathetic companionship into love-making—lots of us men have done it—perhaps some will find, to their sorrow, though each man says "That will not be me." Not the least pleasurable part of it was a friendship I formed in hospital with a man whom chance placed in the bed next to mine.

It was one of those friendships which come into some lives at the first meeting of the eyes, without a word spoken—something that makes one's innermost mind think the words, "At last!"—as if one knew that into one's life had come something hitherto wholly lacking. In this way came my friendship with Percy Hesketh, and as the weeks of our hospital life passed on, we drew even closer, making a compact that, if either should fall on the battlefield, he would endeavour to communicate with the other. The end of my third month in that stately home found me, with my discharge papers, a stiff leg, and a dear little girl, my promised wife.

Elsie did not wish to give up her nursing, so I agreed to wait patiently a while, and when she met me one morning armed with an invitation from her people to spend a month with them to convalesce—adding that she would take her holidays at home during the month—I felt that my lines had fallen in pleasant places.

It was the morning of my departure from the hospital that I noticed the first shadow I had ever seen on my little girl's face. I asked her what was the trouble, and her reply was somewhat vague. "I was wondering," she said, "how you will feel at my home."

"How I will feel?" I queried. "Why, how should I feel, except happy to be there."

"I hope so," was her somewhat vague response, as she walked away almost as if she didn't wish to say any more.

Later in the day, just before I started, she came to me, saying:

"John, you will try and like it all, won't you, for my sake, don't let anything worry you will you. Nothing can really do you any harm."

In the rush of getting away, her few words had not much effect—indeed it was not until some hours later, when my train slowed down at a little wayside station, and an elderly man in livery met me, that I remembered them, and driving along between high hedges of wild roses, honeysuckle and sweetness of many kinds, I failed to attach the least importance to those little words "nothing can *really* do you any harm." Did the little girl mean the jolting of rough roads for my poor leg, or what, I wondered. Then a sudden thought struck me.

Perhaps her people were not well off and she feared a little roughing it for my shattered health, but this thought was speedily banished, as we pulled up at a charming little black and white lodge, where a smiling woman opened a massive iron gate bearing a coat of arms in blue and gold. Elsie had not told me much of her home, or people, beyond that they were an old family and owned all the coalfields round about them. I had paid little or no attention at the time, for the girl—and not her people or position—was before all in my mind.

A long sheltered drive, between giant trees, presently brought us to a broad gravel sweep in front of a beautiful half-timbered house. I had scarcely time to see it, however, before I was hailed by a regular chorus of voices from a deep sunk lawn on the right of the house—it was curiously deep sunken. One is accustomed I suppose, to see a lawn stretching away level with the house or almost, but this one, which I later learnt was always spoken of as the low lawn, was at least five or six feet below the drive; it almost gave one a feeling that if it had been a lake—it would have looked prettier that way—one seemed to have to look too far below for it—the walks and flower-beds surrounding it were so high above it.

At one end of the lawn was a glorious copper beech, beneath which were grouped some seven or eight people near a tea-table, lavishly spread—for war days.

Two people detached themselves from the group and came to meet me—an elderly man with iron grey hair and slightly bent back, and a slim dark-haired girl, perhaps three or four years older than my Elsie. My welcome was warm, as warm as man could desire from the father of the girl he loved, though, man-like, few words were spoken, a firm hand-grip, a keen look, and then—

"I am very glad John to welcome the man our little girl has given her heart to. This is Maude, Elsie's sister."

Maude favoured me with a quick scrutinizing glance, shook hands and turned away to a school-boy brother, who had followed close on her heels.

My ears, keenly sensitive through long nights on O.P. duties, caught the few words she murmured to him, as she met him.

"*He'll* never stand it, Bob, he isn't the sort, but mum's the word."

Bob glanced back at me, and then shook off the sisterly hand on his shoulder, and came up to me with a boyish grin.

"Game leg, Sir? Sorry, lean on me, and come down the steps to Mater and some tea."

"Right! many thanks," was my reply in the same spirit. "I'll be glad of some tea; it's been my first journey since the horrible one back to Blighty."

"Rotten luck, Sir," went on the young voice, "you'll tell me about it sometime, won't you?"

"Not much honour and glory about it, Bob," I replied.

"But you've got a ribbon, Sir, a purple and white ribbon; I know that wasn't got with sitting still in a funk-hole!"

"No, not exactly," I replied laughing, "but lots of chaps who will never get it, have earned that bit of ribbon better than I did. I'll tell you some other time, if you like."

He nodded his head and said—

"Mater, this is Elsie's John, dying for some tea."

"Mater" made the usual little fuss mothers do make, when something in khaki steals into her flock, and wants one of her lambs, and I was soon in a comfortable chair, my game leg on another, while I was refreshed with tea, war scones, honey, and strawberries as I surveyed the rest of the group—Mr. and Mrs. Falconer, Maude, Bob, a Captain McKlean and his sister Nora, staying in the house, a fair-haired girl in a dark severe-looking frock, whom I subsequently learned had charge of the three boisterous younger members of the family; the Rev. L Roberts, a middle-aged man, who had evidently dropped in for a cup of tea, and the three young members, who lay sprawled on the grass beside their mother—Lottie a cherub, aged six, with red-gold hair, and impish blue eyes, Alec and Ken, twins, just at the knickerbockers stage and brimming over with every conceivable mischief—composed the group, of which, for the moment, I found myself the centre.

Talk drifted along from war to rations, and back again; from battles to the keeping of pigs, and the price of eggs; from the scarcity of jam; to my purple and white ribbon; and so on, from grave to gay, until the sun, hitherto blazing in glory on lawn and flower beds, gradually began to sink behind the trees, in a pink glow, that lit up the house as if a pink limelight were thrown upon it. I was intently watching it, enjoying the beauty of it, when my attention was arrested by a sudden move among the group of people, as if with one accord they were seized with the same idea at the same moment.

Mrs. Falconer got up, and trailed away with her knitting in

her hand, her ball of wool dragging behind her, I made a move to retrieve it, but was stopped by Bob saying—

"Don't worry, Sir, if you begin, you'll never stop. Mother's things always trail after her, they arrive at the house in time; we never bother." He softly kicked the ball of wool on its way, with a sly wink at me, adding—

"That's how they get there, unless the twins walk off with them in another direction, among the trees; it's a wonder they didn't spot it; oh! they've cleared, I might have known; it's getting late."

"Late!" I said. "Why it's only just after five!"

"I mean late for the garden," he said.

"Late for the garden?" I asked. "Why, it's the loveliest time in a garden now, when the heat dies down, and the air is all perfume."

"Maybe in most gardens," he replied, "but this isn't one of them."

"Why it's perfect," I said.

"That's all right, Sir, but I wouldn't stay too long, it gets— er—damp and—er—well damp," he said, stuffing his hands in his pockets, as he strolled away whistling.

"It seems an interesting place, Mr. Roberts," I said, turning to face the parson. "I do not know this part of the country at all, perhaps you'll light a pipe, and tell me about my surroundings."

The parson got to his feet—hurriedly, awkwardly—blew his nose violently, and said—

"Yes, yes, my dear major, I shall be most delighted, any time— er—that is, any *other* time, but now I must hurry away, my parish, you see, my work, er—my duties—you'll come and see my library, yes, yes, a fine collection. Goodbye, come very soon,— er—goodbye." And his long lean figure was scuttling over the lawn ere I had managed to gasp a reply.

A circle of empty chairs, a tableful of empty plates, myself, and little Miss Dorcas, the governess, only remained. She was sewing "Comforts bags" for wounded men—the joy of the Tommys' hearts. If *only* more people who can sew, would get on and make thousands more! I lit a cigarette and then said—

"Are you vanishing also, Miss Dorcas?"

"I suppose so," she answered.

"Won't you stay and talk a bit?" I asked. "You see I have to sit still most of my time."

"You will be more comfortable in the smoke-room, or billiard-room," she said, still intent upon her sewing.

"I couldn't be," I said. "A garden like this, a comfy chair, my pipe, and a warm July evening; it doesn't appeal to me to leave it for a billiard-room."

"No," she said, "not yet, but it will."

"Oh! I must go," rising as she spoke, and hurried away folding her work. "You will come in when you've had enough, I suppose."

"Enough what?" I asked, smiling.

"Enough garden," she answered, as she hurried away, leaving me the now sole survivor of the cheery group I had come into, not two hours ago.

Idly I lay back in my chair, puffing away at my war-worn pipe, the drowsy hum of insects lulled me, the scent of flowers soothed, the silence rested my tired nerves and body. I didn't particularly want to think, but my mind kept wondering what was the need of all these good folks to hurry away to other occupations, one and all leaving their rather crippled guest, without apparently a thought as to how I should get my lame leg up the deep grass steps and into the house later. I wished Elsie had been here, but she had decided to come in a few days, leaving me to get to know her family without her helpful influence.

Well! I must make the best of it; at least, I could rest and enjoy the peace of it all. I did my best to go to sleep, but signally failed, though nothing could be more perfect than my surroundings for such a mode of passing a little of the time I seemed destined to spend alone. It was gloriously, warm, and I was pleased to find no trace of damp, such as I had feared, and which would certainly necessitate my moving. No, it certainly was *not* damp, of that I was sure, *then what was it?* For it *was* something, though what I meant by *it,* I haven't the remotest idea. I felt confused, surely I must be sleepy, for my mind, usually alert, seemed dulled, almost as if I were once again under the noxious influence of morphia, as I lay in my chair endeavouring to collect wits that appeared to have a tendency to become scattered, I saw coming across the lawn an elderly man-servant. He approached the tea-table, and with one eye on me, stolidly began to clear away the tea-things. Then he coughed, and hesitatingly said to me—

"Are you thinking of going in, Sir? Can I help you?"

"Well, I wasn't," I replied, "but perhaps I will, if you will give me an arm, when you have cleared away. I am not in any hurry."

"Very good, Sir, but I'll help you first if you wish, though it is getting a bit late."

"Late!" The same word, and again I asked—

"Late—for what?"

"Late—er—for the teacups, Sir," he replied.

"For the teacups!" I said, astonished.

"Yes, Sir, I mustn't be late." Saying which, he gathered them up on his large tray, and set off with his load. He hadn't gone more than five or six yards when he appeared to stumble or slip, staggered to recover himself, and the tray and china crashed to the ground.

"There," he gasped, amidst the wreckage, "I knew it was late."

I regret to say my first feeling was one of idiotic merriment, something about the old man, amidst the debris of china and odds and ends of food, struck a latent sense of 'humour in me, and I laughed unrestrainedly. Not so the worthy butler,—he, with an expression, that baffles description, slowly rose and stood staring at the broken china for the space of a full minute, before turning to me, as if to reprove my merriment. I frustrated him, by saying—

"I am sorry to laugh at you, but 'over there' we somehow learnt to laugh at calamities, and it seemed to help."

"Very good, Sir," he answered stiffly, "I understand, but it isn't *funny,* Sir, not leastways what *I* call funny."

"No," I said, "I can see your point of view. I suppose it means censure for breaking good china."

"No, Sir, it isn't that, for it isn't good china, it's cheap—because any delay means a smash, and we're late today, as I said."

"I fail to understand you, my good man," I answered, "I've seen many queer incidents lately, but I can't see why the clearing of a few tea-things from a garden table should mean they will be smashed if left late, though it is but 5.30 now."

"Quite true, Sir. May I help you in now?" he said.

"Won't you remove the smash first?" I asked. "No, Sir," was his emphatic reply. "I will not, *they* wait till morning, they do."

I shrugged my shoulders, feeling the hopelessness of it—the old man must surely have a slate off. I would perhaps hear further of the smash later. Meantime, I was conscious of a wish for a more cheery spot, so turning to the old butler, remarked—

"I will try the steps now if you will give me an arm, but I cannot go quickly."

"No, Sir," he replied, "you certainly cannot, leastways not here, and we'll maybe get there sooner by going slower."

As an Irishman, that speech appealed to me, and I chuckled as we started our crawl towards the steps. True, I was compelled to move slowly, but I certainly had every intention of moving at least as quickly as I had been able to do during the last few weeks. This, however, was far from the case, some inexplicable "Something" retarded my every step! I found myself trying to put into words my inability to get along, in a joking way. I said to the worthy butler—

"I must have grown stiff sitting still so long, I feel as if my feet were unable to carry me."

"Quite so, Sir," he answered, imperturbably, "lean on me, Sir."

I did, but speedily found I was trusting to a broken reed, for the man stumbled at every other step. To an onlooker we must have had every appearance of a couple of very drunken reprobates struggling home after a wildly dissipated night, and not, as we were, a worn soldier with a game leg, leaning for support on the shoulder of a worthy grey-haired family retainer, crossing a little space of smooth green turf, leaving behind us a heap of smashed china! If I had been asked to describe that march, I should have said—

"Oh yes! I am aware that I was said to be walking across a smooth expanse of velvety lawn, without so much as a croquet hoop to trip me up, but seemingly I was struggling through a close tangle of strong briars, which entwined themselves round me as if they were endowed with sense, and each successive one was struggling to twist and pull harder than the other. That was my impression; yet, on that expanse of smooth green, there was not a single item to suggest such a state of affairs. Slowly, slowly, inch by inch, with the perspiration streaming from us, we reached at last the steps, mounted the first, and were confronted by a heavy pressure, as if to force us back.

"Stick to it, Sir," whispered the old man. And we did, but it took all my limited strength and his combined, to press through that invisible barrier, and finally reach the top. The presence relaxed then suddenly, and I breathed more freely, nor did it need the butler's muttered "Hurry in, now, Sir," to urge me to the greatest speed my exhausted frame was capable of.

I entered the hall, with a word of thanks to my worthy friend, who disappeared in haste through a baize door, mopping his face.

I dropped into the nearest chair, feeling far more done than I ever remembered feeling after long hours in the trenches, and was content to lie back with my eyes shut, until I heard a mocking voice say—

"Drink this, John, you'll be all square in a minute."

I wearily drank what was offered to me, opening my eyes to see the slightly quizzical face of Maude looking at me.

"Thanks!" I murmured, "it's a trying day."

"Very," she responded, "in the garden. I watched you coming in. Rest a few minutes, and then I will take you to the others. They are in our *indoor* garden; we prefer it. Then she went away, leaving me to rest. I must have dozed for a few brief moments for again I did not hear her. until she spoke, in a voice that, to my sensitive ears, still had a mocking note—

"Come along, John, you are quite alive, you know, come to the others."

She helped me up, with a good strong pull,—the kind of pull our young women are beginning to acquire since they metaphorically took their coats off, and gave up fancy work and crochet for making shells, milking cows, and tilling the land—and having got me on to my feet, she calmly tucked my arm through hers, saying, laughing—

"Elsie won't mind, you know." And led me down a long stone corridor with a broad crimson carpet running down the centre, a few old coaching scenes on the walls, one or two heavy oak chairs on either side, and in each of the two windows an old-fashioned flower-stand filled with flowering plants.

"What a ripping corridor!" I said.

"Yes," she answered, "it's rather nice, but this is nicer," she added, throwing open a big glass door and drawing me forward into what I can best describe as a gigantic greenhouse, though Maude's words of "our indoor garden," more aptly describes it. It was immense, having a dome-shaped roof, painted a clear pale blue. Three sides of the place were of glass, through which lovely views were seen, the fourth side was an exquisitely painted landscape of a hayfield and trees stretching away into the distance. For a moment one scarcely realised whether one was looking at real scenes or painted ones, or where one began and the other ended. Clumps of shrubs here and there made secluded corners, where cosy chairs and couches were placed.

A hammock was slung under another tree—one side of the place was trelliswork, with glorious roses rambling over it, and everywhere were flowers or flowering plants. The ground was dull green, like a solid linoleum; in one corner clock golf was marked out; Badminton occupied another place, and under an orange tree was a large round table, with writing materials and many magazines; the dome top could be worked by pulleys and rolled back, the whole idea giving one the atmosphere of a lovely foreign garden.

All the family were present, though each seemed intent on

his or her occupation and no one seemed to have the remotest thought of leaving it for a stroll in the garden *outside,* though a most perfect summer evening was vainly calling.

An hour ago I should unhesitatingly have said they were cranks, or had bees in their bonnets, but now—well—I was not sure what I truly thought.

"Won't you come and sit down, John?" called Mrs. Falconer.

"Thanks!" I said, "I was feeling rather struck in a heap, this is such an unusual greenhouse."

"It isn't a greenhouse," chimed in a little shrill voice, "it's a 'ninside garding, come and see 'noranges," and a moist chubby hand was thrust into my hand.

"I'm very tired, Lottie," I said, "may I come in a minute?"

"That's just like grown-ups," lisped the little kiddie, "vey always say, 'in a minute'—they forgets."

Mrs. Falconer smiled, and patted the chair at her side saying—

"Run away, Lottie, John's tired."

"John is,", I answered, gladly sinking into the cushioned chair. "Why am I tired, Mrs. Falconer?" I asked. "What is the meaning of it all?"

"All what?" she asked blankly.

"The garden," I said, "the difficulty of coming in."

"You've been asleep," she said, "and got stiff."

"And the broken tea-things," I went on.

"Oh! that's Jacobs, he's always having smashes." And the good lady went on placidly knitting her soldier's socks.

Nothing to be learnt there, I thought, as I started chatting about the lovely "garden" in which we sat.

"It's like a wonderful Winter Garden," I said.

"It is," she smiled, "only it's a summer garden as well, after five o'clock."

"Maude!" she called suddenly, as if remembering, "you haven't fed the birds. I'll do it myself." And she moved away, wool as usual trailing in her wake.

I was left to my own devices once more. What an unconventional crowd they were, or is it, they don't want to talk, I was wondering idly as I smoked a cigarette when Bob sidled up to the vacant chair and perched himself upon its arm.

"You'll come in earlier tomorrow, Sir, won't you?" he asked half-shyly, "it kind of knocks one about to stay late."

But I was going to play the same game as others, so answered casually—

"Oh! does it? It didn't knock me about."

"Didn't it, Sir? It did Jacobs," he added slyly, "he's what he calls 'all of a dither.'"

"I saw nothing to 'dither' about," I said.

"No, Sir, I daresay you didn't, but it isn't what you *see* that does it.

"And I most certainly didn't *hear* anything odd," I went on.

"I hope you won't, Sir, I did once, and (lowering his voice) I had brain fever afterwards. You won't catch me out after five."

"Bob, come here, I want you," rang out Maude's compelling voice.

"Oh! blow!" muttered the boy, "they are dead scared for fear I tell you, and you cut off and leave Elsie." With which cryptic 'give away' of his relations he strolled off, hands in pockets. Once more I was alone, and content to be so, to light another cigarette and have a review of the rapid sequence of events—my arrival, tea, the sudden scattering of the group beneath the trees, the broken china and my desperate attempt to cross a few yards of turf. I could not make "head nor tail" of any of it—sufficient for me I was in love and prepared to put up with a good deal to await the coming of the little girl I loved. My musings were interrupted by the sound of a bell in the distance.

"Dressing-bell, John," shouted someone. "I'll help you to your room," called Bob.

"Many thanks, I'll be glad," I said, "I—I'm not very good at stairs alone."

"You aren't upstairs, you're on this floor, Pater thought you'd like it, though I'm blessed if I should—too near the garden for this child to—hang on, Sir, I'm pretty tough."

73

Together we traversed again the long stone corridor, through the hall, along a similar corridor, but of more recent date, being of polished pine, instead of grey stones.

Bob opened a door about half-way down, saying—

"There you are, I hope you'll like it—shout, I mean ring, if you want things. Neither Mum nor Dad ever remember visitors."

"Right," I said, "but I'll manage," turning as I spoke to open the window.

"I wouldn't, Sir," said the lad, "it's beastly—er—damp—"

There were three windows in my spacious bedroom, two on one side, one at a queer angle, in a built-out corner, this latter was heavily shuttered, barred up and padlocked.

"Great guns!" I cried, "Who on earth are you expecting to get in—it's like being walled in— where does it look out? If it's ever opened!"

"It's opened till five p.m.," said the lad, "and it looks on to the low lawn. I'd leave it at that, Sir, it I were you." And he edged himself through the door.

"Alone again!" I thought, lighting the inevitable cigarette. What an extraordinary family they seemed to be, so detached, as it were so self-absorbed, but above all, so skilful at playing into each other's hands—even the smallest of them aiding in the now apparent determination of each one not to remain alone with their wounded guest, and future relative! Why? I wondered. What did they fear? This last thought was a subconscious one, for I had not hitherto consciously thought of *fear* in any form. Well, time would reveal perhaps, meantime, it was a fresh interest—an unusual interest to find myself a guest in a unique house, full of unique people, all doing their best to keep me from finding out "Something"—well—"Something" that so far hadn't a name—it would amuse me to circumvent them, and help to pass the days until my girl came.

And now to dress for another scene; the scenes were certainly following one another in rather rapid succession—perhaps too rapidly for a "convalescent" and yet, I have a firm and fixed belief that the quickest way for a sick person to become a well one, is to keep the mind occupied, busy, interested, to fill up the days and hours, leaving no time for brooding, or speculation as to the why or wherefore of one's apparent slow healing; thoughts of health bring health, just as quickly as brooding melancholy brings depression, and subsequent ills in its train. It has been truthfully said, that the wounded lads who have recovered best are those whose outlook has been buoyant and cheery, those of whom "even a swamp did not depress them," as Mark Tapley would have said. My days certainly gave promise of being full enough.

I had finished my leisurely dressing to the running accompaniment of this train of thought, just as a silver chime of low notes rang through the house. "Pretty" I thought, "and much better than the boom of the orthodox family gong, which always suggested to me the dullest of meals." No one seemed to be passing my way, no cheery voice called out to me their offer of escort. Very well, I would find my own way, since it did not appear to have struck anyone that so far I had not been in any room other than the "Indoor Garden"—if it could be called a room, or that I had not any idea of my bearings.

I switched off the light in my room, and started to locate the dining room. I need not have hesitated, for the whole family were gathered in the Hall, talking, laughing, and in high spirits. There were not any other guests, simply a family party. The Hall was beautifully lighted from above by reflected lights—I mean the actual lights were not visible. The windows—there were three—were heavily draped in a light shade of gold, almost giving the idea of sunlight, as they caught the light from above. I am not a great hand at these things, sufficient to say the place gave one a feeling of brightness and comfort, without glare or striking colour.

I was nodded to as if I were one of them, as with one accord, we moved away to the dining-room. Probably I was expecting the usual sombre dining-room of an ancient family mansion— oak furniture, sideboard like a silver-smith's window, family portraits in gilt frames—but whatever I expected, it certainly was not the gay room in which I now found myself. There were not any pictures, nor did one miss them, for the walls were painted a shade of deep cream, with exquisite flowers, in groups, and sprays upon them; the chairs were of some highly-polished light wood— in appearance like a bird's eye maple—in place of the usual dado round the room, was a curved in recess, filled with plants and flowers with tiny electric lights among them here and there, deftly shaded by foliage and flowers. The dinner-table was a blaze of wild flowers, spotless linen, and shining glass.

I was slightly breathless as I took my seat. Mrs. Falconer smiled, and I explained my rather gasping condition, by saying—

"Your rooms do take a man's breath away, Mrs. Falconer, they seem to transport one into a fairyland of flowers."

"Yes," she said, "I hope they do. You see—" and she hesitated a second—"we cannot enjoy them outside the house, as most people can, so we have them and a gardener inside."

"I should miss a garden," I said bluntly.

"You wouldn't, miss *ours*," she said, as she turned away to speak to Bob on her other side.

I enjoyed my dinner, which was perfect in a simple way, and in the glory of that room of flowers, I did not notice, not until when next I found myself in my own room, that, on an August evening, I had dined in a room hermetically sealed, as far as an open window or fresh air was concerned. Later we gathered again in the Indoor Garden for smokes, games and music. There was not any drawing-room which also delighted me, as I have a wholesome horror of those abominable apartments with their set chairs, cushions of silk only to be looked at. Silver table— neither use nor ornament,—and corners filled with framed photographs of friends, so-called, for whom you care nothing at all, do not miss, and whose pictures you often keep in a drawer until a day when they come to call, when you at once put the right set out, trusting to luck that no one will give you away, though occasionally they have been known to do so!

It was about 9.40 when the sudden need of some fresh air

seized me with uncontrollable longing. I had lived in the air so long, it was impossible for me I felt to remain shut up indoors, especially as there seemed an unwritten law forbidding the opening of windows anywhere. I was idly wondering how I could best escape to smoke a quiet pipe in the fresh air, before turning in, when my worthy father-in-law to be dropped into a chair beside me.

"Getting tired, John?" he asked. "I should turn in early if I were you, we are all early-to-bed folks here."

"No thanks," I replied, "I'm not tired, I was admiring that painted view of the far end of this lovely place, though I should have thought glass on all sides would have better carried out your idea. What would the view be if that end were also glass?

"It all depends upon the time of day," was his reply. "In the morning it would show you the garden, the Low Lawn," he said, "but—now for instance—well, it wouldn't, or if it did, you would rather not see it."

He left me no chance to comment on his explanation, merely stated the fact, leaving me to make of it what I chose.

I didn't make much, needless to say, except to make up my mind more firmly to fathom what they were fast leading me to look upon as a "Mystery," and as I have the healthy Englishman's dislike of mysteries, I did not intend it to be one for longer than I could manage.

"Very well," I thought, "independence is my attitude henceforth, for when I came to think of it, I had been led, influenced, ringed about, as it were in an unobtrusive kind of way ever since my arrival a few hours ago. We would see!"

I rose, shook out my pipe, strolling away as I did so, to where the piano stood under a bank of roses. Maude was playing soft snatches of rag-times. Bob was lounging by her side, Mrs. Falconer nodding over her knitting close beside Mr. Falconer who was reading, while Captain McKlean and his sister Nora, with whom I had not so far had any conversation, were idly knocking the clock golf ball about.

"Come along, John, and sing," said Maude, breaking into the

old familiar "Long, long trail." "All soldiers sing this, so begin."

"I'm not just in singing form at the moment," I replied, "and I'm a little tired. I'm just going to smoke a pipe out of doors, before I turn in, was my calm announcement. But, had I dropped a bomb in the midst of them, the effect of my few words could not have been more startling. Mr Falconer dropped his paper, with a muttered "God bless my soul!" Maude crashed into a jumble of wrong notes; Bob said but one word—"Golly!" and Captain McKlean and his sister dropped their putters, joining the little circle hurriedly. Mrs. Falconer woke—I don't mean she merely opened her eyes—she seemed suddenly galvanised, as she rose, saying—

"John, as my future son-in-law, I ask you *not* to leave the house tonight!" There was a tense silence for a brief second, but I was determined.

"I'm sorry, Mrs. Falconer, but I see no reason to comply with such a curious request. I am a soldier accustomed to be out and about in all weathers. I am *not* a hot-house plant, and if I do not breathe some fresh air, I shall neither rest nor sleep; my little evening walk is my best sedative, and I must ask your kind indulgence of my whim—Fresh *air* I must have."

Bob's was the sole reply—

"If you could get it fresh, Sir, it would be all right."

Mrs. Falconer seated herself again, without further words. Mr. Falconer had disappeared.

I bowed, wished them all "Goodnight," moving way feeling like anything but an *honoured!* guest. I wended my way back to the hall; it was empty, so, slipping on a coat and my hat, I made for the front door, beneath the golden curtains. I pulled one back and stared idiotically at the solid wall beneath it; there wasn't the faintest suggestion of a door, yet I had entered by one— that, I knew. I walked all round. An unbroken carved cedar wood panelling ran right round to a depth of four feet.

There wasn't a chink nor an opening, except the way to my sleeping corridor and the stone passage I had just come along. I felt as if I should lose my temper in a minute, but determined as I was, I retraced my steps to the Indoor Garden, meaning to ask where was the door, or any door. I reached the place only to find it dark, silent, empty; one and all must have gone to their rooms by some other way, probably suspecting exactly what *had* happened, *would* happen. Annoyed and irritated at being thus foiled in my desire, I had no choice but to go to my bedroom. The whole house seemed sunk in the silence of sleep, though it was but 10.30, and I shut my door with a rather vicious slam that echoed and re-echoed along the corridor.

"Now for my windows," I murmured, "for a breath of fresh air I must and will have—"

"Futile wish! unattainable longing! my windows were thick plate glass, minus fastening of any description—"Foiled again!" I murmured, as I began a minute inspection of the iron-shuttered window, which was some three or four feet above the floor, with a broad window-sill. A bit of a risk to get on to that I thought, with a lame leg. I'd best leave it for tonight, but it worried me to be beaten—so with a good deal of pain, I dragged myself up on to a chair, from whence I could at least feel and inspect the shutter. My inspection brought forth a prolonged whistle! I had discovered a weak point—true it was padlocked—but the hasp through which the padlock passed was thin, and needed only a good file and a steady hour's work to cut it through, when, so far as I could see, the shutter could be rolled back to its socket.

"Right-o!" I said gaily, "that is for tomorrow. Tomorrow, I will buy or steal a file, and then—"

Feeling more settled in my mind now, I got into my bed, determined on two points—tomorrow would see that window open, and that I would to all intents, play the game, nor appear conscious of what was an actual fact, that after 5 p.m., I an able-bodied—or fairly so—member of H.M. Forces, was a prisoner.

I did not expect to sleep, lacking fresh air, but as I got into bed, the coolest breeze blew round me, and I noticed for the first time, that at either end of the room, high up, were steel electric fans, moving silently and rapidly.

"Then the 'Prisoner' isn't to smother," I thought, as I dropped into a profound sleep.

I awoke feeling rested, refreshed and fit, in spite of a night of closed windows, to which I was quite unaccustomed; tea was brought to me at 7.30 and I rose, feeling ready for whatever the day might bring; it was not going to bring my little girl, alas! though she hoped to be with me within the next day or two. In my heart was a lingering feeling that it was just as well, for she might, probably would have, interfered with my plans. I joined the family party in the hall a little before nine. All were in the best of form, the hall door stood wide open though I carefully refrained from taking any apparent notice of the fact.

Breakfast was served in the dining-room, which had undergone a slight change—there were fewer plants, fewer flowers, and two large windows were thrown wide open to the sun and air. The same detached spirit was plainly seen, as last night, all were intent upon their own devices. It struck me as unusual that the three guests—one of them a cripple—should not be consulted in the smallest degree, as to their tastes, ideas or wishes for the day. Not a single comment was made as to the previous day, its doings, or the evening of it. It gave one a feeling that "sufficient for the day" was a saying ably carried out. I waited for a kindly suggestion, such as—"Would I care to drive? Would I prefer a lounge in the garden?" *Nothing,* however, was forthcoming, so I asked blandly—

"McKlean, are you coming to smoke a pipe in the garden?"

"Captain McKlean is coming with me," answered Maude. "I have to go to town for some things."

"Town," I might mention, was a small market town, called Singletown, consisting of a main street, a bank, and in the high street, varied shops of a small mixed kind, and boasting quite a good ironmonger's, a lending library and hospital, up to date.

Now this began to look awkward, obviously *I* should be *de trop,* yet reach that ironmongers I must and will.

"I wonder if you would take a passenger to town, as well?" I asked. "I have a little shopping to do, and cannot walk far."

"We are only going to be an hour," replied Maude. "Can't I

shop for you?"

"Sorry!" I said, "I am afraid not."

I knew in her heart Maude was hating me for a spoil sport, but I had to get that file, so at the risk of being voted a nuisance, I smilingly asked again to be taken.

I was taken, but I knew in every fibre of my being I was all that I feared, a spoil sport. I had to put my feelings in my pocket, and when duly dropped at the best stationers, slipped from there into the ironmonger's without delay, the moment their backs were turned. Joyfully I selected three good files, stowing them away in an inner pocket, while ostentatiously carrying a library book and packet of stationery as well as a box of toffee—of a war kind—as a peace offering for the huffy lady. We reached the house again, well before lunch-time.

As before, I was struck with the total lack of exchange of news, none seemed to know or care what the other had been doing; it was perhaps as well, for I might now spend my time as best suited me, irrespective of anyone else.

I was deep in thought when Mrs. Falconer made the only remark as to any arrangement.

"Tea will be on the Low Lawn, John, at four o'clock. We all come in at five."

"Oh! do we?" I thought. "Well I for one don't. I'm not being imprisoned a second time, from five until bedtime, if I can help it." So I just murmured—

"Thanks, I will have a rest first and join you there for tea."

Then I sought my room, ostensibly to rest, in reality to study the lie of the land, and the iron shutter. I carefully made a mental study of the position of the house, its windows, their outlook, and so on, as I went to my room. I hated my room, hated its big shut-up windows, hated its ugly iron one, above all hated the imprisoned atmosphere of it. I studied the view from those windows. They overlooked a walled fruit garden, beyond which stretched a belt of trees. I craned my neck, squirming violently in my endeavour to locate the part of the grounds the iron window would overlook; finding by my memorized plan of house and grounds that as it was a jutting out angle of the house, it would, as I more than half expected, command an uninterrupted view of the low lawn.

"What a pity I could not begin my work now," I thought, "and have a view of that lawn about 5.30." But alas! that could not be. Very well, I would endeavour to possess my soul in patience, meaning to retire early on a plea of tiredness, I spent an hour on the couch in my room, dozing lightly under the pretence of reading, and 3.30 found me wending my steps to the Low Lawn but with a dire thought in my mind—

"Suppose my iron window should be barricaded outside as well!"

I had not long joined the group on the lawn before my misgivings were put to rest. I had spotted the iron windows, also immediately above it a similar one, it was an odd angle in a house, though, if left *as* windows, might have made an attractive corner in the rooms. I would for once, question, but whom? Mrs. Falconer would rise grandiloquently to the occasion flooring me with a single terse reply, that was a foregone conclusion. Maude, not yet having forgiven my intrusion in the morning, would probably loftily disdain to reply at all. Bob was most accessible, so I rose stiffly from my chair, saying—

"Come and be kind, Bob, my leg is worrying me and needs a little gentle exercise. Will you lend me that strong shoulder of yours, in return for a war yarn?"

"Won't I just," he answered, springing to his feet, and placing himself ready for my encircling arm to rest along his shoulders. I kept my promise during three turns slowly up and down the lawn I spun out my yarn a little, making it end about the centre of the lawn as we faced the house.

"Half a second, old man," I then said. "I must have a breath." We stood, and I gazed at the house.

"Jolly old place," I said.

"Yes," he answered. "Are you ready, sir?"

"In a jiff," I replied. "I'm trying if I am clever enough to spot my room. I'll bet you a bob I can."

"Right!" said the lad, all eagerness now. "Try, sir."

I made one or two feeble shots, which were received with yells of derision.

"I give it up," I said at length. "You've won your bob, so tell me."

"Why, there," he cried, pointing, there with the blank window looking this way, with another window like it higher up.

"Of course," I said, "how dense of me. I remember now— that dull window spoils the pretty room."

"Might spoil it more, sir, if it wasn't dull," he replied.

"Oh, I don't think so, Bob," I went on, "look what a picture the lawn would be from it."

"A pretty picture—I *don't* think! I guess you'd jolly quick pack up your traps and quit, if you saw the pretty picture, sir."

"Look here, Bob," I began, in wheedling tones, "let's be chums, and you tell me all about that picture in return for my yarn."

Scornfully the young voice answered me.

"I didn't think you were a rotter, sir. I thought you were a sport, but a *real* sport would see this old shop is dad's nightmare and play the game. I'm a boy scout, sir, and I try to play the game, it isn't the game for a soldier to try and make a scout fail to be a sport."

Humbly, I begged his pardon, feeling about three inches high as I did so, and wondering what his opinion would be of me if it transpired that I had broken open the window—though I hoped to defy detection. In silence we retraced our steps, but I had fallen from my high estate in Bob's eyes, and could feel I was not any longer a hero, even with a purple and white ribbon—so do our youthful judges censure and condemn!

Tea was somewhat more of a rag than previous meals, possibly because little Miss Dorcas, with her three charges, joined us at tea, though their other meals were taken in the seclusion of the schoolroom.

I was keeping a furtive eye on my wristwatch, and wondering which of the party would make the first move, when I saw Mrs.

Falconer nod to Miss Dorcas, who promptly rose, calling the children to come as she went. I wondered by what means such obedience had been taught and enforced since nine out of every ten children would have begged for "just ten more minutes." "The kiddies trot in early," I remarked, to no one in particular.

"You bet," answered Bob, "they always go through the fruit garden to the schoolroom, and if they get there before the sun leaves the apricot wall, they can pick one—you bet they don't miss!"

I smiled, thinking to myself how apt it all was—seemingly so natural—though every move was planned.

Maude and the McKleans were the next to go—Maude talking volubly about finishing the badminton set begun last evening.

They had barely gone before old Jacobs hurried up—this time with a trim maid in attendance—the two cleared the tea things, and departed without loss of time. There was not to be any delay this evening, that was plain.

Mr. and Mrs. Falconer only remained, they were going to sit me out, so to speak! I would alter that plan. I rose, saying— "Might I, too, venture in search of an apricot."

Mrs. Falconer—a barely perceptible shade of relief flashing over her face—answered—

"Yes, surely, and go in by the schoolroom door, from there you can join us in the Indoor Garden."

Mr. Falconer rose, as if to accompany me, but his wife's glance restrained him, evidently it was a little further than even they could, with courtesy, go—to accompany a guest to the fruit garden, as if fearing wholesale robbing of fruit trees. So I was permitted to go alone.

My idea was, of course, to visit the fruit garden, but *not* to enter the schoolroom door, joining the caged-up company, from then onwards, until bedtime. Oh! no, I was merely going to get an apricot—dawdle a while until the coast was clear and retrace my steps, almost to the low lawn, but instead of descending to it, skirt right round the top of it, and so indoors, when I felt disposed.

I reached the fruit garden, took my apricot, waved gaily to little Lottie in the window—disregarded the beckoning hand of little Miss Dorcas, who was gazing at me through the long window, with almost a look of fear in her dark eyes, and retraced my steps to the path which led right round the sunk lawn.

I walked along it on the far side from the steps leading down into it, half-way along past the group of fine trees, where the tea was usually put. I paused—paused because I *had* to—I knew that, but tried not to think it. I wasn't exactly held up, nor was I conscious of briars tripping me up as last night—I had merely stopped—stopped to breathe. Yes, that was it, only I wasn't out of breath—there just wasn't anything *to* breathe; foolishly I found myself saying this idiotic sentence over and over again "not out of breath, but nothing *to* breathe."

I had been once in a gas-cloud in France, but this wasn't like that. *This* was like nothing; 'I struggled a few more yards, and gazed. The house seemed to have receded, the lawn seemed further below me, and appeared veiled in a bluish haze, thicker and thicker it seemed to get, and as I gazed, I fancied I could discern swiftly, hurrying forms moving to and fro. I struggled on again, intent only on reaching the house. As I advanced, the bluish fog dosed round me, shutting me in, in an impenetrable wall. In vain I struggled, in vain I peered; at last, even beating the fog with my hands, as if to force a passage through. Nothing availed me, and ever and *anon* I could see the hurrying forms below me. Terror struck me!

Would that I were safely in the Indoor Garden with its warmth and light and beauty, instead of here, enveloped in fog with other forms of which I dared not think, hurrying below me. Would that I had been guided instead of going my own obstinate way. Vain were such repinings now. The shapes seemed more defined, the atmosphere more dense. Feebly, I struggled to see the time by my luminous watch—Eight o'clock! Have I been wandering here so long—it seemed incredible! I must, and will, reach the house, but now I seemed to have lost the house, all trace of it had vanished.

Last night I grumbled that I was a prisoner— indoors. To-night I was to be kept "Outside the House."

Denser and denser grew the appalling thickness of the air. I feared to move a yard in advance "If only it would lift a little, just enough to enable me to go forward in safety." Even as I spoke, the atmosphere grew perceptibly clearer. I took one step forward, to find myself standing on the edge of a precipice or what seemed like one. I was now facing the sunk lawn— sunk indeed!—for it seemed far, far below me, with a drop from where I was standing of I dare not contemplate what depth, where shapes were ever hurrying to and fro. Cautiously I bent nearer, in a way almost glad to gaze on some movement, rather than into the impenetrable wall before me.

As I gazed, a figure seemed to come close up to me out of the void, stretching its arms towards me as if to drag me with in. I saw no face, no definite shape, beyond the shadowy outline, and the arms. I shrank back, and back, to find myself pressing against the shrubs. "Could I keep in that position without losing my bearings?" I wondered, for if I could, I was then backing away from lawn and house. How far the fog extended, I could not guess, but to press back from the lawn seemed the only thing to attempt. I was weak, spent, almost done, but I threw my last ounce of strength into this move. *Crash! crash!* went branches behind me, my weak leg was failing me, and I found myself feebly trying to pray for help. And now the shadowy forms seemed to follow me, closer, closer, they pressed forward, as I pressed back. Suddenly, I fancied I *heard* a faint shout, then another. I tried to answer, but was powerless, terror had made me dumb. Another shout—

"John, where are you?"

I could not answer, but gave one last push, and fell.

I opened my eyes to find not a search party, not a feverish gang of people, fussing over me, but merely Mrs. Falconer, with a flash of brandy in one hand, a light rug over her arm, leading a magnificent hound by a long chain. His acquaintance I had not made; he was licking my face and hands, when with a long shudder I sat up.

"Mrs. Falconer," I said.

"Yes, John, Gelert and I. Do you feel able to walk? We have some way to go, before you can rest."

"Are we far from the house?" I asked.

"The house, as far as we are concerned, has ceased to exist until daylight," she answered.

"I do not understand," I said.

"Of course you don't," she replied, "and were not content to be guided."

"No," I said ruefully, "but how topping of you to come."

"No one else can," she said, "only Gelert and I can come. But now you must try to move."

I took a little of the brandy, and struggled to my feet, to find I was on the extreme edge of the shrubberies, beyond which appeared to be meadows. With my final twist back, I had landed on my back into the meadow, nothing resisting my strength, and, of course, fell.

"How deep is the shrubbery I backed through, Mrs. Falconer?" I asked.

"A matter of perhaps thirty or forty yards," she said. "Fortunately it occurred to you to back."

"Why?" I said.

"Never mind why, just now," she replied, "we must hurry. Look."

I looked, and saw the fog creeping after us. Gelert growled menacingly, ever and *anon* turning to face the way we were leaving, once, springing as if to grasp something, his eyes like fire, saliva dripping from his massive jaws. A few moments passed, and Mrs. Falconer breathed—

"Hurry John, you must."

"I can't," I gasped.

"You must," she said. But even as she spoke, I felt the impress of a hand heavily on my shoulder. The hound growled, prepared for a spring, I thought, at my throat, as with a quick word and sudden jerk, Mrs. Falconer dragged me through a gate, sinking down on the roadside with a whispered "Thank God!"

I suppose I lost consciousness for a few moments, for when next I opened my eyes, I was covered with the rug, my head on Mrs. Falconer's knee, Gelert beside her, with his great paws close to her.

A faint, grey light, as of coming dawn, was visible, the atmosphere was clear and balmy, and very silent.

Mrs. Falconer rose, and her voice was once again the cold, unemotional tones of my hostess. I vaguely wondered if it had been all part of a horrible nightmare, and had I dreamed that across it I heard her voice, anguished, distressed, calling, calling. There was nothing now, in either her voice or bearing, other than the lady I had hitherto known.

"If you are rested, John, we will go home," she said, in slightly ironical tones, "you will no doubt be glad of a bath and sleep."

"Thank you," I answered, in the same off-hand way. "I shall."

I was deadly tired, sick with pain, and now, in the quickly-coming dawn, felt, and I should not hesitate to say, looked, like a truant schoolboy, caught out of bounds, and conveyed home to receive due chastisement. I felt cowed—no other word describes it, yet deep in my heart lay a feeling of annoyance, that I had been found. I was quite conscious of *not* feeling nearly as grateful as I ought, and of being still a long way from discovering the why and wherefore of strange and terrifying happenings.

That I had seen, things, not of this world, in the ordinary meaning of the word, I was well aware. Nor was I unduly fearful of them, the horror lay in the suffocating fog, and in the apparent wish to haul me into some abyss. I was *not* afraid of mere forms. Some of us out in "No-Man's-Land" were not unknowing of other forms being present as well as our comrades in the flesh. There are those of us, who, in spite of the jeerings of scoffers, still say, that the Angels of Mons were *not* the phantasy of unhinged minds, nor even a mirage due to a tot of rum.

Therefore, I, among many others, have learned to be less sceptical and not to take nonunderstandable things as impossibilities.

The truant schoolboy feeling clung to me all the way home. I shouldn't have felt surprised had Mrs. Falconer taken me by the hand and bidden me trot along. As we neared the house, I observed smoke from one or two chimneys. What time it was I did not know, nor greatly care. In silence we entered the hall, hearing a large clock boom five as we did so.

A small round table was drawn near a blazing freshly kindled fire, a kettle steamed on the hob, toast, and bread and butter were there, but not a sign of any person.

Still in silence, Mrs. Falconer threw off her fur coat and cap, and warming her hands at the blaze, she uttered one of her usual terse remarks—

"When you have had food, John, I advise a bath, bed, and a still tongue. The household are aware you remained outside when you had better have been in. Details of your experience are not desirable, and for Elsie's sake, I do not advise a repetition of foolhardiness, I also ask you to conform to the house rules, which, are made as little irksome as possible."

I did not reply beyond a mild bow and she went on—

"I am going to lock Gelert up now. I counsel bed for you, and the doctor to see your leg in the morning, Goodbye."

I had prepared an elaborate speech of thanks for her timely help, but she cut me short, saying—

"Your best thanks, John, will be to conform to rules; no one else has ever tried to kick them over quite so deliberately before."

She left me then, and I dragged my throbbing limb to bath and bed, too weary to think or conjecture further.

When next I awakened it was 10 a.m. No one apparently had been near me, so I rang my bell. Old Jacob answered it, looking at me reproachfully, as he asked if he might bring breakfast because " 'Madam' has 'phoned the doctor to call."

"There was no need," I said—"he may even order me to lie still."

"Yes, sir," said Jacobs, his tone implying "that's it."

A plentiful breakfast tray speedily arrived, and with it Bob, who perched himself on the foot of my bed, eyeing me as one who wished to know without inquiring. I vouchsafed no information, so he started off.

"Rotten luck, Sir, but only your own fault—quite instructive and very thrilling—Hurt your leg, Sir?"

"A bit," I answered.

Then lowering his voice he whispered—"Anything touch you? Fog, I suppose, and people."

"Oh, no," I said, "at least I don't think so."

"Think so!" he ejaculated, "there would not be any *think* about it.

"What's it all about, Bob?" I asked.

"Better ask the gov'nor, Sir, not me."

"P'raps so—clear now, Bob—I'm going to dress."

"Right-o, Sir," said he as he lounged away.

Fearing a doctor's visit to maul me about, I dressed and tubbed quickly, and was just about to put my jacket on, when I noticed a long tear in the shoulder, also the shoulder strap was missing. "Then someone did touch me," I said aloud, staring aghast at the ripped shoulder, dismayed to think what a giveaway it was to the household as it was my only available coat for day. I had better concoct a yarn to account for it, and get a maid to mend it, while I dressed. I rang the bell and a plain-looking person with glasses and a long nose answered it.

"Did you ring, Sir?" she asked, in rasping tones.

"Eh, yes," I said "I've had an accident and torn my coat, I shall be obliged if someone will mend it."

She took it without answering, and I continued dressing until she reappeared saying—

"I've done what I could, Sir, it's a tailor's job, but it may do until you leave."

"Until I leave?" I said, somewhat startled.

"Yes, Sir," she replied. "You'll be leaving I expect. It's no use staying, Sir, when things like that begin to happen," pointing to my coat as she spoke.

I was about to try a question, softened by a half-crown, when there was a sharp knock at the door, and another maid entered with a salver on which lay a wire. With a murmured "Thanks" I ripped it open, reading—

Coming today, why don't you do as you are told. Elsie.

Forgotten were the horrors of last night, forgotten torn coats, rules, regulations, everything, in the delight of my little girl's coming. I thanked the two women, flung on my coat, whistling like a schoolboy, as I tramped to the hall on my way to breakfast.

A curious restraint met me—something indefinable, a kind of lack of genuineness in the "Good-mornings" I received, which gave, me a feeling of being in disgrace, but no amount of that was going to damp my spirits, so I ignored it, though don't mind admitting the chill rather spoilt the morning, and I was not sorry to escape with a pipe to have a look at a timetable. Mrs. Falconer did not appear during the morning which did not unduly worry me, but when Mr. Falconer asked me to be good enough to follow him to his study, I had visions of the birch-rod, and my footsteps lagged as befitted my part, when I obeyed his request. He asked me to be seated, but instead of a whipping, he mildly said—

"John, Elsie will arrive at 12.40, will you drive to meet her?"

"Thanks very much, I was hoping to," I answered.

"She knows," he went on, "that you—er—that you—had an unpleasant night. I regret that you do not seem able to take us as we are obliged to be, and I admit it is difficult to make one's guests understand and respect our arrangements for their welfare, without explanations, which we are not permitted to give; for Elsie's sake, I warn you, less worse befall, to conform to rule." This was a whipping without a doubt; and I felt a qualm of conscience as he spoke, knowing, as I did, my pig-headed temperament and determination to know more.

I thanked him, offered him a cigarette, but evaded any promises, though he eyed me questioningly as if he awaited something of the kind.

The next few hours I passed aimlessly, wandering about alone, since one and all of the party seemed bent on avoiding me. I had a stroll to the low lawn; though, bathed in sunshine, it looked peaceful and serene, making me wonder vaguely had I dreamed the horrid fantasy. I was glad when the hour came to meet my little girl. I enjoyed the swift run. I was glad beyond measure to see her bright face at the railway carriage window.

"You are looking fit, old boy," she said; adding, without any hesitancy, "in spite of your silly tricks last night."

"How did you know?" I asked.

"Mother wired me to come," she replied, "and take charge of you, as you had been out too late. I knew all *that* meant;" she said, with a shudder.

"Will you tell me about it, Kiddie?" I coaxed, but her little face took a graver look, as she answered:

"No, John, I can't; you must just trust us and do as we do. Stay with me, dear, this evening; never mind trying to fathom things, others have tried before you. Promise me you will not think of it anymore."

"Dear child, I'm a man with a thinking machine. I can't promise not to think," I said.

"Well, promise you won't stay out after time," she said.

"Very well," I assented, "I'll promise that."

She nestled to my side in dear content at that, and our drive back was a happy one.

Elsie was greeted with happy comradeship on our arrival, so lunch was a more cheery meal, and the afternoon was passed as usual, in a rest, a stroll, and tea beneath the old trees on the low lawn. At five, as usual, a general move was made to the house. Elsie held out her hand to me, merely saying: "Come, John;" but, man-like, I wanted to remain, and was reluctant to obey that little outstretched hand, but gave in with a good grace, consenting to be imprisoned for the rest of the summer evening within the glassed garden. To a man accustomed to be out of doors, the enforced imprisonment palled, despite the games, music, gay talk, and general attempt to keep things cheery.

Little Miss Dorcas and her charges joined us for a while; and I had an idea, that if I could get her alone, she would perhaps give me some information. I would try; so invited her to a putting match, leaving Elsie to chat to her mother.

"You are playing wildly, major," said my partner, in a few moments.

"Yes," I answered, "I'm afraid my thoughts were 'outside,' and not in. I had a strange evening last evening, you know."

"Yes," she said. "I hope it is one that will not be repeated."

"Oh no," I answered, "I'm not likely to repeat it."

"I suppose not," she replied, "at least not in that way."

"That way?" I asked. "What do you mean, is there any other way?"

"Unfortunately, yes," she answered, gravely. "Oh! Mrs. Falconer as watching us," she said, suddenly—"play, oh, do play! I'll try and say something while we play. I don't think it is right to keep you in ignorance of your danger; they do, and no one will warn you."

"Tell me," I muttered, as I played.

"I can't," she whispered. "She is coming across, look in the books on your shelf tonight. There! I've won," she said, in the same breath, as she waved her putter in triumph, just as Mrs. Falconer came up.

"Don't overdo it, John," she said. "Elsie is waiting for you, and the children are getting tired, Miss Dorcas."

So our game and little talk came to an abrupt end. From then on, I was given no chance for talks, except with Elsie; but when we separated to dress for dinner, and I found myself alone, I pondered deeply over a quiet pipe. "Warn me of my danger" Miss Dorcas had said, then there was there danger, whether I ventured outside or not? And the bookshelf, that probably meant a note. Surely I was safe inside, I thought, for I was fully determined to get the iron shutter out of my way. Well, I would leave it now, and, as they say, "wait and see."

Dinner was cheery, but I was rapidly beginning to detest the Indoor Garden, with its continual constraint, and made up my mind to press for an early wedding and take my little girl to more congenial surroundings. The evening drew to a close at last! though I was happy with Elsie, and, in a secluded corner, had asked and carried my point of an early wedding.

By 10.30 all had dispersed; indeed, I am certain all hated the enforced seclusion as much in their hearts as I did. I bid them all "Goodnight!" and, with a sigh of relief, flung myself into the armchair in my cosy bedroom. My eyes suddenly fell on to a book, slightly awry on the shelf, and I sprang up as quickly as my lame leg permitted, and took it down; a tiny note which lay between the pages read thus:

> You have given a loop-hole and are waited for, take care you are not taken 'outside the house.' Keep from your windows.—J.D.

"Ho! ho!" I said; "'keep from my windows.' That little warning gives me a clue, but surely, if I do not open them, all will be well. I only desire to *see* through them, and what's more, I will." I took my coat off, mounted a chair with difficulty, managing to seat myself sideways on the broad window-ledge, armed with my files, and a soft cloth, to dull the sound as much as possible. Luckily the file was sharp, and the metal soft, and in a short time I had made a deep dent. It was now 11.30, all was silent, presumably the whole house was wrapt in slumber. Steadily I worked for another half-hour; the hasp was almost through.

I paused for a brief rest. As I paused, there sprang into being, probably from my subconscience, the thought: "Suppose real danger did lie in wait for me, suppose some horror undreamed of should cost me my life, or, worse, my reason, and none knew of this attempt of mine to lay bare a secret so carefully guarded." I prolonged my rest sufficiently to climb from my window-sill, add a few lines to my carefully kept notes of events since I came here, put the bundle of papers in a long envelope, sealed it, and addressed it to Captain Percy Hesketh. Having done which, I remounted the window-sill and endeavoured to complete my task. There seemed some slight hesitancy in my movements, probably because I was now nearing the goal I had set out to win. I braced myself and started again.

How still it was, though the wind seemed to have risen a little. I could hear it moaning round the corner of the house, fitfully, as if a sudden summer storm was coming up. The hasp bent, gave way, and came in two in my fingers. Gently I moved the heavy shutter, an inch—it creaked—creaked, it seemed to me, loudly enough to wake the "seven sleepers." Did I imagine it, or did I hear a step overhead. I must hurry. I scrambled down, switched off all lights, climbed up again, and waited breathlessly. All was silent. Carefully I slid down on to the chair below me, and cautiously drew the shutter back a couple of inches more, then waited,—still all quiet— swung it wide—*CRACK!*

I dimly remember calling Percy, calling with my soul more than with my voice.

★★★★★★

When next I remembered anything, it was to become conscious that I was in a bed in a bright, lofty room, a white-capped nurse was by my bed, holding a glass. Percy Hesketh was sitting by my side—a fact which gave me joy without an atom of surprise. It was as if I had expected him to be there.

"If you swallow this, you may say a few words," said the nurse.

I swallowed it, and gave my hand into the warm grasp of my friend.

"John," he said, "I have your papers. Try to tell me what followed the cracking of the pane of glass."

Feebly, haltingly, I tried, as I stumblingly, shudderingly, told him:

"Following the crack, the window splintered before my eyes, from top to bottom. I bent back, expecting to be covered with falling glass. It did not fall, but a pale, unearthly light illuminated it, lighting up to my horrified-gaze, faces pressed against the window peering in upon me, but faces such as I never in life beheld. They were dark, almost black, with sunken, fiercely gleaming eyes, the cheekbones protruding, flesh sunken, looking almost like living skeletons, save for the skin which stretched

95

tightly over the bones; anger, despair, ferocity, hunger, terror—all were depicted upon those awful faces.

"Through the cracked glass, deadly fumes began to steal, my room seemed cloudy, I was as if transfixed, unable to move, to call, to reach the lights, to do aught but stand staring, tremblingly. The faces pressed closer and yet closer; they reached the glass, it cracked again, and more fumes poured in; long arms (there seemed hundreds of them) reached wildly up, skinny hands, like those of skeletons, were held out as if to grasp. I tried to step back to get away from the window, as with a terrific crash, the glass fell in. Arms and hands stretched through, faces came nearer, nearer—I felt myself seized, held, lifted, drawn upwards.

"I was on the window-sill again, held in an inexorable grip. I felt myself lifted through, felt the cold air on my face, was just able to discern the hurrying figures in the thick mist, and to know, beyond all doubt, that I was being borne swiftly, by claw-like hands, towards the low lawn."

(*Continued by Captain Percy Hesketh*):

As my poor friend uttered his final words, he sank back into my arms in a state of unconsciousness, from which he never fully recovered, though in the many hours of watching over him, which were permitted by the hospital staff, I witnessed again and again the agony of mind and horror he passed through.

My painful task it was to bring the girl he loved to his bedside, to witness her grief, as he failed to remember her name, or face, all my life I shall remember that afternoon.

The sun was shining on the floor of the ward—lighting up stray corners and patches, as I gently led Elsie Falconer to my friend's bedside. He was sitting up, laughingly pointing to the sunny patches, babbling about the funny light. He took no notice of the girl, beyond asking me:

"Why does that girl cry?"

"Do you know her, John?" I asked.

"No," he replied, "but she is pretty, tell her look to at the funny patches, then she will laugh. Take her away," he added, "she cries."

Nurse led the weeping girl away, and I was thankful she had gone. One or another came to see him, it was always the same, no glimmer of memory seemed to return, though at times he would make a little more sensible remark.

One day he spoke to me, saying:

"Who was the old man who called me 'John'? I'm not 'John.' I wish my brains wouldn't keep running round and round like a glass ball full of colours. I could listen to people if the glass ball would keep still," he rambled on, and, uneasy and fearful, I called the nurse. I saw by her face, it was the end, as, with sudden strength, he flung himself against the pillows, shouting as loudly as he could:

"Hark! there are the guns, at it again, are they—give me my rifle, I'll show them. Now boys, come on—over the top, and at 'em." They were his last words, and the day after the following notice appeared in the papers:—

On September 30th, at the Hospital,
Singleton, Major John Longworth, M.C.,
after four years' service, from shock, following
an accident, aged 39.

★★★★★★

Some years later, I ventured to read through my late friend's notes of the experience which cost him his life, and to rewrite them to the best of my ability, for this, I believe, was what he wished done.

It cost me an effort to revisit the scenes of such horror; even after a lapse of years, but I desired also to learn, if I could, what really was the story of the place which my friend—bravely, though foolishly—gave his life to discover.

The landlord of the village inn gave me the story, as told to him by his grandfather, who knew the former tenants of the house. It seems the family had owned all the coal mines round, for generations, growing more and more wealthy as the years passed. The former owner, grandfather of my friend Francis, was an avaricious man, hard and grasping.

There was warning given, one day, of danger in the mine

nearest to the house, warning that it was unsafe to permit the men to descend. Old Falconer, with his greed for money, preferred to risk men's lives rather than lose by delay, and ignored the warning—in fact had it contradicted— and the men went down—to their death—some four hundred of them. Old Falconer added to his crime, by refusing to spend money for rescue work, saying it was useless, that the earth had closed the mine completely. Apparently it had, though there were those who told of groans and shrieks coming from the bowels of the earth.

Falconer went on his way, disregarding all that was said, and in time the ground above the buried mine was cultivated, and turned into a lawn, below the level of the house.

When the old man died, he passed on the dire legacy to his sons, leaving them the whole of his fortune on condition that they lived in the house, making them promise that none on the premises would be out of the house after five in the evening, stating that the entombed men haunted the place.

None ever knew what the old man had seen or heard, but it is said that the miners had slowly starved to death, and could have been rescued at the time, but now haunted the place, intent upon finding victims to drag below with them. There had, said the landlord, been one or two sad happenings, but the worst trouble was the most recent, when a Major Longworth, M.C., who was engaged to Miss Falconer, and who had been severely wounded in France, came to stay with the family, and did not rest until he had witnessed the whole of the awful happenings.

Mr. Falconer was awakened in the night, it is said, by the sound of shattering glass, and rushed into Major Longworth's room in time to see him borne away towards the ill-fated lawn. The big hound, kept on the place, was loosed, and dashed across the lawn, in which a vast crack had appeared. Mr. Falconer described a furious fight for the body of Major Longworth, between the hound and something unseen, but that the hound succeeded in hauling the body out of the crack in the ground, into which it appeared to be slipping, dragging it, mauled and bleeding, back to the house.

"Major Longworth died in the hospital, here, sir," went on my garrulous host, "and Miss Falconer entered a nursing sister-hood. "People say the house will collapse someday—have a look at it, sir, if you've time, before it gets late."

I thanked him, and went my way. I found the house, desolate and dilapidated. The vast glasshouse on one side of it, full of dead plants and broken chairs—dirty beyond description. The gardens were a tangle of briars and weeds, the paths had become mere grass tracks. The Low Lawn, grown rank and rough, its greenness marred by a vast blackened crack right across it, as if a subsidence had taken place.

A brooding sense of mystery and disaster hangs over the place; nor do I hesitate to believe when I hear on all sides how the place is shunned, still less can I doubt my friend's written words of all that befell him in spite of all warnings to conform to orders, and not venture—

"Outside the House."

The Wind in the Woods

To say I was an artist would be giving myself too high-sounding a name, yet my days were spent in trying, and at times succeeding, in depicting scenes as I saw them—not people! I never attempted portraits, for the expression on human faces more often irritated me, than interested— every nine out of ten wore such a worried, harassed look, as if, in the race for gain, or pleasure, they had lost sight of all things conducive to rest or repose; I had no wish to paint such things, nor did I wish them to come and pose in their best garments, with a smile such as one and all would, I knew, adopt.

Fortunately for me, I was not dependent upon my efforts with brush and pencil, though I confess I made quite a nice income by them; but it was always joy to me to remember, if I did not want to paint, I need not, for my meals were forthcoming, whether I made the price of them or not.

I was the owner of a charming flat in London. This was my anchorage, and here I was looked after and cared for by an old family servant, a woman well on in years, who had been for long years a faithful friend and servant in my family, and now, in her later years, had constituted herself my factotum, ruling my small domain, and incidentally myself, with a firm hand, never by any chance seeming to realize that I really was grown up, but bestowing the same thought upon the changing of my socks on a wet day as she had done when I was nine or ten. Her name was "Merry"—Mrs. Merry. As children, we had all adored her; as a middle-aged man, I respected and looked up to her, glad to ask and take her wise advice on many issues of the day.

Mrs. Merry was well used to my vagabondish ways, though at times she was wont to say I should be much happier if I married and settled down! I always laughed at her, for my only love story was buried fathoms deep in the dust-heap of forgotten things; and the very words "settle down" sent a cold shiver down my spine—it, the "settling down" process, would mean a wholesale giving up of all those ways I held so dear. No more sudden trekking at a moment's notice, or coming home any day or any hour, as sure of welcome as I was sure of being safe from questions as to my doings. Mrs. Merry *never* questioned, though she was always delighted when told where I had been, or what I had done. Sometimes I had sketches to show to her, but as often I had none; in either case, she was convinced of my talent and ability, and her faith and loyalty never wavered.

It was early in July when a sudden desire for trees, rivers, and growing things caused me to drop the work I was on, call Mrs. Merry, and request a small Gladstone bag should be packed as quickly as possible, that I was going away. The old lady looked at me keenly, remarking—

"You don't look ill!"

I laughed.

"Nor am I," I said; "but it is hot in the town; also, I feel as if I must see trees instead, of people for a while."

"That will mean strong boots and knickers, I suppose, sir?" was her next remark.

"Yes, Merry, dear, it will; also plenty of pipes, baccy, books, and a stick. I may paint, or I may not; in any case, expect me back a month from tomorrow, for sure, unless I send you word; and if you don't hear, why then," I added, laughing—"someone had better begin to look for me."

"I do wish you would settle down, Mr. Wilfred," was the old dame's parting shot, as she went out to do my behests.

Settle down, I mused, filling a much-used old briar, never, now, though my thoughts went back to those days of joy, when I and a sweet-faced girl with dark eyes and a little fair head just reaching to my shoulder, talked in, twilight hours of a home that was to be. If she had passed to the "Great Beyond," I could have borne it better than the tale of treachery and cunning, which ended in my dark-eyed love leaving me on the morning, which should have been my wedding day, merely announcing, by wire, that she had married my best chum, Kirk Compton, in London, that morning.

Trouble of that kind takes one of two lines, it either sends a man, or woman, to the bad—that is, to drink, gambling—anything of a wild, riotous kind of existence to, as they think, help them to forget—or it sends them into themselves, to more or less live a life of solitude, finding companionship in books or hobbies, fearful of making friends, lest they, too, should prove unfaithful; one's faith in goodness shattered, it is years, if ever, before one comes into one's own, realizing that there is infinitely more in life than the shallow so-called love of one girl. And so, as I was not addicted to drink or cards, I became a recluse, or almost. I had a few friends, was voted a good chap, but a cynic, and gradually left to my own devices. I was happy as the years went on, finding my books and work all sufficient, while my fervent love of nature proved the healing of my sore, and I was content.

July 20th stared me in the face from a large lettered calendar, as I woke for my early cup of tea, on the day I was starting for a whole month, somewhere in Wales.

There is not any object in making a mystery of my destination, except the small fact that my chosen haunt was a very well-known district, within only an hour's journey from a large manufacturing town; therefore, it is possible that there are people who might recognise and locate the district if I gave more than a mere hint of its place on the map. It has been for years a very favourite corner of mine; the hills which surround it are not so high as to be unclimbable, they are heather clad, though here and there one came upon an oasis of sprongy turf and golden bracken—what I call, in my own mind, "kind hills"—high enough to lift one up from life's little worries, but not high enough to be awe-inspiring, or to frown down upon us puny mortals.

The rivers are fishable after rain, otherwise one can inspect the stones, which form the beds of these mountain streams, and decide among the dry stones which place might best conceal a trout, when the next rain comes; personally, I am quite willing to believe that once there were fish in plenty in the stream, but that lean years had driven the farm folks to catch them the best way they could. Perhaps the chief beauty of the place lay in the charm of its many and varied woods—at least, this was to me the magnet which drew me here generally once or twice in a year.

Up on the hillsides the woods seemed to open out, one into another, ever revealing fresh beauties of trees, from the tender green of the sapling birch to the hoary old beech or oak of many years old; beneath their green arms, the ground was carpeted with soft tiny wild thyme, wild mint, and little flowers of many kinds whose names were unknown to me. Most of my hours were spent deep in the heart of these woods, which never failed to hold me entranced with their ever-varying lights and shades.

Below, nearer to the river, there were woods also, but of quite a different nature, there, high pine trees of sombre hue towered above you, each one seeming to say: "Let me stretch up to the blue sky and leave the gloom of this wood beneath me." For gloom there undoubtedly was, yet I have liked that gloom; sometimes, on a hot summer's day, I have enjoyed lying on a soft, dry heap of pine needles, listening to the gentle coo of wood-pigeons, nesting high above me. "Silent Wood," as I called it, was always sheltered from wind, for the pine trees were close together, and beyond a soft sighing wind in the tree tops I never remember feeling the wind from any quarter. The sunlight seldom penetrated the "Silent Wood," save only in single shafts between the pines, or, maybe, in some clear patch where a tree had fallen or been cut down; but, even lacking sunshine, it was always warm and dry.

One side of the wood was bounded by a path, the other side by the stream—at least in autumn and winter it was—for in summer it dried up or trickled away to reappear a mile or so further on, as if it had tumbled into some old mine shaft; and later, changed its course and returned. "Silent Wood" was *not* my favourite, but it had a fascination for me, difficult to describe; and on this July morning, when I bid farewell to dear old Merry, and started for my holiday, "Silent Wood" was much in my mind as a quiet place to rest in, before I tackled longer, steeper walks, or began to think of taking canvas and paints with me.

My journey was long, also suffocatingly hot, dusty, and tedious; many people were travelling, and my compartment was well packed with bundles and packages, as well as people, so I hailed my last change with a sigh of relief, for soon the hills and trees would surround me instead of the bricks and mortar I had grown so tired of.

A broken-down trap, drawn by a fat Welsh pony, met me at my station; from thence we crawled up four long miles of hill ere I reached my favourite quarters, an old farmhouse in which I was always a welcome guest, and where two cheery rooms were always at my disposal. The peacefulness of that first evening will linger in my memory for many a day to be able to gaze around, seeing nothing but hills, fields, trees, and sky, instead of houses, chimneys, motors, and people, was pure joy to me; when, after a simple meal, I lit my pipe, I felt intent to linger in the warm, hay-scented air indefinitely.

There are those to whom the contemplation of such a holiday, as the one I thought lay before me, would have been a dire penalty, those to whom solitude and nature would spell boredom and weariness; and I pity all those natures, for they know not what they miss.

I passed a gloriously restful night, and was up early, with a long day of golden sunshine ahead of me. I had never been here in July before, early spring or September had been my usual seasons; but to be here in July, in radiant warmth and beauty, was a treat I was prepared to revel in.

Day by day slipped away, in almost complete idleness, until a week had vanished, almost unnoticed by me, for calendars had been left behind me, and I, more often than not, forgot to wind up my watch—I had no use for time. I ate when I felt hungry, and slept when I was tired; but the end of this week found me thinking of brush and canvas, so I decided to take lunch in my pocket, trusting to luck for some tea if I desired it, and prepared for a long day's sketching. "Which way do you think of going, sir?" asked my hostess, more, I fancy, from politeness than from any real interest in my goings and comings.

"Oh, I don't know," I answered, "but probably I shall wander to the woods."

"Which, sir?" she next enquired, a little to my surprise.

"Probably the shadiest," I replied, smiling, "the one below with the pine trees, and silence, is the one I most fancy today."

"The higher woods are nicer, sir, don't you think?" was her next remark.

"No, I don't," I said. "I like the pine woods, they are always so intensely silent; one never feels any wind there, and there is a breeze today."

"That is true, sir," said Mrs. Hughes. "There isn't any wind there—as a *rule.*"

"As a rule?" I echoed. "Why, I've never felt it there, not even in autumn."

"No, sir, you wouldn't then, but you may now; and I'd go to the upper woods if I were you." Now Mrs. Hughes had never, to my knowledge, taken the slightest interest in my doings pre- viously, and her persistence this morning simply had the effect of making me feel perverse, as is the way of men; so, smilingly, I bade her good morning, determined, in my own mind, that "Silent Wood" should be my destination for that day. The good lady ventured no further remarks, but turned away to busy her- self with farm duties, leaving me to set off without further ques- tioning.

There was a slight breeze, just enough to make walking more pleasant, but rather more than I liked for sketching purposes, so I was glad when I dipped down from the path by the river-side to the edge of my pet woods. They were, as ever, still, dark, and airless, just as I had pictured them many, many times as I smoked my pipe beside my studio fire while busy London surged on, beneath my windows.

In those woods, I have always felt as if I must tread softly. I do not remember ever to have sung or whistled there; yet, there was never anything to disturb, for I have never seen even a rabbit, it seemed too sombre a place for animal life; moreover, there was nothing but dry pine needles for them to eat. I don't remember ever *seeing* the wood-pigeons I occasionally heard above my head; so, lacking animal life, the place was even more silent than deep woods usually are.

It suited me in my present mood, however, and in the intense silence lay its greatest charm. Somewhere in the world there are a few kindred spirits, I have no doubt, to whom such perfect silence and freedom from every jar would appeal, as it appeals to me—those who often crave for just one hour's unbroken silence, and who find it one of the most difficult things to attain; those to whom the incessant opening and shutting of doors, clattering of things, ringing of bells, voices, and the coming and going of people have to be endured with a smile, though every nerve may be on edge, and the aching for quietness is almost—more than can be borne—those people, and those only, will enter into and fully understand the intense charm to me of "Silent Wood."

I entered it, as usual, on this morning as on many previous ones, walking softly as if not wanting to disturb its peace by so much as a snap of a dry twig, and as I walked deeper and deeper into the shadows it seemed to grow stiller and more silent. The scent of the pines was soothing, and the warm, dry air seemed to draw it out and intensify it.

About the centre of the wood I paused to look and listen. Not a sound broke the stillness, save only the faintest cooing of the wood-pigeons; so there, in the patch of sunlight, I drew together heaps of pine needles to form a couch, stretching myself on it in complete enjoyment, canvas and brushes idle by my side.

The natural outcome of such an environment and such quiet calm was to fall soundly asleep—a glorious, restful sleep—

knowing that there could not be any early knocking at my door, no engagements to keep, nothing, no one for whom I need wake until I had slept all I desired. I woke at long length, with the softest of breezes blowing gently on my face; so softly as to make me wonder, in my half-asleep state, if it also were part of my dreams; but no! there it was again, soft and cold, and this time a little stronger. I opened my eyes. Surely it must be night! I thought. How many hours had I slept? It seemed dark, yet high up between the pine-tree tops I could catch a glimpse of blue sky.

Then it is not late, I thought, but how dark it is here under the trees. I must see the time, and shake myself into a more reasonable state of mind, for, truly, I feel almost nervy! So my thoughts ran as I raised myself from my pine-needle couch, and stood up. I glanced round and could scarcely believe it was my beloved "Silent Wood," it seemed so chill and dark, not the soft gloom I was accustomed to there, but an eerie darkness as of a gathering storm; but ever and *anon* a little moaning wind swept past me, each just seeming more chill and dank.

"Horrible!" I murmured, fastening up my coat before preparing to pick up my little knapsack of odds and ends, "horrible! I never thought the place could be so chilly; I'll get out as speedily as I can for it must be late."

I peered at my watch, which was difficult to see in the gloom, to find I had, as usual, forgotten to wind it.

"It is probably about four!" I said aloud, "but it's like night!"

I spoke aloud, and my voice seemed to come back to me in mocking echo from the far side of the wood, "like night"

"I never knew there was an echo," I thought. "I'll try again tomorrow," I said clearly, and back from the distance came the echo—"tomorrow"—and a hoarse laugh came with it.

I started, I had not laughed! Then, who?

"Oh, you idiot," I murmured, giving myself a shake, "it's some country yokel answering you back, making a fool of you; pull yourself together and get off home—you require your tea."

So, with a last look round, I turned my face towards home,

and tea, but my feet seemed weighted, and seemed as if I could not leave the wood, eager as I was to reach the daylight. I seemed to have already dragged myself double the distance I had to go ere I found myself at the edge of the wood, shivering in every limb, chilled to the bone, unnerved, as I could not believe possible, over—nothing at all! In the warmth of the sun I speedily recovered, and was ready to laugh at my own stupidity; to prove this to my own satisfaction, I gaily shook my fist at the woods behind me, calling back—"tomorrow," and, far away in the distant darkness, I fancied—for it could only have been fancy—I heard a mocking echo and a faint sound of laughter, as if the word "tomorrow" floated back to me; fancy or not, it served to hasten my steps, and the farm kitchen with its cheery tea-table, which I hurried to reach, quickly dispelled any lingering fear I might have felt.

For the first time, since my holiday began, I passed a restless night, burdened, when I slept at all, by dreams of mocking voice and laughter. My first thought on waking was one of dire vengeance, on someone, for causing me to lose a night's precious sleep. I would repay them, I vowed, as I sprang up, preparing to dress as rapidly as possible.

"Will you be in, sir, for lunch, or will you take it out?" asked my hostess as soon as I had finished a wonderful breakfast of home-cured ham, fresh eggs, scones, and home-made jam.

"I will take it out, please, Mrs. Hughes," I replied. "Some of that fine ham, and some bread and butter, if you will be so good. Don't make it into those abominations called sandwiches though, it would utterly spoil both bread and ham. I never can enjoy food done up in that way, the bread tastes of ham and the ham only tastes of bread, and both are dry and worn out by the time you want your lunch; so separately, please—if you love me."

Mrs. Hughes eyed me as if uncertain whether to laugh or scold at what she termed my oddities—the laugh triumphed, and she went off chuckling over the ways of faddy men-folks.

Presently, the good lady reappeared with a neat parcel, which she handed to me, with the remark—

"There you are, sir, *separately,* and I hope you will enjoy your lunch. Which way will you be going, sir?"

So again my destination seemed to be of interest to the worthy dame, but this time I wasn't going to let her off so easily.

"Why do you ask, Mrs. Hughes?" I enquired.

"Well, sir, it's Tommy, it's Tommy," she said hesitatingly. "Seems like the lad likes to be on the look-out for you, sir, and always pesters me to say which way you've gone, sir.

As the good lady was speaking she edged nearer and nearer the door, and her final words were uttered as the door closed between her and myself, leaving me looking rather blankly at the door, and quite unable to reconcile Tommy's present anxiety as to my whereabouts, seeing the lad had not apparently noticed my existence up to now.

However, they were none the wiser—no one, save myself, know whither I was bound, and if I changed my mind, no one would know, or care.

I debated a few moments as to whether to burden myself with sketching materials or not, and, finally, a happy thought struck me, I would take my Kodak, it was ready loaded with new and highly-sensitive films, so, if I liked, I could take special bits and later, if I wished, sketch or enlarge from them in the quiet of my studio. So with my camera on my shoulder, my lunch in a handy pocket, I set off, prepared for another happy peaceful day in "Silent Wood." Yet now I had started, I wondered if it really would give me the pleasure I had anticipated to fulfil my vow of vengeance on Him, Her, or It, who had mocked me the previous day. I was *quite* determined, on one point, that I would discover the hiding place of my mocking friend, and rid myself of the disturber of my sanctuary.

To begin with I would not enter the woods by my usual path, I had a fancy to inspect the far side of it, which was as yet unknown to me, and which I had often thought of exploring, but so far had been too lazy to do so; it had been sufficient for me to get into the still warmth, and there to stay—resting, dreaming, or reading; but today I felt energetic, braced up, ready for anything, so instead of taking the lower path by the river to the woods, I struck off higher up, crossed a few fields and some tiresome fences, heavily loaded with barbed wire as if to keep out some invading enemy and not the three or four cows it guarded.

My plan had led me higher than the woods, which now lay stretched below me in a triangle, thick and dense, possibly half-a-mile in length, not more, I shouldn't think; looked at from where I stood it appeared quite an insignificant patch of dark trees surrounded by fields of waving corn, or haycocks, late in being carted home. Here and there, men and women were working in the fields; I could hear a reaper busy somewhere, and voices of children at play sounded clearly in the distance.

It was gloriously sunny, not a breath of wind stirred the leaves or grasses, yet, in spite of its beauty and brilliance, the dark trees lying below seemed to call me. I could see the waving branches of the pine trees, as if they were arms beckoning me to come, to rest in their shade. I knew I had to go; I knew in my heart I wanted to go, yet I lingered, drinking in the beauty of fields and sunshine as I strolled along, until, descending gradually, I found myself near the edge of the woods, at exactly the opposite corner from my usual point of entrance.

One more fence, a thick one of briars, thorns, and undergrowth, and I was in my beloved woods. It wasn't quite so dark on this side as the other, let it felt more desolate, more cheerless somehow, possibly fewer people came this way, which might account for it; anyway, here I was, and now to explore. First, I quietly skirted the wood for a little way, but this proved uninteresting, so I struck in under the pines, and almost at once was conscious again of the warm scenty feeling of the air.

"Glorious," I murmured; "how peaceful, how still, but I will not rest yet, I want to look round first." Presently, I caught a glimpse of what appeared to be a building. Funny place for a house, I thought; I wonder if anyone lives there, if so, my friend of the mocking laughter is now unearthed; so, with a smile at my own smartness, I marched on until I reached the building, at least what I thought was a building—now, alas! a ruin. Two ends and one side were almost intact, the rest, except one chimney, was just piles of rough, grey stones. It had every appearance of having been deserted many years, for the tumbled-down stones were moss-grown, with here and there little ferns protruding between the crevices; the spot must once have been a lonely corner, though now it looked utter desolation.

Laying my camera and lunch down, I strolled to have a nearer inspection of the lonely ruin before I sat down. There was not any trace to be found of how many rooms the cottage had once contained, though probably three or four was the limit; what must once have been a fireplace faced me as I entered, and on one side, about two yards from the ground, were five stone stairs; evidently there had been a stone staircase or steps leading to an upper room or rooms; though no sign of any floor above remained now. I couldn't imagine a stone house falling to pieces so completely, it gave one the impression more of having been hurled down stone after stone, nothing else would have demolished it so utterly.

There being nothing more to inspect, I strolled back to my belongings, but the sight of my camera reminded me that, after all, I could get a picture of so battered a domicile without the fag of sketching it; it would be interesting, I thought, to have a photograph of those five curious stone steps, and battered walls, so I quickly found my focus, taking the picture from a little distance to get a big pine in as well. It was a curious tree, at least half of it had apparently been shattered at some time. I then went closer, focussing for the stone steps only. It was shady within the walls so I gave a little longer time, and hoped for success, though I felt sorry I had not even yet succeeded in getting exactly the point of view I wanted. I had one film left; I would wait until the sun lit up the far side, and would take that also. That was enough for now, and I had earned both lunch and rest.

Somehow, my moss cushion did not give me the comfort I liked, though to try to say why, was beyond me, apparently it left nothing to be desired, my back was against a pine as I faced the deeper shade the woods in front of me. There was not any wind to disturb me, and no sound of any kind, all was quiet, serene, peaceful, and yet—

Again, and yet again, I found myself involuntarily turning to look over my shoulder at the heap of grey stones behind me. I didn't *want* to look at it, I had seen enough of it, yet turn I must and did, I was getting fanciful, for I could have sworn I saw a shadow of some person flit past the onetime doorway. Surely I had not missed a part of the place in my search, and there was someone hiding there. I would make sure. To this end I walked right round the place, looking well among the old bushes and holly trees—no sign of life—so I went back to my cushion and my rest.

One pipe I smoked, falling asleep ere I had finished it, to wake with a violent start, springing from my seat, sure, positive then, as I shall always be, that someone had laid a hand on my face. I tried to imagine a crawling thing had wandered over my face, I imagined a leaf falling, even tried the effect by closing my eyes and dropping a leaf on to my cheek, it was useless, no amount of thinking could make me believe that touch was aught but a hand.

Ghosts! I didn't believe in, I always looked on yarns of such things as the results of too heavy a supper, or a too vivid imagination, so was inclined to laugh at what I struggled so hard to minimize. I tried to whistle, but if you try to whistle with the corners of your mouth turned down, you will understand that effort ended in failure. I tried to hum a song, which resulted in a species of quavering dirge, I got up, I stamped, I beat the soft, unoffending turf with my stick, I did everything I could think of to shake off a creepy feeling that was fast getting a firmer hold of me, anything to avoid turning round as I felt impelled to do— all was useless, I might as well give in, but had now quite made up my mind I had had enough of the remains of the cottage, I would leave it to its solitude, first taking one more photo, then I would go on straight through the deep shades I loved, and out at the side I knew best.

Just once, I admit it, I looked towards the fence and back

down which I had come, almost furtively, I glanced that way, as if in my heart I would rather have returned by the same path, but it was only momentary, for I knew that through "Silent Wood" was the way I should go.

I picked up my camera for my final snapshot, choosing the far side of the ruined place, now in the sunshine, and exposed my film. As the shutter clicked, the sunlight vanished, as if a heavy cloud had suddenly obscured it, and the camera in my hand shook, as if it had been hit—*my* hands were perfectly steady, I am positive of that, yet I had all but dropped my precious toy! Someone must have thrown a stone I decided, but who the someone was, or where they were, I did not venture to look into, enough for me that I had got my pictures, and was ready to start through the woods, and so home to tea.

I was probably half-way, having long passed out of sight of the ruins, when I remembered my long forgotten ham and bread. I had better eat it, I supposed, so feeling happy again, now I was in the warm gloom of my favourite place, I made for myself another cosy seat, and proceeded with the now somewhat belated lunch. I was just about to bury the paper wrapping, as is my way, when it suddenly whisked away in a sudden gust of wind.

"Wind!" I ejaculated. "Here! Impossible!"

As I spoke, another little gust whirled past me, scattering the pine needles, and whirling a little crowd of dried bits round my feet. It really is most remarkable, I murmured to myself, the times without number I have been in these woods and never felt the smallest breath of wind until yesterday and today. I'd best be moving, it may rain, though I'll be dry enough here if it does, all the same I'll go. As I rose, another and another draught of cold air swept by me, and then a sudden quietness fell, and all around me seemed to be growing darker, and still darker, little whispering winds seemed chattering above my head, and colder and more chilly it seemed to grow.

I started off hurriedly, only to find, in the gathering darkness, I had missed my way. On and on I plunged, deeper and deeper the blackness grew, colder and colder the wind, now rising almost to a gale, *anon*, dying away with a moaning sound. Bravely I struggled, wildly endeavouring to locate one familiar tree or stone.

The wind, now icily cold, seemed to lash me, buffeting me, as if I, strong man as I was, had been but a weak puny child.

Suddenly I stopped, determined to find my bearings, determined I would not be driven along as I was. I raised my face; my eyes were streaming with water, in the smarting cold of the lashing wind.

Gloom, black gloom, met me on every side. Pines, once familiar, now seemed twice their original size, standing out rigid, gaunt, and black, no glimmer of light anywhere.

"My God, I am utterly lost." I said, aloud.

"Utterly lost," came back a voice from far away, and with the words, making my blood freeze and heart stand still, a shriek of hideous laughter.

With a valiant effort, I steadied my voice, and shouted aloud:

"Who are you? Come to my help."

"To my help," rang out the voice, and I shuddered as a shrill peal of laughter followed it.

"Won't you come?" I cried once more.

"You come," echoed the voice, and the laughter that came with it seemed of many voices—the gruff, hoarse laughter of a man, the shrill, cackling laugh of women, and even, I was sure, the laughter of children.

On, on, I plunged! gasping now for breath, praying, hoping for deliverance; lost, but blindly struggling to reach some haven of refuge. A more vicious bang of the tearing wind suddenly sent me forward, and I seemed to have reached grass at last. With a sob of relief, I raised my eyes, thinking to see the grass at the edge of the wood, but was frozen stiff with horror and amazement, to find myself on the clearing, with the ruined cottage before me.

"Ruined cottage," I called it, ruined no longer! To my amazed eyes it appeared intact: a door stood ajar, a window on each side of it, through each of which glimmered a faint light; two win-

dows above, from one of which peered a white, tearful face—
a man with an evil, sinister face, stood beneath the lone pine,
holding a wailing child by its hair with one hand, and in the
other—Oh God, the horror of it!—a long, sharp knife, which
glistened as the glimmer from the windows struck it.

I didn't faint, I didn't fall, so rooted to the spot was I, I seemed
as if made of stone. The wind had all but died away; and, but for
the fact that, in my now frenzied brain, I *knew* I had seen the
place desolate and ruined, I should have thought I was faced
with a workman's dwelling, peopled by real beings. I *knew* it
was *not* so. Fascinated, horrified, I gazed. The man moved, with
a muttered curse, dragging the child with him up to the door;
as he reached it, the wind redoubled its fury, howling, shrieking,
like every evil let loose. I fell on my knees, powerless now to
even pray; and hiding my face in my hands, I waited, for some
awful thing, I knew, was to come.

It came, with a wild scream of awful horror, the scream from
an upstairs window! and then a second, the shrill, awful scream
of a child! Agonized, I knelt, and saw the man lurch through the
door, reeling, join a group of waiting people hitherto unseen by
me. As he came up to them, one of the women spoke to him,
and then began to laugh. Oh God! the unspeakable horror of
that laugh. One after another of the group spoke to the man,
and each, as they moved off, laughed or chuckled, even two
small boys who were with them burst into shrill laughter. I cannot describe it, save only in one way, it sounded like fiends from
Hell, so vile, so malicious, so diabolical were those awful sounds.

As I knelt, unable to move, I struggled to keep a hold of
myself, I found I was striving to explain away what I knew in
my heart was totally inexplicable. I whispered to myself, "That
laughter *is* real, *is* human, hideous as it is," but I knew it was neither real nor human. Always, to my dying day, it will ring in my
ears, laughter such as no human creature could be responsible
for.

Quite suddenly, there came a lull in the wind, a stillness in
the air, the laughter died away. Could I, dare I move, rise, and

venture to look? But even as I thought of it, the wind, with re-doubled fury, broke forth again, causing me to crouch still lower as it swept over me. An awful crash sounded, a crash that echoed and re-echoed through the woods. The wind had seized and felled, as if with giant hand, the pine that had been standing at the far side of the cottage.

So terrific was the blow that the end of the cottage, where it hit, fell like a house of cardboard! To demolish the rest of it seemed but child's play, as, with one whistling shriek, the wind tore beneath the now shattered roof, ripping it off, and almost the remainder of the walls, with a deafening roar, high above which rang out peal after peal of hideous laughter! until it, too, died away as now the wind was dying, dying fitfully, with an angry gust, and then a sobbing wail, until at length a long low wail seemed to pass through the woods and fade into silence, a long silence.

At last I moved, raised my head, looked, listened. Nothing, no sound broke the stillness; the ruined cottage was as I had first seen it, just a worn, weather-beaten heap of grey stones, a semblance of a fireplace, five stone stairs, that was all. I ventured nearer, try-ing to persuade myself I had dreamed the horrible scene. I must have dreamed it, for it had been dark, pitch dark, when the wind had begun to rise, and yet, by what light then had I witnessed this awful thing, for light of some kind there surely had been. Who were those people I had seen, from whom came that awful laughter? I was trembling yet, shaken, feeling desperately ill, no dream had brought me to this pass—then what?

Visitants from "Beyond?" But to what end, for they and their works were evil? I turned abruptly, with one thought in my head, to get out of the wood, and home. I glanced at my watch, having made a point this time of winding and setting it right—only five o'clock. I must be mad, I had gone through hours of dark night; how could it possibly be but five! I supposed, long afterwards, when I reviewed these hours, that it was the knowl-edge that it was only five o'clock, and not perhaps, as I expected, many hours later, that gave me the fillip of courage, which led me to linger still another moment near the ruins, and gaze, as if to print the thing on my mind. I stood possibly three yards from the ruined doorway, and said aloud "It was a murder!" Away through the woods came the mocking answer "A murder."

"Oh God!" I gasped, "not again, for they are fiends from Hell!"—"From Hell!" came back the answer, and again the awful sound of laughter of many voices—

I turned and fled, holding my hands over my ears as I strove to run. I remember knocking violently against something, and falling, falling, falling, endlessly, or so it seemed, and then nothingness—until I opened my eyes three weeks later, to find myself in bed in my quaint room at the farm, and beside my bed, placidly knitting, sat Mrs. Merry.

"Merry!" I whispered, and the sound, or want of sound, in my own voice startled me.

"Yes, it's me, sir," answered the dear soul, "and high time too; but we are not talking, sir, if *you* please, it is medicine time and then you'll sleep."

I only too gladly obeyed, unquestioningly, as I obeyed for many weeks, the quiet, though firm, commands of Mrs. Merry. I was far too weak to fight, even had it been of the slightest use; indeed, it was very little less than six weeks ere I was permitted to ask a question or have my own way in anything; but at length a day came when I was allowed to sit in a chair by the window, from which the view was something only expressed by colour, words could not do it. I gazed for a long time in silence, then said:

"I am well now, Merry, tell me what brought you, what has been wrong with me, where was I, everything—I must know."

She looked at me, then put her glasses on—she always did that if she meant to talk severely, then she said abruptly:

"You'd been missing for two days when they found you."

"Missing for two days?" I asked, incredulously, "But where was I?"

"You were at the bottom of an old lead mine," she answered, "on a big heap of dead leaves and ferns. Luckily, it wasn't one of the deep mines, and also the leaves and ferns saved you, though how they got there is a mystery," she added.

"But how on earth—" I began.

"Quite so, sir," she went on, "that's what we all want to know, how on earth, unless you were mooning along and wandered into a weak place in the ground above the mine. That's where you were, anyway, in one of the small shafts close to the old ruined cottage. You were quite unconscious; you must have had your camera in your hand, sir, because it was beside you, though how it wasn't broken is another mystery."

"Bring me my camera, Merry dear," I said.

"Very well, sir," she answered. "That can't do you no harm"; and off she went, to return presently, gingerly holding my Kodak, as if fearful of it.

She was right. By some marvel it was unhurt; moreover the number of the film it had last turned to stood clearly forth. I would have them developed at once. I felt curious, but I had not yet asked all my questions:

"Who found me, Merry?" I next asked.

"Tommy Hughes, sir."

"Tommy Hughes!" I said. "What made him look for me?"

"Well, sir," answered the old lady, "they do say as he found another gentleman once in the same place, and when you didn't come home, he set off to look for you."

"Was the other chap hurt, Merry?" I asked.

"No, sir—at least not hurt, sir, because he was lying on ferns and leaves just the same. Oh no! he wasn't hurt, sir, not his body!"

"What do you mean?" I asked. "Tell me, please."

"Oh, dear sir, how you do worrit, and it's time for your soup, anyway."

"Tell me first, Merry," I said.

She glanced at me, to see if I was in earnest, and then, seemingly, decided that for the moment, at least, I was boss.

"His body was all right, sir, it was his head, at least his wits, sir; he's been in a lunatic place ever since, so they say," she amended, with a sniff which, I knew, meant utter disbelief in gossip or village yarns.

I did *not* so entirely disbelieve, for, as the fragments of memory began to join together, I shuddered as I recalled my experience, and could only too readily believe that a very, little weaker minded individual than I would very easily lose his reason if he went through all I had done. I would, however, leave further questioning until the next day, for I had observed the snap with which my dear old Merry had closed her lips.

The following day my doctor paid me a visit, one of his many, but this time he came in less professional manner, in fact he had every appearance of spoiling for a gossip, I could have wagered my last *sou* on it, so wasn't surprised when he accepted my offer of tea, and a smoke, with alacrity. The tea disposed of, he did not beat about the bush, but asked me if I could give him any light at all on my accident.

"I am curiously interested," he said, "because you are not my first case to have a very similar accident."

"Did your other patient make as good recovery, doctor?" I asked, instead of, as politeness demanded, answering his question.

"No, he did not," he replied. "He never recovered and never will in my opinion. He is mentally deranged, though all searching has failed to reveal a cause. He is quiet generally, and peaceable, but in a high wind he becomes frenzied, utterly distraught, his attendants are unable to cope with him, often he shrieks and yells, for the most part unintelligible rubbish. One night, in a furious gale, a man was blown over in the grounds, and the attendants were laughing about it when, without apparent reason, the poor insane chap fell on the luckless attendant and half-killed him, shouting all the time:

"Stop laughing, will you!" It's always the same if the wind blows. They take him to a more sheltered room when it blows hard now.

"Tell me, will you, what preceded your fall—there must be some sort of link between the two, because, in your delirium, you raved of the wind, though we've had no wind to speak of

119

since your arrival."

"I'll tell you the story, doctor, though you will be inclined to put me with your other patient, *unless* I can convince you, and this I may perhaps do, if my camera depicts what I saw."

I told him my experiences during two days in the woods I loved, I gave him every detail, even to the taking of the snapshots of the place, and he listened, silently puffing at his pipe, until I ended by telling him of how I struck something violently and fell, remembering nothing more until I found myself in my room.

There was a long pause as I finished, he seemed unable to speak, so I asked him how Mrs. Merry came upon the scene.

"She arrived after you had lain long unconscious, saying you had said if you were not home in a month to come and look for you—not hearing, she came and found you, as I have said, and has since nursed you devotedly.

"What does it all mean, doctor?" I then said.

His answer disconcerted me.

"I do not know, though I have heard strange stories told of the pine woods, which you are pleased to call "Silent," but I confess I have hitherto put them down to an extra glass or two of beer. Now, for the first time, I am bound to think more seriously of them, having on my hands first, the strange maniac, and then you, found in the same spot, under similar conditions, and—strangest of all—on *the same day* of the year!

"I don't know the tale, but no doubt your worthy host does, ask him; and, meanwhile, develop your snapshots, though I do not hope for much in the way of proofs from them."

"I will look in tomorrow, you had better rest now," and my matter-of-fact materialistic doctor picked up his hat and departed.

I sat at my window for a long time, thinking much, hearing again, in fancy, the roar of wind, the laughter of fiends, the crash of the tree. As it grew dark, I was possessed with the desire, at all costs, to develop those films, so, calling Mrs. Merry, I told her I was tired, and was going to bed, that there was nothing I required, so, bidding her "Goodnight," I made my rough and ready preparations, lacking all the essentials of a proper dark room, but in these days, tabloids of developers, a jugful of water, a candle-lamp, with a crimson silk scarf tied round it, would serve me very well.

The first negative came up beautifully, just an ordinary common or garden broken-down cottage.

The second was a different story, and I watched it fearfully. There was distinctly, unmistakably, a form of a man going into the doorway!

The third film, taken from the other side of the cottage, showed me a lower window, more or less unbroken, in the frame of which was the face of a man—so much I could see, but to me that meant much, for *I knew* that I was alone, horribly alone at that moment of taking the photo.

Next morning, I was up earlier than had been permitted for some time, and a very few minutes sufficed to print a rough print from each negative. I stared at them, stared, with my eyes nearly starting from my head. They were good photos, clear, sharply defined, no woolly-looking details, so easily mistaken for other than the actual things I intended to take, except the figure, and the face. Those I neither saw, nor intended to portray, yet there they were, and, as is so often the case, the camera lens depicted what the human eye did not see.

The figure, tall, gaunt, seemed as if going into the house, but the face! the *face* in the frame of the window was unmistakably the face of the man who passed me, who entered the house, from which issued those screams of agony, the man who later joined the group of people to whom he spoke, the people who made the air hideous with their horrible laughter.

I kept my own counsel, hiding the photos also, until late in the afternoon, the doctor made his appearance. He studied them carefully, and then said:

"I should have laughed at your story, my friend, laughed at your photos of your so-called empty cottage, last evening, but tonight I cannot. I made a few enquiries after I left you, and the outline of what I gleaned was this:

"The cottage was built when the lead mines were working, for the use of the men, and was subsequently taken possession of by a foreman. He was a glum, taciturn brute, given to drink and gambling. He brought with him to the cottage, known as Leadmine Cottage, a very pretty young girl as his wife, though gossips say she was not. He seemed passionately attached to the girl, and also to a little child of three, said to be his niece's child. The man, by name Woodrow, led an almost double life, one half of which was spent with a gang of men and women, with whom he was said to drink and gamble; and who used to jeer at him for what they spoke of as his milksop life, in the company of his so-called wife.

"When with her, he was simply a devoted husband, and when sober always refused to associate with the gang who other times attracted him. Finally, the gang of criminals—I can call them nothing better—tried to embitter him against the girl, whom they thought was getting a firmer hold on him. One or other of them started to fill his mind with suspicions of the girl, telling him that chance visitors found Leadmine Cottage attractive. They used to follow him home, for the fiendish joke of hearing him abuse the girl and threaten her with worse things if she was untrue to him.

"These fiends finally plotted, and eventually sent a young doctor out there, saying someone was ill in the cottage. The unsuspecting doctor called late one evening, and Woodrow was persuaded to hide in the trees and watch. It was, I am told, a wild, stormy evening, one of those sudden storms that come in these mountain districts in summer, and break down corn, lash rivers to fury, and hurl trees and branches to the ground.

"Woodrow watched, and saw the doctor enter, saw him speak to the girl, saw her smile at him, and laughing, give him her hand as she might do to a doctor, who desired to feel her pulse; though this was apparently not the construction put upon her innocent action by her husband, goaded to madness by drink, as well as by his uncontrollable jealous nature. He waited until the doctor had gone, and then entered the cottage, murdered his wife and child, afterwards rejoining his fellow-criminal, whom, it is said, received his news with jest and laughter, glorying in the success of the vile plot which they guessed would give him wholly back to them and their evil ways.

"The cottage and all trace of the crime was effaced, so 'tis said, by the sudden rising of the wind, bringing down a tree, which fell athwart the house, shattering it to bits. The gang are believed to have fled the country, all but one, who later died in hospital after giving the story to a medical man there, whom, by a curious coincidence, if indeed there be such things, wrote it to a colleague of mine, whom I met last night at a dinner. It is a strange story, and one, in the light of your recent experience, not to be gainsaid. The story goes on to say, that in the same month every year, the murder takes place, with every detail complete, even to the rising wind; and that those who know the story and the wood, shun it as the plague, during that month. At any other time, I believe, it justifies our name for it of 'Silent Wood.'

"That is the story, my friend, make of it what you will. I have also taken the liberty of asking an aged miner to look in this evening. I want you to be good enough to start chatting casually of the wood, your fall, etc., and show him your photos. Don't give him any other lead. Now, I will see if he has come. He is very old, but can see pretty well. His little grandchild is bringing him to see me here, to save time, and the old boy wants a dose for a cough."

With this, the doctor vanished, to return almost at once, leading an old man by the arm. They tell me folks live long up here, and surely it must be so if this is a specimen, for the old man looked ninety, and hale at that, though bent and withered. I gave him a chair and baccy, but instead of filling his pipe, he stared at me with clear, penetrating eyes, and mumbled:

"So you're the gent that fell down the mine."

"Yes," I said, "I'm that unfortunate man."

"Did you fall, or were yer put there?" he questioned, sniggering to himself.

"I don't know," I said.

"No, my boy, but *I* do," he wheezed, pointing a claw-like finger at me. "I do, yer were put there, my lad, put there, look you, and so will others be, if they do not keep away from the pines in July!"

"I took a picture of it," I said, after a pause.

"A picture—whatever—" answered the aged being, "show me the picture. I once worked there."

"Hurry," whispered the doctor, "he quickly fails.'

I handed him the picture, holding a powerful magnifying glass over it as I did so.

"Aye, aye! there's Johnny Woodrow's house," he muttered, "all in a heap, all in a heap."

"This is another," I said.

"My God!" burst from his shaking lips. "My God, there's Johnny Woodrow, Johnny Woodrow, my old pal. Why, I thought him was dead, he is dead, I knows he's dead, how could he live after murdering his wife and little child—murdered them, he did, in the cottage by the pines, and them as interferes with the cottage, he'd put 'em down the mine—he said he would put 'em in the mine to starve, if they move a stone or meddle with wot 'e calls her grave. He told me he'd do it afore he went away, 'is very words were 'Living or dead, I'll do it, Bob,' and wot Johnny says he'll do, he *will* do."

His old head fell forward on his breast as he finished speaking, so we did not speak, save in a whisper.

"He sleeps," said the doctor. "Presently he will wake, but will not remember. We will leave him. Mary will take him home, and I'll send him some stuff in the morning. The old boy is nearly through," he added, "but I am glad he was here to give you what you wanted—proof!" though proof of what, or for what reason, I cannot pretend to fathom.

We parted a little later, my doctor and I—he to go on with his work for sick humanity; I, on the morrow, to return to my studio in London, back to the turmoil of town, back to live among the haunts of men, to leave the beauty of hills and rivers;

but in some quiet hour in my studio, maybe during some winter night of wind and storm, I shall hear again the hideous laughter, shall dream of the scent of the pines—nay, perhaps I shall even try to forget the horror of all I went through, and may memory, sometimes kind, only recall the peace, the scent, the perfect still quietness of the woods I loved best, when I knew them only as

"Silent Wood."

The Twins

The tragedy of my life is summed up in these words—"Basil and I were twins!" It doesn't sound tragical, it doesn't sound even interesting, but hear my story, and pity me.

From the hour of our birth we were remarkably alike: both were dark, both had brown eyes. In fact, so much alike were we that the usual tricks were resorted to by both mother and nurses to distinguish us, and if, as once happened, my blue-ribboned rattle got changed for Basil's pink one, why, then, I swallowed a nauseous dose of medicine, intended for him. That was the start: from then onwards, my brother's misdeeds were laid at my door. *My* indolence, *laziness* my father called it, was put down to my brother.

If our parents had been *really* interested in us, they would have studied our various temperaments, discovering that only in appearance had we the remotest resemblance; and, knowing this, if they had guided us, taught us, and led us, all the sorrow that eventually fell to me would have been non-existent. But parents differ so; some give all their thoughts, time and money to their children, ours gave none. They were wrapt up in each other, and in the gay social life they led. We were more of a bother than a joy, our bringing up depending chiefly on the ministrations of our nurses, and the rough tutoring of an old Scotch gardener, aided by stable men, odd boys about the park—all and sundry, in fact, who could do us harm instead of good!

The difference between us in appearance was so very slight that even our coachman had been known to bring a pony ready saddled for *me,* who at heart was an arrant coward, whereas Basil would ride pretty nearly anything on four legs. I have seen him try to ride a pig, a sheep, and a cow. He was fearless where horses were concerned, adored animals of every kind, being kindness itself to sick or maimed ones. The kink in his character being love of self, he would stoop to any lie or subterfuge to escape deserved punishment, never having the least scruple about letting me suffer for his misdeeds. He rarely opened a book, except French ones—prohibited—and these were usually found on *my* shelf, or in *my* drawer, never in his.

In our school days, it was Basil who went out of bounds, for sweets, cakes, etc., to the tuck shop, but it was *my* cap, and very likely *my* jacket, that he wore, and *my* room the stuff was stowed away in, until he had time to eat it! In holiday time, it was Basil in *my* pyjamas who acted "Ghost" and terrified the maids; Basil who lamed my father's famous hunter, but *my* whip that was found in the paddock; Basil who was seen drinking beer in the village "pub," but *I* who was kept a prisoner in my room, and not allowed to go to the skating carnival in a neighbour's park; Basil who enjoyed the society of Esmé Simpson, the doctor's daughter; and so it went on.

Occasionally the truth would be found out, and then folks said to me:

"Why don't you assert yourself, give Basil away, and let the right shoulders bear the blame?"

My reply invariably was:

"Too much trouble; besides, it is difficult to swear away the evidence before people's eyes." It was *my* whip, it was *my* cap, they were *my* pyjamas. No one could get away from those facts, my and nature was becoming warped and morbid through long years of injustice, from which there was no redress.

Later, Basil grew more and more unscrupulous, and several times feigned my handwriting, using my notepaper, etc., writing notes, purporting to come from me, to Esmé Simpson; until, at last, the old doctor, called on me to know if I intended asking his girl to be my wife! To Basil, all this was a huge jest; to me, it still further embittered my life. I was only twenty-four, I did want Esmé; our comradeship, which began in our childhood, was really, in my mind, just a sweet chumship, without a deeper note; but the letters shown to me by the doctor were masterpieces of love-making, and so it came about, as usual, my denials were unheeded, and I was forced into an engagement with Esmé, whom I did not love, and did not want.

She was a dear girl, and an ideal wife for some country doctor or lawyer; was a capable manager, possessed a clear, clever brain; but to me, "Bossiness" aptly described her, and her love of meddling in other folks' business was to me a perpetual worry. A new baby, she was there, lecturing the mother; a wedding, she was there, to dress and buck up the bride; a funeral, she was there, to put things in order and boss generally. It wearied me at first, and made me frantic at last, for my dreamy temperament wanted tranquillity, peace, softness.

My ideal wife was a very different being from this girl, chosen by fate to be mine. I *had* met my "Dream-girl," met her in the only spot in all the world in which, so far, I was free from my brother: a friend's studio in Chelsea, where I made one of a happy Bohemian crowd on the rare occasions I could escape alone to London. So far, Basil had no trace of me there, for my friends of the studio faithfully kept my secret, all of them remembering a single sentence, which I invariably announced my arrival in town with, proving to them *I* was Dal and *not* Basil.

The words were these, though I fear to put them on paper, lest Basil should one day see them, but so far all is safe, and the words "The lotus flower is in bloom" was sufficient to call together my kindred spirits in the Bohemian corner I loved, the atmosphere of which suited me, and where I was known and was myself only, and not the dual personality I so often seemed to be.

There were one or two artists, a few writers, a few musicians, no terrific overwhelming talent amongst them, but sufficient for each to peg along, paying their way, enjoying a little simple amusement, though the charm lay in the happy-go-lucky spirit of "never crossing our bridges until we reached them," coupled with the ever-ready hand of friendship and help, which one and all never failed to hold out, if needs be.

This was my paradise, my oasis in a world that was using me ill, through my twin brother's evil character.

In my paradise there was an "Angel;" at least, to me she was one, though most people only saw a little elf-like girl, with clouds of dusky hair and green eyes, a small compact little person, with tiny feet and wee, capable hands. She was usually enveloped in an old greeny-grey painting pinafore, when she was not helping someone who was sick or tired, then the pinny was cast aside, and a practical little person, in well-worn, though well-cut blue serge, with a string of jade beads round her throat, would take the place of the dreamy, fanciful little being of her studio up in the roof of an old house.

She made enough out of her dainty water-colours for her needs, and to supply those of a few other folks, she occasionally did a small amount of illustrating for papers or magazines, to help out, but this latter work was necessity, and not her wish. Sometimes we did not see her for weeks, but a call to a "Lotus flower" meeting usually unearthed her. She held my heart tightly in the hollow of her little hand, and just to be near her brought out all that was best in me, leaving all that was bitter and wrong far outside. I intended to marry her, as soon as I had an assured position, but this seemed still far distant. So our happiness consisted chiefly of teas in her studio, or walks in unknown bits of old London, with the stars above us and love in our hearts.

My "castle" came crashing to earth with my forced so-called engagement to Esmé Simpson. I told the whole story to Alys, as I told her most things, sure of her understanding and sympathy; but, on this occasion, the only one in my life, she did not hear me with that wholehearted faith in me which usually characterized her attitude towards me. She listened, that's true, but listened standing stiffly, coldly, aloof, not curled up on her favourite cushion on the floor in front of her fire; she listened silently, she always did, but oh, what a difference there can be in silence! There is the "silence" of warm understanding love, which seems to envelope you, bringing its own sweet helpfulness and sympathy, but there is the "silence" of cold criticism, which chills you through and through, making you hesitate and falter in your tale, as if indeed you were guilty.

It was this unusual "silence" which encompassed me, as I struggled to tell Alys my woeful story, causing me to stumble, to halt, and finally to burst out with— "Oh, you don't understand, you can't! It seems an impossible yarn to ask you to believe that love letters written by someone else should be the means of *my* getting engaged to someone else."

Alys only looked at me steadily for an instant, and then said:

"It is almost impossible to think that *you* did nothing yourself to put into Miss Simpson's mind the idea that you cared for her."

The words were slowly, carefully uttered, but they raised the devil in me, and I spoke words which a lifetime has been all too short in which to regret. We parted silently, without so much as a hand-clasp—we who had been all in all to each other for four years; we who had so repeatedly said, could not live without each other—parted, bitterly, and month of trials, and troubles were my lot ere the sunshine of my little girl's smile burst upon my sorrowful life, bringing in my latter years the love, the peace, and happiness, that I had thought was within my grasp. On the day we parted, we never meant to meet again, but our lives became interwoven in a manner which left no room for doubt as to our love for each other.

My existence after this was a round of subtle cruelties, practised by my seemingly fascinating brother, and it made of me a morose and gloomy being. My engagement to Esmé was proclaimed far and wide by her worthy, though mercenary, old father. I fulfilled to the best of my ability my duty of an engaged man, but refrained from marrying, hoping always that something would happen to prevent it. Nothing did, and I could see Dr. Simpson was of opinion that the time was surely come for his daughter's wedding to take place. Especially as Basil and I were now well off, owing to the death of our parents at sea—an occurrence, I am sorry to say, which left us unmoved, being, as we were, almost strangers to them.

It was a lovely morning early in May, on which I received a visit from my future father-in-law, a visit which blinded the sunshine, leaving me feeling as if now, in very truth, my last hope had fled. I listened to all he said, and was obliged to agree, that short of playing the villain, there was nothing for me to do but marry the girl, whose name, he said, was suffering through my neglect, and whose health was becoming undermined, owing to her great love for me, and my coldness in responding. So it was settled, the wedding day fixed for six weeks ahead, and it was arranged that, as stated in my father's will, the first of us to marry was to live in the old home. This arrangement flung Basil into a rage; he did not see why I should live in the home that belonged equally to both of us, so, in a fit of generosity I said:

"Live here as well!" and, rather to my surprise, he joyfully agreed. I repented of my rashness—only once, and that was forever!

Towards the end of the six weeks' freedom left to me, I went up to town, and spent a quiet afternoon in the Art Gallery. I was strolling idly through the rooms when I came upon a little group of people. I only noticed them casually; but, as I passed them, something compelled me to raise my eyes and I looked straight into the green eyes of my one and only love.

"Alys," I murmured, but a cold stare and a quick movement showed me I was not even to be considered a friend of the girl I loved. I moved away, hearing as I did so, the gay voice of her attendant swain say:

"Come, it is 4.30—tea-time, and I'm starving!" Something made me pull out my own watch, as one so often does, and compare the stated time with one's own. True, it was exactly 4.30. I also would go and find tea, but alone!

I landed back home after the short railway journey, but alighted at the station before our own, intending to have a tramp home after the stuffiness of a London May-day. The walk would take me almost an hour, and the woods and fields appealed to me, so, lighting my pipe, I set out. It was almost dusk when I reached "The Park," and lights were beginning to twinkle here and there amongst the local cottages, though "The Park," as our house was called, struck me as looking particularly bleak and dark.

I entered quietly, and was slipping upstairs to my own rooms, when I was suddenly confronted at the top of the stairs by Smithson, our butler and factotum, accompanied by the village policeman.

I thought they were cronies, and perhaps had been having a quiet smoke, and was passing them with a curt "Good evening" when—

"Please stop, sir," burst from Constable Gill.

I stopped.

"Anything wrong?" I enquired.

"Yes, sir. Miss Simpson has been found murdered in the old Spinny, and it is my duty to arrest you for murder."

"Don't speak, sir," he added, in kinder tones, "everything's against you."

I was powerless, speechless, and suffered myself to be led away to the village gaol, where I sat, dazed, able to think. Only the merest details had been told to me, simply that about four o'clock, Esmé Simpson had been found shot through the heart lying among the ferns in what was known as "The Little Spinny." A book was lying close to, a walking-stick—which she generally used—lay a yard or so from her, and the revolver, with one chamber emptied, was at her side. It was, I need hardly say, *my* revolver. More than this I did not know, any more than I knew how I was going to extricate myself from such a predicament. I was known to have been absent the whole of that day, but no one knew where I had been, even my ticket to London was no guarantee that I ever went there.

I was *not* seen leaving the train at my own station, and I question very much whether anyone noticed my departure from the station before. I *was* seen crossing the fields beyond the Spinny, however, yet, surely, no one in their senses could think I would murder a woman between three and four, and hide in the woods until six, the time I reached home. A sudden thought came to me—

Alys! She had seen me, she knew me, at 4.30, in London. Could I send word? Would she come? Would she say she had seen me? Surely, surely, I could trust her, but would she believe or would she doubt? The more I thought, the deeper and darker seemed the abyss before me. I could not see one solitary gleam of light anywhere.

At the inquest, it was proved to the satisfaction of the neighbours that I, Dallas York, had wilfully murdered the girl I was about to marry, using a revolver, proved to be mine, because it had my name on it. I was committed for trial at the County Assizes, and, so far as I could see, my life was ended.

I do not propose to dwell on the awful weeks which followed. I had able lawyers from town to aid me, and to them I told my story. I could see, while doing their best for me, they had little hope, especially, as they found the studio in Chelsea, where I had directed them to seek for Alys, empty! and none knew where the lady had gone. Then I implored them to send my brother to me, for surely he would speak; he could not really mean me to be hanged. If he would only come, I would plead and beg for my very life.

Alas! for my last frail hope, my brother was missing, had not, in fact, been seen since the day of the murder, and village rumour had it that he had said he would not live in the same county as a murderer!

After this the days went by in agony. Time sped, and my trial was upon me. I was tried, by twelve good men and true, and I was found guilty and condemned to death.

The last day of my life had dawned. I was past all feeling, as I sat in my cell, waiting the sound of the keys which would herald my doom.

I heard the heavy footfall of my jailor coming, coming, nearer, louder. I heard the jangle of the keys. I heard the key turn in the lock, and the grating sound as the door swung open, and then— I fainted—

When I came to myself, I opened my eyes on familiar surroundings. I was in my own bedroom at "The Park," so much I was sure of, and then followed another blank. Slowly, very slowly, I came to complete understanding, and learned that it was to bring me a pardon that my cell door had been opened, and *not* to take me to my death, for my brother had, at the last moment, given himself up as the murderer of Esmé Simpson, and was hanged instead of me. He told all before he died, how all his life he had hated me for my superiorness, he called it, and had planned and schemed to injure me always, even to ransacking my desk, and learning of Alys, to whom he had gone, purporting to be me, using our "Lotus flower" code; and finally taking her away to lock her up, and so prevent her giving, as she intended, evidence in my favour.

It was a sordid, horrible tale, ending with the murder of Esmé, whom he confessed he had always cared for, and whom he killed in a fit of temper, vowing I should not have her, since she would not have him. Poor fellow! he did the only brave deed in his evil life when he confessed, and took the place so wrongfully allocated to me. His last message was given to the chaplain to give me—

> Tell my brother Dallas I have done right by him, but that time will show him his life will not be a calm one in spite of my death to spare an innocent man.

I did not understand the message then. I *do now,* and daily, hourly, the full horror of all he intended to convey comes home to me!

After the whirl of tragedy which had enveloped me, I lay ill and weak for some weeks; at times bordering on brain fever, and again just lying ill and spent, waited upon by a hard-featured nurse, whose aim appeared to be business and *not* comfort; a woman to whom I represented two guineas a week, and disturbed nights; a woman whose very voice grated in my ears, and whose pursed-up lips, as she took my temperature, made me long to shake her, upsetting the stiff set of her appalling cap, and putting a few creases in her starched apron. She was an automaton, and I question much whether, in her stiffly-held head, there was any other knowledge than the measurements of a medicine glass or the reading of her precious thermometer. I was thankful when, at last, I was able to leave my bed, and try to pick up the shattered threads of my life. The dismissal of my nurse I hailed with thanksgiving, and celebrated the event by going downstairs for my small dinner, after which I intended to pass a few hours in the library with a book and pipe, or my thoughts, for company.

I had successfully managed to dispose of a grilled sole, and was idly playing with my wine glass, when it suddenly snapped in two pieces. How stupid of me, I thought, and what a mess!

"Smithson," I called, as the butler hovered near, "tidy this up, will you; I can't think how I was so careless."

The man eyed me gravely, as he set about removing the debris, but did not speak. As he was moving away, my chair jogged violently.

"Don't hit my chair, Smithson," I exclaimed, irritably.

"Sorry, sir," he answered, "but I didn't; sir."

"You must have done," I snapped, and again there was silence.

Left to myself, I played with the food put before me, feeling weak, tired, unnerved, and unable to eat. I was chilly, too, in spite of a big fire of logs; a curious chilliness, it seemed, but I put it down to all I had gone through, and my subsequent illness; so wended my way to the library, as being a more cosy room than the huge dining-room in which I felt so solitary and alone.

Alone! did. I say, or rather think, yet, even as the word crossed my mind, I was conscious that it was wrong, I did *not* feel *alone!* Would to God I had! Some other presence was there, I knew it, I felt it; I knew it when my wine glass snapped, I knew it when my chair shook. It needed not the feeling of chilliness to impress me that as I sat at my apparently lonely table, some other being was there also!

I resolutely turned, my steps to the library, switching on all the lights as I entered, so that no gloomy corners or shadows could aid my imagination. Taking a book, I drew up an armchair, lit my pipe, and prepared for a quiet read. As I seated myself, the chair similar to mine, on the opposite side of the hearth, wheeled softly towards the fire! and I heard the soft thud, as of a person sitting down, followed by the clatter of the fire-irons. Then I knew! for Basil had invariably sat, feet on fender, usually preceded by the kicking away of the fire-irons. I knew I was ill, but I also knew definitely that *this* was no phantasy of an enfeebled mind. *This* was real, vivid, I was *not* alone, my brother Basil bore me company!

Steadily I tried to read, never for a single moment unmindful of the fact that the opposite chair was occupied. When I could no longer keep any attention on my book, I rose, determined to go to bed. As I rose, so did he, pushing back his chair as I moved mine. Something—call it fear if you will—made me pause, hesitatingly, as I reached the light switches. "I will send Smithson to put them out," I murmured; but a faint soft chuckle fell on my ear as every light was instantly snapped out, and I felt someone pass me.

I managed to keep some sort of grip on myself as I sauntered through the hall, and leisurely made my way upstairs. Even as I did so, I heard the soft steps, always furtive as they had been in life, follow me to the top, along the corridor, stopping only as they reached my door. Quickly I entered, slamming the door behind me, foolishly thinking here, at least, I should be free and alone. Alas for my hopes! I speedily learnt that not even here could that be so, no matter where I turned or what I did, those furtive steps followed. I tried to pray, to voice some feeble petition that this haunting presence might leave me. It was useless, or I was too powerless.

Half frantic I sought my bedside where stood a small table on which was a framed photo of Alys. I picked it up, to gaze longingly at her sweet face, but the picture was seized from my hand and dashed violently on to the floor. With a smothered sob of grief and anger, I bent to pick it up, but ere I could do so, a hand was pressed heavily on my shoulder, and I raised my head to see a faint illumination—almost, it seemed to me, like a ring of light, in the centre of which stood—my brother! Pale, drawn, silent, he stood, with a faint mocking smile upon his lips, and a mark as of a rope showing plainly round his neck.

I remembered nothing more until I came to myself with Smithson bending over me, holding a glass, containing some spirits, to my lips.

"Smithson!" I gasped. "What is it? Where am I? What has happened?"

"I heard you call out, sir," replied the imperturbable Smithson, "and I came, fortunately you had forgotten to lock your door, I found you on the floor, sir, with this broken glass picture alongside of you, sir. Did you slip, sir? Or were you ill?"

"Neither, Smithson," I said, wildly. "I—I—oh—I can't explain; you'd have me locked up as insane."

For a moment Smithson eyed me, and then, in a voice more human than his "butler" voice, he said:

"I understand, sir, I understand, it is an awful thing, sir, but you are not alone in it, sire Mr. Basil has been with me too."

"Been with *you?*" I echoed. "How do you mean, explain please, Smithson."

"Yes, sir," answered the man, "he, Mr. Basil, follows me about, has done ever, since he—be— you know, sir—he breaks things, upsets things, turns pictures face to the wall, rings bells, and if I answer them, I've heard him give that laugh of his, sort of mocks one, he does, sir, same as he used. He goes along to his own room, sir, and times I've gone in, and found the bed all crumpled up like as if someone slept in it, I don't know if anyone else has heard him, and I've kept me mouth shut, sir, you know, beggin' your pardon, sir, that Mr. Basil was never my favourite, and he seems to be set on paying me back for telling a few things I knew he had done, and blamed *you,* sir. One of the stable hands did tell me, someone had been playing pranks with the horses one night, though, and that all the beasts were uneasy and fidgety, but I said nothing, and now, sir, here are you, on your first

137

day downstairs, bothered same as I've been."

"Smithson," I said, "you're a brick, don't let us be beaten, be my friend, as well as my butler, and see this thing through together if we can."

"I'm with you, sir," answered the man, "there's my hand on it, if I may make so free, you've been kind to me and mine always, sir, and I'll not desert you. Shall I bring a camp-bed into your room, sir," he added, in his usual matter-of-fact tones, "until you are well, Sir,—I'd better, I think."

That night passed quietly, and I was awakened by Smithson at my side with a cup of tea, imperturbable as ever, all trace of his camp-bed removed ere he wakened me. I felt tired, yet in a sense alert, feeling as if I must get up in spite of weakness, for I had work to do which I intended to accomplish.

Gone, were the fears of last night, gone, the shaken nerves, I intended to win—I was *not* going to be beaten, trampled on mentally—if I may put it so, rendered unfit, by the haunting of my brother. Surely if his tricks were to be confined to the senseless jogging of chairs, breaking of glasses and such like, they were means of a paltry description, and I would speedily show him I was unaffected by them. So determined a clear brain, in a room full of brilliant morning sunshine! I spent a quiet morning, resting and reading, and decided I would after lunch, try what a gentle ride on my favourite horse would do towards restoring my former health and strength.

It clouded over towards noon, but I rather liked grey clouds with a warm wind, and started off with a smile and nod to Smithson, who watched me start with rather a solemn look on his face, and a caution "not to overdo it, sir, first time." Sultan was a little fresh at starting, but gradually settled down and we jogged along peacefully for an hour, when I thought, possibly by the time I got home, I would *not* have overdone it, first time. As we turned towards home, I noticed Sultan stumble.

"Steady, boy," I murmured, "that is unlike you," and bent to pat his satin, smooth neck. Before I touched him, he shied violently, nearly unseating me.

138

"I see nothing to shy at, boy," I said, but my voice had no effect, and he suddenly stopped dead, beginning to quiver and shake.

Surely the beast's ill, I thought, preparing to dismount and lead him, but he suddenly seemed to steady down and impatiently shook his head as if to loosen my restraining hand.

"Very well then," I said, "go ahead," and he started off obediently—probably a couple of hundred yards were accomplished when again the same sudden stop and quivering. My temper was rising, and I brought my whip down pretty sharply on his haunches. Instantly, he reared, and with a wild snort, set off at a gallop, heading for home; half a mile we galloped, when he paused again, but evidently with the recollection of my whip, did not stop, but giving a wild, terrified squeal as of terror, he took off and jumped probably nearly six feet high, as if over a high fence, and tore on down the road home, not stopping until he pulled up of his own accord at the front door, where he stood quivering in every limb, with the sweat in gleaming patches staining his satin coat.

My return was greeted by a keen look and a profound silence on the part of Smithson, that is, until the library door closed behind him, as he followed me in. Nor did he then wait for me to speak, but his quick "What is it, sir?" seemed almost wrung from him. I answered somewhat curtly, feeling almost too worried to reply at all, describing the whole scene to him, seeing as I did so, that his opinion was also mine, my terrified horse had seen, feared, and finally jumped over something in the road, which I had only sensed and *not* seen—it was easy to visualize it, however, I had no doubt at all, nor do I think had Smithson, what or who stood in my way. There seemed little to do, and less to say, so we parted, silently, Smithson to get me some tea, I to sink into a chair, light a pipe, and wonder—what next?

I was not left to wonder long, for Smithson, bringing in my tea tray, was followed diffidently, by Mary Higgs, my housemaid.

"Mary wishes to speak to you, sir," murmured the man.

I looked up sharply, for this was an unusual proceeding.

"What is it, Mary?

"Please, sir, I must leave," gasped the scared-looking damsel.

"Oh?" I queried, "aren't you comfortable?"

"Oh, yes, sir, very, it's not that; I'm quite comfortable as far as the house goes but it's the goings on, sir.

"Goings on!" I said.

"Yes, sir, it's awful."

"What is?" I asked.

"Well, sir," she went on, growing garrulous, as these girls do, given an opportunity. "It seems like as if someone else was always where I am."

"Someone else always where *you* are?" I questioned. "Please explain, Mary."

"Well, sir, if I'm doing your bed, someone pulls the sheet out of my hands, sir, and if I'm cleaning, my brushes and things are knocked down; and—and the worst is, sir, when I'm going upstairs at nights someone walks up behind me, and once, sir, a hand touched my face—a *cold* hand, sir; and, please, I must go, I couldn't live here, it's all so like Mr. Basil and his tricks, sir," saying which, she burst into tears.

There was nothing I could say, so I paid her wages, murmured I was sorry, and sank back into my chair, feeling too exhausted and worried to go up and change.

"Bring me a bite to eat later, Smithson, here; I won't change, I'm dead tired."

"Yes, sir," he answered, moving away with a backward glance at me, almost as if asking if he might stay; but I did not speak.

Daylight faded with a yellow gleam or two as a parting shot from the setting sun, and the room, which in ordinary times I had loved best in the twilight, now seemed to grow sombre, shadowy, eerie, or was it my imagination? I thought not, for I was conscious of a feeling of chilliness as I bent down and threw another log of wood on the fire.

I had every wish to get up, turn on all lights, dispel the gloom, but it seemed foolish, for it was still twilight; moreover, I felt a disinclination to move, or *was it inability?* Slowly the shadows deepened, immovable I sat, wanting to get up, yet fearing to attempt it, without knowing why; there I was, a fairly able-bodied man, to all appearances, comfortably-seated in a big armchair, before a glowing fire, in a room of which the appointments left nothing to be desired, surrounded by every comfort, needing but a touch to flood the room with brilliant though tastefully shaded electric light, but that touch—I could not give, I knew it, was conscious of it in every sense and nerve; knew that, free man as I appeared to be, I was bound in my chair as surely and safely as if I had been fastened with iron bands—I could not reach the bell.

My tea was a thing of the past. Smithson, knowing my love of firelight and quiet, would probably leave the tea things unmoved for an hour, unless—and there lay my one and only hope—it occurred to his brain to come with some excuse, or without one, to see if "things" were all right. It was ridiculous, I argued with myself, to feel compelled to remain here; I would not, I would assert my boasted will-power and get up. As I determined this, a growing sense of weight oppressed me, I struggled to rise, but invisible hands kept me down; invisible but plainly felt, their cold clamminess touching my face, my neck, my hair; I sank back, still with all my wits about me yet terror stricken, shivering.

I felt something pass before my eyes, I can best describe it as a wet cloud; and, before my horror-stricken eyes, my room seemed to alter, walls seemed to fade, bookcases to recede; I seemed to see only high stone walls, a scaffold! God in heaven! and my brother hanging by the neck. I screamed, as I fought with my hands beating the air, as if to push this awful horror from me. Some maid must have heard me, for Smithson rushed in, to find me, fully conscious, panting, struggling. Instantly he raised me, carrying me to the window, which he flung open.

It was an hour later ere I could tell him the awful thing I had seen.

"Will you give it up, sir?" he asked, "and come away."

"No!" I said, "not yet, though I may have to unless something else settles it; though what can, I do not know, for as he tortured me in his life, so my wretched brother is determined to torture me still."

Rather to my surprise the remainder of the night passed quietly. I was correct, I think, in calling it "torture," as, evidently, the torture was to be intermittent and just enough at a time to keep me perpetually in a state of nervous tension.

The day following my twilight horror I never saw nor heard anything unusual, but my household, stablemen, etc., were all subjected incessantly to discomforts and annoyances. Another maid gave me notice, and fled; a stable lad, with eyes all but jumping out of his head, shaking knees, and stammering speech, tried to tell me a garbled tale of the horses all taking fright and lashing out; all but Stella, my brother's mare, who "whinnied, rubbing her soft nose up and down for all the world, sir, as she did when Mr. Basil petted her; and, please, I can't bear it, sir, I'm off." That left me with Smithson, my housekeeper, a pert kitchen girl, who boldly acclaimed she cared nought for spooks, and two men for the garden and stable. We all by this time were fully alive to the trouble, but so far were all determined to see it through. I had my doubts.

The next day came, still quietness; what did it portend? For I could not think it meant *peace.* I knew my unhappy brother too well for that, still I was thankful for small mercies. What should I do with my quiet hours so long as they were left to me? thus I mused over my after-breakfast pipe. Should I ride? I thought not; that was to court trouble. Should I walk? I did not think so; for, though honourably acquitted, the village folks, and others, too, still looked at me askance, nor seemed anxious to rush to me. I would not give them the chance to cold-shoulder me. The other direction from the village? No; I could see the spinny from every side, some day I might walk past it, but not yet; there was therefore nothing left but a prowl in the grounds, read, or write. I was just about to get my cap, when a sudden ring of the front door bell made me hesitate. I would wait a minute, just in case a friend had called to look me up; but alas! for my hopes, it was only a telegram, brought up by Smithson.

"Any reply, sir?" he asked. I opened it, read it and reread it.

"I don't understand," I said. "You know I've never left the place, Smithson, but this is from a friend I had once in London—

The wire read—

Don't ever come to see me again. I wanted to see you—I would have made friends—but you have spoiled it coming like that.   ALYS.

"Say 'No reply,' Smithson," I managed to say, "and don't come until I ring," saying which I closed the door, once again reading my wire. "Alys!" What did it all mean? "I would have made friends"—oh, how my heart beat at the thought of such happiness—"but you have spoiled it coming like that." Like what? I wondered, for full well I knew what had happened. Alys must be back in her studio. Basil must have shown himself to her as of old pretending to be me. But how? What had he done? Oh, God! show me a way out of my misery. What will quieten the unrestful spirit of my brother; will nothing make him cease his persecution of me—living or dead?

Long I sat, with my head bowed on my hands. I saw no way out, I was helpless. Even my loved little girl could have come back to me, but he had prevented that. It would have been better if my life had paid forfeit, for to live in such misery was beyond my power.

Should I go to Alys, throw myself on her mercy, tell her the whole story; let Smithson do his share. Could we convince her; and if we did, to what end? She had failed me in my hour of dire need, but that it was not entirely her fault had been explained. I would go to her. This decision made, I was restless for daylight so that I could go at once.

Next morning I was up early, catching the first train up to town, carefully avoiding, as far as possible, those of my neighbours who were likewise bent on London.

Usually, I enjoyed walking through the streets, having a look at shops and people; but today I was too intent upon my errand to loiter by the way, so hailed the first taxi, bidding the man drive quickly to Chelsea, when I would further direct him. As we neared the block of buildings where the studio was, my courage began to ebb. I almost wished I had not come, as, with trembling knees, I climbed the worn stairs, halted for an instant before the dull brown door with its old knocker, noticing, as I did so, that the copper plate with Alys' name on it was shiny and bright. Then she *is* here, I thought, and knocked my own familiar knock. The door opened slowly, and Alys stood before me, wearing an old green overall as in days gone by. She stood an instant looking at me before she spoke, then asked in ice-cold tones—

"Why have you come?"

"Let me come in," I said, "I have much to say; be just if you cannot be kind, for the sake of old times.

Something in my voice must have touched her, for she drew back, motioning to me with her hand to enter.

I did so, and felt the same restful calm steal over me, as I had ever done in her quiet studio, here, shut in from all sounds, save the dull rumble of the busy world outside.

Fear left me, cares seem to lessen; for a brief moment I even forgot what had brought me here, so happy and at rest did I feel. Quite quietly, just in her low, sweet tones I had loved so well Alys spoke to me. Will you please sit down, she said, and then, as if she too remembered, her voice altered, becoming cold, as if she spoke to a stranger, as she added: "And kindly explain why you have come in spite of my wire, telling you *not* to come again."

"Again!" I said. "I have not been before, not since my trouble."

She laughed a little mocking laugh.

"You are pleased to add untruthfulness to the rest of your horrible behaviour," she said.

"I am telling you the truth," I answered, "absolute truth!"

"Truth!" she replied. "You don't, apparently, now the meaning of it. You came here, you gave me the Lotus Flower signal,

I let you into the studio, where you stood laughing at me; I thought you must be drunk, until you touched me and your hand was as cold as death. You walked round my room, you upset my things. I begged you to go, you did not answer, only looked at me with the expression of a fiend, your eyes sunken, your face ghastly. And then you held my face between your two horrible cold hands, and I felt myself going faint; I screamed, and my charwoman came in. You must have slipped out as she came in, I did not see you go; and now you sit there telling me you have not been here, and you talk about 'truth.' *Why are you here again* I ask?"

"Will you hear me patiently?" I said; "hear my story, and then judge me. I will prove to you *I* was *not* here."

She seated herself some little distance from me, merely inclining her head to tell me to proceed.

Carefully, without exaggeration, I told my tale. She listened unmoved, for a while, but gradually I saw a dawning interest in her eyes, when I told of the receipt of her wire after the morning I had spent of indecision, and for which Smithson could vouch; she seemed to become suddenly alert, and rising from her seat, came swiftly to me.

"Your story," she began, "sounds an improbable yarn. There are but two small items that make me even half inclined to believe you. The first—I know it was *not* you who sent me the false telegram, which resulted in my being kept a prisoner until your trial was over. I will tell you about that horrible time later on. The second item—whoever it was who came here, purporting to be you, did not give your signal on the knocker, and tonight I heard it; I felt I *must* open the door'. I am glad I did; but, oh! your story is too horrible to believe. I must prove it; I must know. May I return with you; your housekeeper will, I know, look after me. There are things I *must* find out; will you let me come?"

Would I let her come? Dear heaven! how my heart beat at the mere thought of it! Alys, *my* one and only love, under my roof! But I must not frighten her, so merely said—

"Yes, come, my housekeeper shall look after you; come by all means if you are not afraid."

So within an hour we left together, managed to find a quiet place for some food, sent a wire to Smithson to order the car to meet the evening train from town, and to tell Mrs. Goodson, my housekeeper, to prepare rooms for a lady. We caught a train about four, arriving at our station somewhere about eight, where the run-a-bout met us. The short distance to "The Park" was soon covered, though it, like the rest of our journey, was almost passed in silence. I helped Alys out, handing her bag to Smithson, with the remark—

"All well, Smithson?"

"Fairly so, sir," was his reply.

"Miss Stainton," I said, turning to Alys, "if you will come now, I will take you to Mrs. Goodson. Dinner will be ready when you are, unless you prefer to have some sent up to your room."

"Thanks," she answered; "I will come down."

I bowed; and seeing Mrs. Goodson coming towards us, I gave Alys into her capable charge, merely saying—

"Miss Stainton is an old friend, look after her well."

It was about half-an-hour later when we met at the foot of the stairs—both, apparently, intent upon our own thoughts; both trying to keep up a chilly reserve, and more or less succeeding.

Mrs. Goodson, so I learnt subsequently, was inclined to be censorious on the subject of my having a lady guest in the absence of what she considered a proper chaperon, possibly it was unorthodox, but so were the circumstances; moreover, I could not well explain that this visit of Miss Stainton's was by her own desire to see if I was, to put it baldly, telling her yarns by way of clearing myself in her eyes; I could see she was only half inclined to believe me in my denial of going to her studio and behaving strangely; I was also pretty certain that she did not believe at all my story of the wretched brother's haunting of me—to this end she had come as my guest, to prove me. I knew it, felt it in her gravely-disapproving green eyes, as she faced me during dinner. It remained to be seen whether or not anything would happen to upset the theory, which I was convinced she held, that I was either bad, or mad.

It was a farce of the first water, that *tête-à-tête* dinner of ours; conversation was impossible, long silences hung with oppression over us. I, at least, could not help comparing it as it was, with the might have been, if things had not gone so much awry with me.

Smithson waited upon us with much solicitude, and had just put dessert upon the table, lowered the lights round the room, leaving only the softly-shaded little lights in the centre of the table, then withdrew, with his usual manner of—

"I will put coffee in the library, sir," and closed the door softly behind him, leaving us alone, at least, I suppose so, though I was not by any means sure.

"Will you excuse me, Mr. York?" asked Alys, rising hurriedly, as she spoke; " I—I am rather cold."

"It is cold," I said; "but please come for some coffee, the library will be warmer."

"Not unless you insist," she replied.

"I cannot, of course, insist," I said, "but I do ask you to give me all the help you can."

"Very well," she murmured, "for half-an-hour I will come, but—I do not believe your tales." I bowed in answer, as I held the door open for her to pass through, steps, other steps than hers were plainly audible.

I noticed a startled expression flit across her face, then she paused, looking at me, as if questioning. I smiled, endeavouring to be reassuring, and we crossed the dim hall side by side, her little high-heeled shoes making a click on the polished floor, my heavier tread beside her, and close behind us those other steps— unmistakable. We ignored them by tacit consent, and entered the library. I pulled the armchair close to the fire for her, heaping cushions at her back, and asked if she would pour out coffee while I got my cigarettes.

In spite of all I had gone through, I found myself hoping that the horrors might be repeated, if only to convince Alys of my truthfulness. I even felt it would be happiness if, in terror, she looked to me for help, already I knew she had heard the steps, what else might she not see, and hear. My spirits rose as I pictured her face, when she really had to believe me and knowing her generous heart, I felt it was only a matter of time ere we were once more lovers, without a cloud between us. Having possessed myself of my smokes, we sat in silence, one on either side of the fire, with the coffee tray between us. It was a unique situation, for, to all intents and purposes, we were host and guest, and yet we sat there as strangers, so far as any attempt at conversation or interest in each other went.

One hour passed in almost total silence! Uneasily, I watched her as she sat cold, immovable, each moment, as it passed, seeming to add a harder, sterner line to her pale face. Ten o'clock sounded as she rose to her feet, saying, as she looked at me with scornful eyes—

"I might have known. But I felt I must give you what appeared to be your one, chance—the chance to prove you were telling me the truth. I disregarded conventionality, I have braved the gossip that must follow me; I came to your house, and I learn nothing. Not one thing which you have put forward as your plea has happened; I do not believe in your story of haunting. I believe you to be an unscrupulous man, and I consider you have added insult to the rest of your horribleness. I refuse to see or speak to you ever again!"

In silence I held the door open for her, but as I watched her go slowly up the stairs I heard her little laugh as she spoke to Mrs. Goodson, and the laugh hurt me more than all. Perhaps I had not yet learned that women can, and do, laugh and jest with breaking hearts; laugh until none could dream that beneath the gaiety lies sorrow little dreamed of. I learned it later, but then, I believed that Alys truly felt nothing more than distrust and dislike of me, or perhaps even amusement. I returned to my chair, as sad a man as one could find, frantically cursing my brother, that he could even withhold what I needed, to help me to happiness.

I groaned aloud: "If you had shown yourself tonight, I might ever have forgiven you!" burst from my lips almost involuntarily. I was answered from the opposite chair by a low, ironical laugh! It was my last straw. I felt I could not endure anything more, so made my way to my room, determined if sleep as well as all else forsook me, I would drink until oblivion came. *I,* even I, who all my life had been abstemious would now drown my troubles in drink—was my mental state; and to what it would have led me, I dare not think, but for the simple fact that, as I passed the door of the room where Alys was, my steps were arrested by the sound of low sobbing, such sounds as few men could hear unmoved, and yet to me it brought a rush of joy, checking once and for all my idea of weakly drowning my trouble in drink.

I dare not knock or whisper a word, as with a full heart I went on towards my room, sure only of one thing, the laugh I had previously heard had not meant either indifference or amusement, it was, I felt sure, only to hide her real feelings, which I had discovered unwittingly, and which I must therefore ignore.

The following day, after a sleepless night, I was not awakened by Smithson until almost ten o'clock, and then he told me Miss Stainton had gone by the early tram, bidding him tell me she would write, and regretting her hasty departure. This I knew to be a polite fiction for the benefit of the household, nor did I ever receive the promised but unexpected letter.

I wrote once to the studio, but my letter was returned through the dead letter office, which seemed the ending of my brief love story. I made many attempts to discover Alys's whereabouts from some of our mutual Bohemian friends. One and all these so-called friends ignored and finally cut me, and my life was one endless weary round of trouble.

All my staff had now left, except Smithson and Mrs. Goodson. We shut up most of the house, and I lived through days, weeks, months of brooding isolation.

Once the neighbouring clergyman called, but he was a man of narrow views, and his visits were hours of torture to me; and I think he always left me sure in his own mind that either I was mad, or that my house was possessed by evil spirits, brought there by my own evil thoughts. In my distress I asked him could he not pray and thus help me to rid myself of the persistent haunting of my brother. He listened, with a pious face of horror, as I told him a little of my story, but assured me, with a pitying smile meant to humour me, that; so far, he was not aware of anything abnormal! This was true, horribly true; my wretched brother appeared to take infinite care that nothing abnormal should occur, if ever there was anyone present likely to be of help to me.

Even Smithson, with earnest desire to help me, had on several occasions asked his crony, Constable Gill, to smoke a pipe with him; but, invariably, the house was silent on these occasions, except in my own rooms, and Gill would leave, believing me mad, and admiring Smithson for his assiduous care of "the poor gentleman." And so it went on—by day, I was tormented; by night, it was even more hideous. It sounds so little as I tell it, yet imagine yourself for even *one* day always conscious that you were *never* alone.

At my meals I always heard another chair drawn up to the table, as I moved through the house those other steps kept pace with mine, at nights I was disturbed in a dozen ways, and an unusually calm day was invariably followed by a night of horror. The chilliness of my room, causing my teeth to chatter, always heralded the arrival of my wretched brother, and if, as sometimes happened, I felt resigned to my fate, and more or less inert, it was then I would not only hear him, but see him, pale, shadowy, with a mocking smile upon his lips, and always the awful mark as of a rope around his neck. I realized, to the full, now what he meant by his words to the chaplain of the prison:

"Tell my brother his life will not be a calm one, in spite of my death to spare an innocent man."

And I knew also what I had done when I asked him to live in the house with me; *that* was the meaning of his mocking smile—he did dwell with me, I was *never* free from him. I had tried, as time went on, absence from home; I had even gone abroad; nothing availed me, so I returned where, at least, I had the material comforts of my home.

Thus, one year passed, solitary, isolated, alone, except—always except—for the company of my brother. I lived the life of a hunted animal, daily seeking sanctuary but finding none, my health undermined by days of torture and sleepless nights, all pleasure long since gone; my stables were empty, I could neither keep horses nor men in any semblance of peace; my gardens were mere wildernesses, for no man would remain to see his work mutilated and spoiled. It had even happened that when I once found a book which held my attention to the exclusion of all else for a few brief hours, that same book was removed from the table whereon I had placed it, and I found it battered, torn, illegible, on the floor.

I had resolutely kept my vow, I had not degraded myself by drink, but at last, after a severe nervous breakdown, had given Smithson the excuse he had long sought to call in a medical man. I permitted it because the local doctor, a man well known to me and my family, was, I learnt, absent from home, his place being filled for the time by a young man from London. Knowing him to be a stranger, trusting also that there had not been sufficient time for him to have heard the local version of my affairs, I permitted him to be called in. He did not stay long on the first visit, nor did he allow me to talk but left me some medicine and the assurance that it would bring me needed sleep.

It did, but it brought me more—it brought me a man to whom I could open my over-burdened heart, sure of his understanding. I asked Dr. Willis if he was not afraid of administering sleeping drugs to a man in my condition, but his repeated assurances that I must have plenty of grit to battle as I had done, heartened me, gave me confidence, and he acceded to my request to spend all his leisure with me with whole-hearted alacrity.

As usual my tortures ceased when the doctor entered, to commence again the instant the door closed behind him, but on one never-to-be-forgotten day he came prepared to spend the whole day. We lunched, and I, as ever, was at once aware that my constant visitor was close at hand, but I was surprised when Dr. Willis suddenly exclaimed—

"How cold it is, York!"

I smiled in answer, and he at once understood that we were *not,* as he supposed, alone! Colder and more icily chill grew the room, until our teeth chattered. At last Dr. Willis rose.

"For God's sake, York, let's get out of this," burst from his lips.

"Very well," I said, "we will try the library." As ever, the room looked the acme of comfort.

"Ah! this is better," said Willis, drawing a chair nearer to the fire, sinking into it with a sigh of relief, only to spring from it with an oath, as he gasped—

"There's someone else sitting in it."

"Of course," I murmured; "there usually is."

"Man!" he said. "It is a marvel to me you are not a maniac."

"I should be," I replied, "save for one fact—my never slackening desire to prove to a woman, whom I love, that I am neither a maniac nor a liar!"

"You shall prove it," he said, "for I will help you."

As he spoke, there was a crash, splintering the mirror behind us into a thousand fragments.

"That is a mere nothing," I assured him; "nothing is safe."

"But," he said, "I don't understand."

"Nor I," I answered.

"I mean, I don't understand the reason, the wherefore," he said. "I am as hard-hearted as most men, harder than a good many, but I suppose even the hardest of us have a soft line somewhere, some dim recollection, maybe, of stories told at our mother's knee, of angel guardians, stories of good folks who died, and went to Heaven. One reads, of course, that people claim to have seen the spirits of those departed come back to earth. I have even read of pranks played in old houses, but that any spirit can come again and carry on a systematic degraded existence, be it here or on some sphere, I can't grasp. Where can such a being dwell, to whom practices of this kind are of the slightest satisfaction?

"I don't know," I answered. "I am almost as much at sea as you are, doctor. I say *almost,* because during these last months I have abandoned my former studies and have read and studied every book on occult matters I could lay my hands upon. There is, I find, a theory amongst certain students of the occult, to the effect that 'the very lowest planes of the Astral world are filled with souls of a gross type—undeveloped and animal life, Who live as near as possible the lives they lived on earth.' Also the particular book in which I read this goes on to say—'About the only thing they gain being the possibility of their living out their gross tastes and becoming sick and tired of it all, thus allowing them to develop a longing for Higher things. . . . these undeveloped souls cannot, of course, visit the upper planes, etc.. . . .they often flock back as near to earth as possible.'

"There is a good deal more, but something of this kind may control, so to speak, the actions of my unhappy brother. His life here was *not* an elevated one, his tastes and ways were of a low order, and I take it that his hurried passing from here to wherever he has gone, left him no time for either repentance or desire to become a better man. It's a horrible theory, but I can find no other. The only chance for him and for me then, seems to be, that something will so sicken him of his present life, that he may be moved to long for some higher plane, and therefore attain it; but what must it be that will help him? and where can I turn to find it?"

The doctor shook out his pipe, and refilled it, before he spoke; then, to my amazement, he said, quietly, and in most matter-of-fact voice:

"Love might do it. You spoke of a woman you loved; there was once, long ago, such a woman in my life. She died, but the love she scattered lives on, and many people still bless her dear name. I often chided her for working too hard amongst the poor souls where my earlier work was done. She never spared herself, early and late she nursed and toiled amongst the sick; and when I would have checked her, she would answer brightly—'We only pass this way once, let me help all I can.' She died six months later of diphtheria, caught from a child she nursed devotedly; and if your theory is in any way correct, then there are men and women too, whose lives hereafter will be on a higher plane than they would have been, but for the example of her unswerving unselfishness, and noble aims. Can you not get this girl you love to help you?"

I answered him sadly enough, by giving him a *resumé* of my happy days with Alys, and my subsequent meetings and disappointments.

"She must be made to understand," he said. "Sooner or later she must realise the truth. I will think it over, and now, 'Good night'; I must leave you, although I hate to do so."

Left to my loneliness once more, I pondered deeply over my friend's words—"Love might do it." Aye, it might, if only it could! Here my reflections were broken in upon by the steady knocking, as of a hammer, on first one, then another, of the chairs or tables in the room, followed, as always, by the icy chilliness of the room. This hammering was a recent form of torture, generally occurring when I was either in deep thought or reading.

It effectually put a stop to either as a rule; but tonight, I was determined to continue the thinking-out process, so sat apparently unmoved, though fully conscious that the room grew perceptibly colder, and that the dreaded presence hovered close. I was correct in my surmise, for now, two icy hands passed themselves over my eyes, encircling, as it were, my head also in their cold grasp. The pressure was intense, as if my head was in a vice of marble coldness; the sweat began to break out on me, in awful fear, as I sat there, failing now to think at all, conscious only that in another instant I should faint or scream— tighter, tighter, grew the clasp, gradually moving lower, lower, lower, so gradually, that I did not realise at once that the vice-like grip was now over my nose.

Then my mouth and ears were covered and held, lower—and oh, God! the grasp was at my throat; tighter, tighter, that awful icy clasp; on my throat the pressure seemed now to concentrate into a tight line round my throat, as of a rope. I knew it, knew in a brief moment of horror, that it was a hangman's rope that I was held by! Slowly I felt myself lifted, my feet no longer rested on the ground, I was suspended by the neck in mid-air. I was being hanged, though gradually, to spin out as it were a torture that would in ordinary event be swift. I felt myself gasping, choking—and knew no more.

I learnt later that Dr Willis had returned, having forgotten his pipe, and had found me rigid, cold in my chair, my collar and tie lying on the floor, and a blood-red mark round my throat. When he left the house again, he took me with him, and for some months nursed me back to life, in his own house in London, where he took me the instant the local doctor returned to his own duties. In Dr. Willis' pretty home I recovered some of my former health; and though, at times, I was still subjected to persecution by my brother, I had help at hand, and was no longer alone to endure it.

At last came one never-to-be-forgotten night. Willis had been out spending the evening with friends, leaving me alone. During those hours, I endured every conceivable torment from my haunting brother, and I was reduced to a quivering bunch of nerves by the time Willis returned. He saw at once that all was not well with me, nor did he need any spoken word to show him I was in the last stage of exhaustion.

"Doctor," I began, but he cut me short—

"Don't say it," he ordered. "I can see you are at the end of your endurance, but you will not end your torture by taking your own life."

I stared at him, for though I had never hinted such a thing to him, this end of my trouble had lately been much in my mind.

"Cheer up, old man" he went on. "I have another solution, but first I must give you a dose to pull you together, then I have something to tell you; and when I have told you, don't put me down as an interfering ass. As you know, I have spent the evening with some friends, but they are an unconventional crowd, mostly artists or writers. I am an outsider, but more or less am one of them, at heart, at least, and they dub me their Medico. To-night the talk turned on ghosts, and hauntings. A young fellow, gave us a strange story of a man he knew, who was, so the man said, 'haunted' by the spirit of his brother who had been hanged for murder. Do you follow me, old man. I found myself listening to *your* story, as seen from another point of view.

One or two present believed it, and pitied you; several derided it; and a little girl, who had listened silently and attentively throughout, announced that she believed it to be a fabrication right through, that she had reason to know this haunted man, as he called himself, was an untruthful, unscrupulous man, but added she would like to prove his story true, for several reasons. I saw at once that chance, Providence—call it what you will, had led me face to face with the girl you love, and put into my hands, perhaps, a better way of helping you than with my drugs.

To cut my story short, I managed to get introduced to Miss Stainton, and in a very few moments I had interested her in a case of haunting which was in my care. She listened, open-eyed, believed me, and then rather falteringly asked me could I not get to know her friend and find out if he also was truly, as he believed, haunted. Little by little I led her on, until she confessed to me that she loved this man, but had no reason to believe him, and every reason to distrust him. Then, and then only, I, too, confessed, told her it was you; and at this moment she awaits a sign or message from you, telling her you forgive all her doubt of you.

Gone were my fears, gone my wish to end my life!

"Doctor," I said, grasping his hand, "you give me hope, but, alas! I am a broken-down man, I dare not ask a girl to share such a life."

"Try it," he answered. "Who knows that love and all the inspiration it brings, may not help, try it."

That night, my brother stood beside my bed until early dawn, the old mocking smile upon his lips, I closed my eyes, his cold hand was laid on my face; I opened them, to see him always at his post beside me. As my thoughts wandered to Alys, he shook his fist menacingly at me, his expression seeming to say:

"Do not dare to get the better of me."

With love in my heart, I dared it all. I rose early and sent a messenger to the address Willis had given me, then waited.

She did not keep me long in suspense, for shortly after breakfast was over the maid announced:

"Miss Stainton for the doctor."

Willis looked at me, motioned me to go, and with faltering steps I entered his study.

"Alys," I murmured, fearing almost to put out my hand, "you have come."

For an instant she looked at me, then, with a sob, was in my arms.

"Do you believe me?" I asked.

"Can you ask?" she answered. "I should not be here unless I did. Dr. Willis convinced me that you spoke the truth, and that I had wrongfully judged you. I am here because I love you, here if you love me, to help you."

"I have never ceased to love you, dear," I answered. "But I dare not ask you to share my haunted, troubled life."

"I *am* going to share it, however, and it may be neither troubled nor haunted, we will see."

About a week after this meeting, a quiet wedding took place at a Registry Office. It was not the wedding I would have chosen for my little girl, but we judged it best, as she insisted upon my not going back home alone. We two, and our friend Willis, had a merry little luncheon later, and then my wife and I travelled home.

Once again my home became a real home. In it love ruled and reigned supreme. Alys' life, her ideas, her aims, were so pure, so true, so noble, that gradually the evil sounds in my house began to grow less and less, until one winter's day, she had been out all afternoon, I did not know where, and I had been alone; she came in about five, and found me in the library, deep in thought; and, kneeling down on the hearth rug, began to tell me where she had been.

As she began, I suddenly saw the old familiar, queer light begin to appear in the dim room. She saw it, too, and raising her head, looked before her, with shining eyes.

"Basil," she called, "have you come to say you are sorry?"

I gazed at her, wonderingly, for, as she spoke, the form of my brother stood before us, one pale hand was laid upon her little head, the other was outstretched to me, as with a sorrowful smile he softly vanished, leaving behind him for an instant, a glowing radiant light, in place of the cold, chilly gleams which formerly came and went with him.

Then silence fell upon us.

"Tell me where you have been," I asked her, in a few moments.

Shyly she answered:

"I went to put flowers on the grave of Esmé Simpson," she said, "and I got permission from the governor of the prison to lay a tiny wreath on the earth where your poor sinning brother lay."

Probably it is an unknown thing, I have never heard of it being done, that someone could so think of a murderer as to pity him and softly lay a flower upon so dishonoured a grave; but maybe the very act of love would inspire the unhappy soul to long for better higher things; and in the eyes of his Maker, repent and struggle to atone in the Great Beyond for the sin he committed on earth. I may, or I may not be right in my theory, but I prefer to think that this act of tender love on the part of my dearly-loved little girl was the means of aiding my unhappy brother, as her tender love and devotion helped and strengthened all with whom she came in contact.

Be this as it may, from that day onwards our home and ourselves were free from all trace of haunting. As the years passed, they only served to hold us firmer in our endeavours, as they held us more and more securely in bonds of love, faith and comradeship.

Nothing could shake our trust and love for each other, devotion seemed almost a weak word to express all that we lavished on each other. Dr. Willis, our most valued friend, stayed with us often, and had been heard so say, jokingly, he wouldn't mind being haunted, if it brought such happiness, though he and I knew it was love for "all things great and small" that brought happiness to us, as it must to all.

Sylvia

It was just one of those days when all the world seemed to go awry, or it appeared so. Probably, I was over-tired or worried, for war news and rationing were both beginning to leave their mark: war news, because one must wear a smile, no matter how long the casualty lists grew; rationing, because I was rapidly becoming worn out, perpetually struggling to feed us all somehow. All this is really not sufficient excuse for nerves at the point of breaking, as mine were; and I, for once, welcomed a severe attack of "flue," followed by my doctor's advice to go away for a couple of weeks to pick up. Without the "flue," I should have felt compelled to ignore his advice in these strenuous times; but, triumphantly armed with that evil germ of "flue," I felt I was justified in taking it.

As usual, I took my ticket for a little-known spot in Wales. I say "as usual," because it was the one spot I loved best—a spot which will ever hold my happiest memories, as it holds some of my saddest.

I felt uplifted, invigorated, merely gazing upon my beloved mountains as the train ran down the long incline before it stopped at the station—names are unnecessary, so few people know it. Alighting, I made my way to the old inn which stood in a large open square at one end of the village street—a street composed of little houses, about four nondescript shops, two better shops, and a post office. I did not care what the shops contained—I loved them all, and the people were my very good friends.

There was a tiny shop where I could buy a morning paper, as well as fishing tackle and flies; and there I paused, just to see if my friend, who dwelt there, remembered me. He did; so I went on my way, to receive the welcome I was always sure of from the good people at the inn. A bright fire was burning gaily in the sitting-room (always called mine) although it was June; for up here in the hills, evenings were chilly until perhaps August. I did not pause by the fire, my steps took me straight to the window, to gaze on a view which to me, has not an equal in this or any other country which I have seen.

I have stood at that window times uncountable. I have looked at these high mountains when they have been snow-covered; I have watched the mist and driving rain lashing down them until every trickling stream was white foam. I have watched them with tears in my eyes; I have stretched out my arms to them and laughed. I loved them, and the valley beneath them, as I have loved few things in this world; and this June evening, I think I loved them best of all, as they stood serene, steady, grand, far above the worries of the day; seeming, by their great peace, to sooth my jangled nerves, bidding me look up, be hopeful, and not cast down. A faint purple haze hung over them, giving promise of a glorious day tomorrow, and I watched until one or two stars were visible, and lights began to twinkle here and there from distant farms; then, with a sigh of happiness I turned to my evening meal, which I had entirely forgotten.

A peaceful night in my quaint bedroom found me early next morning, feeling already tons better, and quite ready for a tramp. I knew before I started, which way my feet would inevitably turn; I could not help it, up the valley following the little river up and up, I knew I must go, away from the cottages, past where the river narrows and falls in a mad rush for some twenty feet, up, and still up, until I reached the wild moorland, where I knew I should find a patch of mauve, *scented* orchids.

It has always been a source of wonder to me how such things as scented orchids came there, on that rough wild moor; but I always found them there in June, and revelled in their beauty and scent. I was not by this time, more than three miles from the village, yet I might have been a hundred, so still, so solitary was it. The crying of baby lambs, and the rushing sound of the river, now left below me, were all the sounds to break the silence, of the everlasting hills, and here I stayed for many hours, resting, idling, dreaming; the world, war, rations, all forgotten.

I supposed I dozed, for when I came back to earth, I found it was nearly four o'clock. Time I was moving I thought, and forthwith began to walk to the nearest farm, where I knew they would gladly make a cup of tea for me. Towards it I wended my steps, carefully carrying my bunch of orchids. The farm I wanted lay a little further up the mountain, off the beaten track, yet not far from a main, if somewhat rough road. I would have my tea, I thought, and return by the road, as being easier walking for my first day.

I got my tea, as also my welcome; and in a little kitchen, rough but homely, I rested and chatted.

"You are late to go down," said my friend of the farm, "are you not afraid?"

"Afraid!" I said. "Never, up here, and I love to go down to the village in the dusk, and watch the lights twinkle on the hills; but I will not leave it any longer, so 'Goodnight,' and very many thanks," and the farm door closed behind me.

How glorious it was, how serene! I couldn't leave it, I didn't care if I got back for dinner or not, the air was so pure, so clean. Some people would say like champagne, though, personally, I always consider that simile a slight on pure mountain air!

I wandered slowly along, humming a little song, drinking in the beauty, until a tempting gate seemed to call forcibly for a halt, and I took my favourite position on its top rail, for just five minutes. Five minutes passed, and then another five, and still I lingered, gazing at the pink light in which the setting sun had bathed the mountains. As I gazed, I heard the distant creaking of wheels, as if some lumbering cart or van was coming up the winding hill. I will just wait until it comes.

I heard the creaking coming nearer and nearer; and the stamp of horses' feet as if they strained pulling up the hill, louder and clearer; until I found myself saying, "One more corner, then I can see them and go." A whip cracked, as a slowly-moving caravan hove in sight.

Two figures walked beside it, a man and a woman, seemingly silent, probably tired. Up the hill they came, a few baskets dangling at the sides of the caravan, the door of which stood open. Now they had nearly reached me, so nearly that I could speak to them. Slowly they passed me.

"Goodnight," I called, but neither answered me. They moved on, unseeing, apparently unhearing.

"Rough road," I said again. No answer was vouchsafed to me. They were past me now, just past me, and I turned to watch them, going along a bit of straight road.

There was nothing on the road! No slow-moving caravan, no straining horses, no man, no woman; the road, clear and white in the falling dusk, was empty—save for myself. Yet they had been there, I had seen them, spoken to them, and now they had gone, gone without a sound; but, as the thought crossed my mind, I was startled by two pistol shots, which rang out clearly, echoing and re-echoing among the hills, and then silence, deep silence, as if the mountains held some secret which they would not share.

I found I was trembling, cold and scared! What did it all mean? Where or what was that caravan? Who were that man and woman who could vanish so completely and so swiftly? I could not answer, but my walk back developed into a run, so eager was I to find myself once more back in the village, amongst friends.

Later that evening, the doctor of the little village paid me a visit, but chaffed me upon my absentmindedness, though he ended by asking me if I didn't feel well, and ordering for me a hot drink. Presently I revived, and ventured to ask him if he had ever met a caravan on a lonely road in the hills?

He met my question by another:

"Have you seen it?"

"I have," I replied; "and if you promise not to certify me as insane, I will tell you about it," and then and there I told him my story.

He listened in silence until I finished, and then said:

"I am unable to explain it; but if you are not tired, I will tell *you* a story."

I give his story as he told it to me, only adding:

"I am not the only person who saw and heard the caravan, nor am I the only person who believes it still lumbers up the mountain road as the dusk falls."

"I will not tell you the story in my own words, my friend," said the doctor, as he lit his pipe. "I would rather tell it as it was written down by my great grandmother, who, I believe, got the story from one of those who lived in it. She wrote it, and a friend of hers later rewrote it from her facts; wrote it, he always said, because even today, as you have proved, the remembrance of that tragedy still remains with us. It is many years ago, and who can tell for how many more years, someone, with a more sensitive nature than others, will see and hear the lumbering caravan. Maybe some will, as you did, speak to the man or woman, meeting with nought but silence—the silence of those long gone, and yet whose spirits live at times amongst their old haunts."

"But now, my story, for the time is getting on."

Many years ago, on such a fine day as this, a gaudily painted caravan was jolting slowly on its way along one of the most beautiful lanes in Wales, lending a picturesque touch of colour to an already lovely scene. High mountains towered on every side some of them with their grand crests bidden in a faint-hanging mist, which only served to give them the touch of mystery which the unseen always lends. Foliage was at its greatest beauty. Banks and fields were gay with wild flowers, hedges sweet with wild roses and honeysuckle.

The heat was intense, dust lay thick on the roads. The mountain rills and little torrents, so rushing and racing in the winter when the snows melted, were quiet now, and only the winding river at the foot of the hill moved on, though even that was in a sluggish way, as if it would rather hang about in pools without making an effort to glide along over the stones towards the sea.

All nature was drowsy; the cattle under the trees idly flicking the flies with their tails, stood, as if even that necessary labour were a toil.

Here and there a group of hay-makers rested under the hedges, glad of the respite, and the only thing which seemed bent on getting along was the slowly-moving caravan. It was evidently the leader of a band of gipsies, for a long way behind it, one caught a glimpse of the roof and little chimney of another caravan.

The first one was gaily painted in reds and blues, the little windows were closely curtained with spotted muslin, and any brass that was visible shone like burnished gold. Two strapping grey horses drew it, the driver walking beside them. He was a splendid-looking man, probably about thirty years of age, dark, clean-shaven, broad-shouldered and muscular, dressed in riding attire, with breeches and gaiters, a blue flannel shirt with a low collar, showing a strong brown throat and neck. He wore a slouch hat, and swung a little switch, though he seldom used it on his horses.

The rest of the gipsies must have been far behind, or resting within the caravan, save one other—a girl—who sat on the steps at the back of the caravan, her chin resting in the palm of her hand, her eyes fixed steadily on the long road they had just traversed.

She was dressed in a dark skirt, worn and patched, and a blouse which had once been pink— now washed and faded to a shade of yellow—her hair was dark, though, where the sun touched it, it seemed almost red, her eyes were dark, a mixture of grey and green, darkly lashed, her face a perfect oval—colourless, except for the brown tinge of sun-burn, her little hands burnt nearly tan-colour, were bare of the usual gipsy rings.

She seemed lost in a dream, and the voice of the driver speaking to her, caused her to give a sudden start.

"Sylvia," he said, "why don't you come and. sit in front and see the glorious view, and the road we are going?"

"Because," answered the girl, with a faint smile, "I prefer to try and look along the road I have come."

"Always the same," the man muttered, "always trying to search into the past. Why on earth can't you give it up, Sylvia, and be content with the future?"

"The future," said the girl, sadly, "holds nothing for me—the past, everything—if *only* I could remember! How long is it Jim, since I first began to live in a caravan? I seem to dimly remember some other life once, and I *know*, I *feel*, I was not always here."

"I do not know," answered Jim. "I had been in Australia and news from England brought me home, and I joined this tribe, because I was soon penniless—you were not here then. I was obliged to go away again shortly. I was away six months, and when I came back, you were here—a little girl of ten or so—and here you have been ever since, and you must be seventeen or eighteen now. Mother Alison expects you to marry her son, Jake, you know—are you going to?"

"No! never!" replied Sylvia. "I hate his coarse ways, I hate his jokes, his talk, his ignorance—everything about him—but I suppose Mother Alison will torment me until I give in," she shuddered.

"Do you remember if Jake was here when you came, Sylvia?"

"I don't know," answered the girl, putting her hand to her head in a dazed way. "I forget—I was ill at first, and when I grew strong, I had forgotten. I don't think I was called 'Sylvia' always," she went on. "Some other name glimmers in my mind sometimes. I must not bother" she added. "I am happy, and even Jake is good to me. He says he has much to make up to me. I don't understand what he means, but he is generally kind—except if he tries to make love to me, then I hate him, and Alison is unkind to me then. Where are we now, Jim?"

"I am not sure, answered the man, "but in any case it's time we had a rest and some tea." He called to his horses, who obeyed his voice and drew up. He and the girl seated themselves on the bank to await the arrival of the rest of the band.

They sat in silence for a few minutes, and then Sylvia rose, saying:

"I can hear them coming, Jim, they must be near, I heard Molly laugh I'm sure."

"No doubt," answered Jim, "since she seldom does anything else—useless baggage," he added.

"Jim!" said Sylvia, in amazement. "I thought you were fond of Mollie. Alison says you love her, and that you are all she thinks about."

"They are wrong then," said the man, vehemently. "I care less than nothing for lazy Mollie; women and woman's love are not for me, either now, or ever. My life was spoilt years ago by a dastardly black lie, and for all my careless life of freedom, I am only a hunted animal, never knowing the moment I shall be called upon to pay the penalty for a wrong that was not rightly laid at my door. But never mind little girl, don't look so woebegone, I'm happy enough under the skies, sunshine or stars, and if sooner or later my freedom ends, well—I must know that at least I leave no woman to suffer." And lighting a cigarette, he moved carelessly away to his horses, to pat and caress them—his chums, perhaps his safe confidants.

And Sylvia, with white face and eyes burning with tears she dare not shed, gazed after him, with an aching heart, murmuring to herself:

"Ah! my love! my bonny brave lad! what is it that darkens your life, and with it, mine? For you love me, Jim; I feel you do, yet, there is some shadow on your life, and because of that you treat me as you do—one day kind, the next cold as ice to me, and my heart is breaking for you, yet I can only be silent."

There was not time for brooding however, for two other caravans now lumbered up.

The first, hung all over with baskets and chairs, made, so thought the simple-minded villagers, by the gipsies; in reality, turned out of factories, probably in other countries by the hundred. A man was leading the horses: a man with a dark, sinister face, though handsome in a rough, uncouth style, and by his side danced his sister Mollie—almost fair for a gipsy, with saucy blue eyes, up-turned nose, add merry mouth.

No dark-browed gipsy this, but a laughing, merry hoyden, who thought the world a good place to play in, and whose greatest trouble was the frequent whippings from her grandmother, for what she called "the lazy idle life" the girl led. If a fire was to be made, Mollie would be sitting threading gay beads, to hang round her pretty neck; if there was washing to be done, Mollie would be away in the woods gathering flowers; never at hand if there was work to be done her mother said, though pretty Mollie was far the best hand at selling a basket, or persuading a bony and angular spinster that a hard, unyielding basket-chair "would be cosy, lady, to nurse your babies by the fire, some day."

Only one person in all the tribe could ever induce Mollie to abandon her own pleasure and do a turn for someone else: Jim alone achieved this, and to him she gave a dog-like devotion and obeyed his every word.

It was quickly decided to pitch their tents and remain where they were for the night, and each one was soon busy with his or her allotted task—all but Mollie, who vanished as usual, leaving who would to do her share.

Tea was soon over, and the men slouched off to pitch tents, water the horses, and make ready for the night; and Alison, "Mother Alison," as the tribe called her, lit a short pipe, and watched from under her low-beetling brows that the others did their work properly. Mollie's mother did the lion's share, and to all appearance was the most fitted for it—tall, strong, muscular, big capable hands, arms which many a man might envy, and a hard, unprepossessing face, from which the coarse black hair was tightly dragged in uncompromising severity. She worked swiftly and in silence, and when all was done, turned to Sylvia, and in a harsh voice told her to "get baskets and begone to the village to sell them."

The old dame, with her pipe, raised her head at this, and said in questioning tones:

"Is't wise, think you, 'Liza?

"Tut!" answered the other. "We may as well face it, Gran, 'tis many years now, and it's as well to know for certain—let the child go."

Sylvia who was used to their abrupt conversations and never joined in, picked out a few of the prettiest baskets, and made her way down to the village, nestling peacefully below them.

From his work with the horses, Jake saw her, and called out: "Where art thou going to, lass?"

"To sell baskets," answered the girl. "Wish me luck, Jake. Something tells me I'll have good luck this evening."

Muttering to himself, "Mother must be mad," Jake turned and swung himself up the caravan steps.

"Mother!" he cried. "Ar't mad to send the girl to the village, after all these years? Must thee tempt Providence in this way?"

"Easy, son, easy," answered the woman. "The girl's mind has gone, never to return—it never has done, it never will—but this one test I must and will have, for thy safety, then I can rest. The girl will never remember, and thou, lad, ar't altered in eight years. She will not be gone long, and it is worth it for my peace. Begone to your work, and be ready for some love-making when the girl returns. I'd be best pleased to see thee wed, and some of her fine lady ways knocked out of the girl."

The man slunk out without further question.

Sylvia went happily on her way all unknowing that she was the object of discussion, and hoping she would meet with a little kindness instead of the usual roughness, and slamming of doors in her face. Half-dreamily she wandered on until she reached the little village.

A long, straggling street—one or two poor looking shops and a couple of decent-looking inns was all it consisted of, and at the further end, it seemed to terminate in a high stone wall, into which were set a massive pair of wrought iron gates with coat of arms in gold and blue, and a little way inside stood a neat-looking black and white lodge. A yard or two from the gates was a quaint door in the wall, which now stood open.

Sylvia, peering in, saw a pretty patch of garden and an old

lady with very white hair asleep in a chair, with a black cat on her knee.

As Sylvia looked, she awoke from her nap, and, catching tight of the girl, cried out:

"What do you want? Who are you? Aye! dearie me, dearie me! it's gipsies, and me asleep! Come here, girl, I hate gipsies, but you don't look bad and I want a basket."

"Which will you have?" asked the girl.

"There, there, I never could choose anything in a hurry. I must chance your being honest. Come inside and put them on the table."

"What a pretty kitchen," said Sylvia. "Do you live here alone?"

"Aye! alone now," said the dame, "unless my lady sends for me to the castle."

"It must be very lonely," said Sylvia, gently.

"It is so, too lonely for me at times, and I weep over the old days—long since gone, and my bonny bairn—the light of my eyes."

"Had you a child?" asked Sylvia.

"No, no, none of my own, but my own in all but name—but there, I'm a stupid old woman, talking to a gipsy girl, but sometimes it is so silent, I feel I must speak. Sit you down, I'll get you some tea; you have a gentle, sweet face."

"Who lives at the castle?" asked Sylvia, as she drank the tea the old lady made for her.

"Only her ladyship—poor dear lady!"

"Is she ill?" asked Sylvia.

"No, no, not ill, except in mind. She has scarcely spoken since the awful thing happened."

"Can you tell me about it?" questioned the girl.

"Yes, I suppose I can," said the old lady, who was not averse to a gossip when anyone would listen. "Anyway, I can try, though it's a gruesome tale."

"Old Sir John Foulks was alive then, and it was always a grief to his wife that they had not a son to come after them; but when Sir John died, he directed by his will that his two nephews—

the sons of his younger brother, should live in turn for twelve months each at the castle, and that my lady was to decide in four years which would more fitly inherit.

"It could not be decided by seniority, as they were twins. They drew lots as to which should come on the first visit, and it fell to Lionel."

"Well," continued the old lady, "Mr. Lionel Troy came, but somehow he did not seem to get on with the people. He lacked the qualities which make men loved: he was weak-spirited, nervous on a horse, did not care for shooting, and preferred an afternoon at the White Arms drinking and playing cards, to a day after the hounds, and he grudged every rabbit and bird shot by anyone but his own pals, and *they* were a queer lot. He wasn't straight even in his dealings with poachers, but uses dirty underhand methods of catching them, and was bitterly disliked in consequence.

"Mr. Max came next, and his first twelve months was a very different thing. He was all that his brother was not—genial, frank, manly, generous, a thorough sportsman—his worst fault being his hot, uncontrollable temper; and though strict, he was just, and not too hard on the men who snared a few rabbits to feed big families with.

"The terms of the will were, unfortunately, well known, and gossip among the villagers caused a feeling of bitter jealousy to spring up between the brothers.

"Well, Mr. Max's first visit came to an end, and Mr. Lionel's second year began; but just at this time, a niece of her ladyship came home from India—her husband died there, and my lady offered a home to her, and her little girl aged ten. Ah! my bonny baby, how sweet she was! my little Chrystabel," and the old dame paused to wipe her eyes, not seeing that the mention of the child's name had brought a strained look to her guest's face, and that, with dilated eyes, she was breathlessly hanging on every word, with white face and quivering nerves.

"That year was a better one for Mr. Lionel, he was softer, more lovable, and was trying hard to win favour; and the reason was little Chrystabel. He adored the child, and her soft baby-fingers could lead him anywhere. Indeed folks began to say he would win through his love of the little girl; but, just getting near Christmas, he lost ground again, through a bitter time with the poachers; and he got one fellow—a stranger—locked up for a month; and it came out that the fellow was a skilled poacher, and was catching game for a man who was ill and couldn't work, and whose wife and little ones were starving. Feeling ran high in the village against Mr. Lionel, and all felt he had lost.

"The morrow was the day for Mr. Max to return; and by some chance, through deep snow, Mr. Lionel was delayed, and the brothers met. It was late at night when Mr. Max came, and little Chrystabel, whom he had never seen, had gone to bed. Had she been about, with her sweet face, perhaps the tragedy would never have happened, but the two young men met in the library—met as enemies, and in bitterest spirit. They were heard with voices raised, and using angry words. Mr. Lionel was twitting his brother for being a saint,' and poor Mr. Max lost his temper, and called Mr. Lionel 'a sneaking cad,' who tried to curry favour; and then there was a scream—a pistol shot, and someone burst into the room to find traces of a fierce struggle—an open window, Lionel dead on the floor with a bullet through his heart—and silence.

"The police were sent for, and evidence seemed all to point to poor Mr. Max as his brother's murderer and a warrant was issued for his arrest, and a search for him was made; but in vain, he had gone, as if the earth had swallowed him, and the most awful thing was, that when, some hours later, I went to see my baby, to see if the disturbance had awakened her, she was not there! Not a trace of her could be found, and never has been.

A sudden sharp scream brought the old lady to a stop, and she jumped up, to see her guest fall suddenly, heavily, hitting her head on the fender.

"Oh! what is it?" moaned the girl. "I—" When she opened her eyes some moments later, after a violent shaking by the old lady, "Something seems to have happened to my head—What were you telling me? Oh, I know. I remember, a library—men—fighting—what does it all mean? Tell me quickly—has that library got red walls with big gold birds on them? Is there a rug with a big bear's head on it? Tell me—tell me."

Trembling in every limb, the old lady nodded.

"Yes, yes. Who are you? How do you know?" she whispered. "My old eyes fail, but there was something in your voice which held me from the first."

"Take me to the house," said the girl. "I must see the house. I *must* remember, but it is all so dim."

"We will go," said the old lady, "but I am weak and frail."

Together they set out, and as they neared the castle the girl shuddered, and gazed.

"Take me quickly to that room," she said, and the old lady led her through a side door along endless passages, and at the entrance to a fine hall she stopped abruptly.

"Go yourself," she said. "See if you know."

And slowly the girl crossed the hall and turned the massive handle of a door, and entered. As she did so, the old lady turned on the lights and flooded the room with a soft glow; and, with a low cry, the gipsy girl sank down on the floor.

"It is," she sobbed. "I am right. I remember the room. Two men—one I knew, the other I did not. I had left my dolly, and crept down in my nightgown with bare feet to get it. They never heard me, and I stood at the door. I can see it all again," she sobbed. "A window flung open, a rough man entering, who shouted something about paying back, and raised a pistol he had in his hand, there was a shot, and Mr. Lionel fell; the other man never moved, never saw me, but the man with the pistol saw me, and called out: 'God! a child!' and I felt a fearful knock on my head, and never remembered again—until now. I found myself in a gipsy caravan later; was told I had been ill, and had always lived there; and life has been one long struggle to remember."

"Oh! where is my mother—my grannie? Does anyone know me?"

Silently, with the tears pouring down her withered cheeks

the old lady put her into a chair and went away telling her to remain; some twenty minutes after, she returned, bringing a frail, white-haired lady, probably not more than forty years of age but looking many years more.

"Will you speak to this girl, please, Lady Maud?" asked the old woman.

Lady Maud turned to the girl.

"Speak, girl; who are you?" she gasped. "Who are you with my Chrystabel's eyes and voice?"

"I am your little girl. O! mother! mother! try to remember me!"

And there in the old library every detail of the tragedy was gone into, and at last the blame was laid at the right door.

"Must I tell?" sobbed the girl. "It was Jake—I remember now, but he has been good to me— must I tell?"

"I fear so," answered her mother, "for poor Max is homeless and suspected until you do. It must be done now—at once. Come, dear."

★★★★★★

A few hours later a carriage drew up by the gipsy encampment, where quiet and peace seemed to reign. A wood fire was burning, and round it sat, or lay, the gipsies.

Old Mother Alison, smoking her pipe, was holding out her skinny hands to the blaze; Jake and his mother were sitting, talking in low tones; Jim, lounging gracefully, silently smoking, and pretty Mollie was twanging two strings of a worn-out banjo.

With a low cry, Sylvia sprang into the midst of them.

"Oh! my friends," she cried, "I did not mean to harm you. I have remembered, and I had told all before I realized all that it meant. Forgive me! Forgive me!"

One quick glance at his mother, and Jake rose to his feet and suddenly clasped the girl to his breast.

"I forgive you, Sylvia. Mother!" And the woman stood before him, rigid as stone.

Into the circle stepped the uniform of the law, but too late! There were two quick shots, and Jake and his mother had gone before a Higher Judge.

And Sylvia was clasped quickly in the arms of the man whose loyal love for her, and those who had sheltered him when a hunted suspected murderer, had always prevented him saying a word to bring sorrow on the girl he worshipped.

Old Mother Alison lit another pipe, muttering—

"It was in the stars. I knew it. None could avert their destiny. Go! Get from my sight all of you," and dismissed them with a wave of her skinny hand.

★★★★★★

Years have gone by, but the natives tell a story of how, when coming to their homes late at night, over the hills, they hear the creaking and lumbering of a caravan, and see it coming along with a man and woman walking beside it.

The vision lasts but a few moments, then—two clear pistol shots ring out, waking the echoes of Snowdonia.

The Star Inn

"What do you say to a change and a bit of a rest, old lady?"

"I'm with you every time, dearly beloved," was my reply.

After this exchange of brilliant remarks, my brother and I sat and gazed at each other in silence; but silence was not an unusual thing between us, we were so essentially two of those people—alas! that they are so rare!—who can contentedly pass long silences in perfect accord and happiness. We were neither of us exacting, and each was sure of the other—sure that no call could be made that would not be answered if possible—sure that if either had a burden, heavy to be borne, the other was waiting and ready to lighten it. Circumstances prevented our being much together, but long absences never wore any thinner The strong link of affection that bound us together; but when, as now, opportunity came for us to spend a few days in each other's society, we were not slow to grasp it.

After his preliminary remarks, my brother puffed complacently at his old much-blackened pipe, while I waited, with a hundred plans flying to my mind.

"Not too long a journey," he next vouchsafed, in answer to my unspoken query, "but somewhere alone—where people cannot find us."

"And telephones cease from ringing," I murmured.

Then he smiled, and the rough-coated dog, stretched at my brother's feet, smiled too. He surely did, for my brother stopped to pat him, with the remark—

"You too of course, old boy." You may not believe me, most

likely you won't, but a deeper glow shone in the loving brown eyes of the old dog! Understood? Of course he understood; it is we, poor, ignorant humans, who do not understand, and are deaf and blind to the sensitiveness, devotion and love lavished upon us, whether worthily or not, by our four-footed pals.

"And now to get our idea into train," said my brother, hauling himself out of the depths of his easy chair, and taking up a position on the corner of the table. "I suppose you don't much care where?" he asked.

"Not a bit," I replied.

Then," said he, "let's open a timetable and race through it for places not more than an hour or two away."

The search ended in our stopping, abruptly, at a station called "Pine Side." Why we selected it we were never quite clear. Dick always said it was the pine that attracted me, but I think both of us imagined a place with a name like that would be a very different spot to the one we subsequently proved it to be However, we decided upon it, and stuck to it, and in our usual rather erratic way, made up our minds to journey there without even finding out whether it was town, village, hamlet, or, indeed, anything beyond a station.

"There is sure to be an inn, and that will do for one night anyway," said Dick; and I, as ever, acquiesced.

★★★★★★

There was an inn. Oh! yes; and I for one am not likely to forget it. But to return to our beginning, we parted that night, far into the night indeed, watched and followed with faithful persistence by Timothy's brown eyes—he poor doggie, refusing supper or bed lest we should slip away with our boxes on our backs and leave him behind. We were not likely to, for he had too warm a corner in both our hearts for us willingly to be without him.

At last our belongings were ready and labelled, and when I finally put into my box Timothy's feeding bowl and rug, his satisfaction was complete, for then, and then only, did he curl up on Dick's bed, and heaving a sigh of relief, settled himself to sleep and dream, perhaps of bunnies, which he raced with and chased—perchance, only to, sleep with one eye and keep the other in ever watchful care upon his master.

Next morning we drove to our nearest station and asked for tickets for Pine Side; obviously, it was little known, for the booking clerk had to go through that ever tedious business of writing tickets.

"So far, so good," whispered Dick. " It isn't a much-sought-after place, anyway."

"How many changes have we?" I asked a weary-looking porter.

"Dunno," he replied; "three or four, I expect."

"And what time do we get there?" I went on.

"That depends," said he. "Sometimes you're early, often as not, late—sometimes very late—it depends on the market."

"The market!" I said. "Where? What market?"

"Pine Side, of course," he answered, looking with an expression that seemed to put me down as a poor ignorant kind of soul, and then he slunk off, leaving me standing with a bundle of sticks in one hand, a bag in the other, and murmuring "market" to myself.

A sudden bustle announced the arrival of our train, and we and our belongings were soon comfortably settled in a compartment, and off on our vague journey. The journey itself was nothing out of the ordinary, except as to the changes of which there were five! and each subsequent train we entered seemed slower than the last. It is unnecessary for me to give the direction of our destination except to say that we travelled north, and that our spirits rose as we drew nearer and nearer to higher hills and purer air.

It was growing dark as our slowest of engines laboriously grunted itself to a full stop at an odd-looking junction. I say odd-looking, because the platform was full of crates of hens and ducks, calves in sacks, with just their sad little faces outside the sack, pigs tied by the leg and squealing their way through the crowds of people; men in big boots, gaiters and rough cord garments with coats of antique pattern; women in clogs, wearing short, bunchy skirts, flapping hats tied under their chins with gay ribbons; most of them also enveloped in large blue and white check aprons, and carrying baskets poised on one hip; many of them leading an animal or carrying a fowl.

I wondered, idly, whether the animals and people travelled together, and my unspoken question was speedily answered by the door of our compartment being suddenly opened, and two stout women entering; or rather, they rolled in, treading on my toes, falling over my brother's legs, and calling forth a decidedly snappish bark from Timothy, who was lolling on a seat to himself, nose between his paws and brown eyes fixedly regarding every movement made by my brother. The arrival of our fellow-passengers necessitated Tim's removal from his seat, which was promptly crammed with bundles and packages, and crowned by two live fowls tied together by a bit of string, heads down, and gurgling as if every breath would be their last.

Tim's interest centred in them for the moment, and he eyed them with an unholy grin on his lips, and the wickedest twinkle in his eyes. I wondered much, if he could restrain his well-known passion for anything feathered, so far as to keep his paws off them; and I know it was only the restraining glance he got from time to time from his master that made him appear the demure dog he looked. Once he raised himself—I waited breathlessly, but a murmured word, which he apparently understood perfectly, made him at once adopt an expression seeming to say: "I am utterly indifferent to fowl, or any other beast, just now!"

The two women eyed us curiously, the fatter one of the two gave me an affable smile, as she remarked—

"''Oneymoon, my dear?"

"No," I replied, "nothing like that, just a pleasant holiday with my brother."

"Oh!" she said, "where, my dear?"

"Pine Side," I said. " What is it like?"

"Pine Side!" she exclaimed. "Why, whit in 'eaven s name will you find to do, my dear, and where will you stay?"

"We shall walk," I answered; "and shall stay at the inn!"

"Lord-a-mussy!" she almost shrieked, "ye'll stay at the inn?" At which the other woman nudged her violently in the ribs, and muttered—

"Leave 'em be, Kate; leave 'em be. They'll be all right seeing they know nought—"

I looked the questions I did not ask, would that I had. The train with many grunts drew up to a wooden platform, and, with a bob and a muttered "afternoon," the two women bundled out trailing their many belongings after them, hurried by Tim, who gleefully snatched a feather from one of the birds and laid it with intense devotion at his master's feet.

"Well, girl we have arrived," and, with a prolonged stretch of his long limbs, my brother got up, shook out his pipe and began to lift our numerous belongings from the rack, and proceeded to alight from the train on to the platform of Pine Side Station—we knew it was the station, because a broken-down board said so—but it was a melancholy spot, and except for the market folks and their animals of all sorts, was utterly devoid of all the usual look and life of a station. We stood for a moment and looked at each other, and then at our surroundings, and then both laughed, for after all, we were together, and little else mattered.

"Hold Tim while I unearth and interview the station-master," said Dick; and, leaving me in the midst of our goods and chattels, he tramped off to emerge within five minutes from a dingy looking corner, followed by a dried-up little man, apparently the station-master signalman and porter, for we saw no other official. He and my brother were talking in a low tone as they approached me, and I caught the words, "You can but try, sir, and say nothing."

"Even', Miss," said the worthy official, touching his cap. "Hope you'll have a pleasant holiday, and be no worse for it."

"Worse for it?" I said, smiling, "that is not possible, I'll be all the better." And he looked at me with keen little gimlets of eyes, from under shaggy white brows, and went back to his dingy room without any further words.

"Come on, Pat, I know where to go," announced my brother, grabbing a bag and rugs and leaving me the rest of the things. My name, I might mention, was Patricia, but "Pat" was the nearest to it my brother ever got, so "Pat" I remained.

"Where are we to go to?" I asked.

"The Star Inn," he replied, with a grin; and we set off.

"How far?" I next enquired.

"Wait and see" was his only answer, as we trudged down the narrow muddy lane leading from the station, and so out into the main street. I should say *only* street, for one could scarcely call the many straggling lanes we passed by the dignified name of street.

"Broad Street" was the name of the one and only; it certainly was broad, though rough, the middle of it being paved with big cobbles. Small compact little houses lined it on each side, and what struck me was the sameness of them and the cleanliness; each had its strip of garden divided from the next house by a low white railing; each had its spotless white step and brass knocker on a dull green door; each roof was composed of some sort of large flag—they were not slates or tiles—the windows were the only thing in any way different from each other, and they showed a decided individuality; some had scarlet blinds, some white, some had pots of flowers, and one or two had singing birds in gilt cages. There was an entire absence of people, so I surmised they lived in the back premises, and the front rooms were for show. Presently, my brother stopped under a dull red lamp.

"Here we are," he said. "This is the 'Star.'"

"Oh, is it?" I said.

A low rambling building with a similar roof and very neat windows, most of them full of scarlet geraniums. Blackened oak beams seemed to support two big gabled windows, a long verandah reaching nearly the entire length, and a white cat on the step washing its face. Such was my first impression of the "Star Inn."

I looked at Dick, and Tim looked at the cat; presumably they spoke, for the cat after one scornful glance, fled precipitantly, and we rang the bell. A little old woman answered it. She had a face like a russet apple, snow-white hair, eyes like little blue beads, and not any teeth; she was dressed in a lavender print frock, and wore clogs.

"Well, what do you want?" she asked.

"We want two bedrooms and a sitting-room, some food and a wash, and we want to stay here for our holidays," was my brother's terse reply.

"Well, I never did!" quoth the old dame; "I never did!"

"Neither did we, I'm sure of that."

"Come in, come an," she said. "Visitors for me after so long!" and, muttering amiably to herself, she led us into a sort of parlour. It was spotlessly clean and uncomfortable, rigid chairs with starched antimacassars, a horse-hair sofa, some bright wool-work mats, a case of decrepit looking stuffed birds, a shining polished mahogany table with a large Bible on it, a stone floor with a deep border of whitening round it, and a grate stuffed full of coloured paper! I shivered and looked beseechingly at my brother; he had taken it all in, and then said to the old dame—

"Haven't you any other sitting-room? This is a bit small."

She looked at him, then snapped—

"No, I haven't."

"I'll pay double for; bigger one," he went on, and the blue beads of her eyes glittered—greed was evidently the old woman's besetting sin, for without further demur, she said—

"You can see it, anyway," and led us along a stone passage, up a flight of stairs to an old oak door. This she opened with a key hung from her waist by a long steel chain. We entered, and stood enthralled, delighted.

"Light the fire, this is ours," said Dick; and, delightedly, I sank into a big old chair and gazed about me.

The room was long and narrow; it seemed to be as far as one could judge, almost the entire length of the house, and except for the passage from which we entered, would have been as wide as the house, or rather as deep. The floor was merely white boards, but they were scrubbed as white as snow; the centre of the room was covered with an old Eastern rug, in faded shades of blue and buff; the walls were only coloured a dull blue, all the wood-work was the same well scrubbed white unpainted wood. There were a few old etchings of coaching scenes on the walls, and one or two old willow-pattern plates.

The hearth was modern, with a quite up-to-date well grate and copper fire-irons. On each side of the fireplace stood deep scarlet leather chairs, artistic in a vivid way. A roomy couch piled with real feather pillows, was pulled up across one of the low windows, and a writing table with many drawers, filled the other; a woman's workbasket stood beside one chair, and a smoker's table beside the other. That was all the room contained, except a large feathery fern, fresh and green as if carefully tended. A soft white sheepskin rug on the floor in front of the fireplace completed the furnishing. This latter article met with the unqualified and instant approval of Timothy, who at once took possession and watched our next proceedings with a satisfied grin.

"You like it, sir?" asked the old dame.

"Certainly we do," answered my brother. "Please let us have a fire, then some tea—a big tea," he added; "we are hungry."

The old dame shuffled slowly away to reappear shortly with her apron full of logs of wood; these she piled in the grate and set fire to, eyeing them complacently as the flames began to leap up the wide chimney.

"The chimney's cold, sir," she remarked. "It is long since a fire was burning here, but I'm glad to see it," she went on, "and trust you'll be comfortable and warm," she added, as she moved away towards the door with a backward glance at our now blazing fire.

It must have been almost an hour later when I heard a quick knock on my bedroom door, and a voice called—

"Your tea is ready; Miss."

"Thanks," I answered, though thinking it was quite time too, although the hour had given me time to unpack my own and my brother's belongings, tidy my hair, and get rid of the dust of the journey. I speedily left my room, and entered our sitting-room. I smiled to see the happy picture which met my gaze. Dick sprawled in his big chair, before the glowing fire, with Timothy beside him, the old dog's head resting on my brother's knee, and those eyes of his, in which you could see his whole soul, fixed on Dick's face in steadfast and loyal devotion. The tea-table was utterly ignored by them both, they were for the moment sufficient for each other, and were, I firmly believe, intent on a conversation, wordless, but perfectly understood on both sides.

If you two have quite finished airing your views to each other, we will have tea," I remarked.

Dick smiled, as he answered—

"We will come, although we were deeply engaged in a problem."

And the problem?" I queried.

"Merely whether in the next world we should be together," he answered.

"And the answer?" I asked.

"We are uncertain, as yet," was his reply, though both of us are inclined to the opinion that heaven would not be heaven to us minus each other.

"Come to tea, goose," I said, and without further remark he came, and the three of us enjoyed the excellent tea of cold ham, scones and honey the old dame had given us. We chatted on many subjects over our meal, and decided that our vague journey had landed us in comfy quarters, and looked forward to our little holiday with much pleasure.

Just as we finished our tea, our old lady appeared, to clear away, first asking us if we would like lights, it struck me then for the first time that there was no gas, or, apparently any mode of lighting, and I asked her what sorts of lights they used.

"Candles," she replied.

"Candles!" I echoed. "We shall want a lot of those to light this room!" She gave me a quick, keen look, but vouchsafed no reply, and went out, returning in a short time with a large and heavy candelabra with five tall candles in it. This she banged down in the centre of the table, and said—

"You'll light it when you need it," and departed. The room was getting darker now, so we drew our chairs up to the fire, which we replenished from a wicker-basket full of logs, left for our use. Curiously enough, with so much to talk about, we had fallen into silence. My brother puffed away at his pipe, and I—as was ever my way—had slipped from my chair and squatted on the rug, at his knee. I always chose to sit on the floor in preference to a chair when there was someone with me who understood. There are not many, and, there are very few people whom it is possible to sit on the floor with.

There are lots of people who *say* they like it, but they only do it because others do it; to me, it is, and has always been real rest—the cosy intimate feeling of squatting or lying before the fire on a rug, watching the sparks on the back of the fireplace, until my fancy pictured them as armies advancing, retreating, joining, fighting, until one side or the other is wiped out. And so I sat lost in my dreams, seeing pictures in the fire, until my brother's voice brought me back to earth again, with the common-place remark—

"Aren't you cold, Pat?"

Now, I have a distinct dislike to being brought back to earth from my dreams, and am always inclined for a moment to cordially detest the disturber of my visions; indeed, had it been anyone but my beloved brother, I should inevitably have answered crossly—if I answered at all! But Dick was different, and occupied a unique position in my life; he could enter where no one else dare, so I detached myself from my army of sparks, and answered him—

"I wasn't cold until you spoke, and yet I have been feeling chilly now you mention it."

"An answer, my dear Pat," he said, jokingly, "quite in keeping with your usual lucid remarks."

"Well," I said, "we've got a fire big enough to cook us, so it

185

really does seem absurd to talk of being chilly," saying which I gathered myself up from my cosy rug and wandered to the now dim outline of the table. "I will light our most magnificent candles," I said.

"No, I will," announced my brother. "Girls never get a light from the first six matches at least."

"Very well, Mr. Superior, light it yourself; but I'll bet you an ounce of baccy to a box of chocs' you will not light them with less than three matches yourself," and I curled myself up in his vacated chair to await results.

He laughed as he struck a match. I did not trouble to turn my head, my armies on the chimney back were advancing, and I was once again deep in contemplation of their manoeuvres. My brother's voice again aroused me.

"Pat! Come here."

"'What's the matter now, old worry?" I asked, without moving.

"You have won your bet," he answered in a voice that struck me as a little queer. "Come here," he added, "my matches are mad, I think."

With a sigh, I pulled myself out of my chair, and moved to his side as he stood by the table—in the darkness.

"Light it," he said.

"'Why, Dick, what's the matter?" I asked, as I took the box from him, "your hand is shaking."

"Light it," was his reply, "and be quick." I struck a match, it flared up, wavered, and went out.

"That's only one of my six," I said laughing, as I struck another; again it flared up for an instant, wavered, and went out. "Two!" I said "But you blew that one—" He did not speak, and I struck my third, it burnt well, I leaned over to light the candles, and out it went.

"You *did* blow it," I said.

"No," he answered, "all mine did that—there must be a beastly draught from somewhere—try another. I did, and as I held it for an instant, it lighted up Dick's face, and the extreme whiteness of it struck me. I bent over again, and this time succeeded in lighting one candle.

"There!" I exclaimed, "and only four matches," but even as I spoke the flame of the candle wavered, flickered, and went out.

There was a moment's silence, broken by a low whine from Timothy, who was trying to shove his cold nose into my hand.

"What is it, Dick?" I managed to gasp.

"I think the place is draughty," he answered, turning as he spoke to where an old-fashioned bell-pull dangled on the wall, but ere he reached it, the door opened to admit our old dame carrying a lighted lamp; she glanced at us and said:

"Maybe this will give a better light."

'Maybe it will," Dick answered, as she slowly withdrew and closed the door.

The glow of the lamp showed the room in a new aspect, though it only lit up a part of it, leaving the corners dim and shadowy. Neither of us spoke as we once more drew near to the fire. Dick was the first to break the somewhat long silence, and his remark was addressed to his dog: "Come here, old boy, I want to talk to you," he said. But Timothy was deep in slumber, or appeared to be, for he took no notice.

"Well if you won't, you won't, so I'll smoke instead," added Dick, pulling out his well-worn pouch and filling his old briar. Whether Tim smelt the baccy or had decided he would join in, I do not know, but at this moment he rose, padded softly to his master and placed his front paws on Dick's knees, wagging his tough scrap of a tail as if to apologise for his recent neglect.

"One minute, boy, till I get a light," said his master, "then I will talk." And he struck a match, ready to light his pipe. One second it remained a steady bright light and then went out. At the same instant, Timothy gave a low growl which ended in a whine, as he slowly drew himself backwards from his master's knee, and still keeping his eyes fixed on him, slowly backed until he was pressing heavily against my skirt. I, too, was watching Dick, and saw his face grow still paler, and the hand that held his pipe trembled.

"You old villain," he said, in a voice he strove to keep steady. "You blew that out, grunting like that. Come here," but Tim only cowered back.

"What is wrong, Dick?" I managed to stammer at last.

"I don't know," he answered, "but I think we are all over-tired, and bed is the best place. Come along, dear, I'll see you to your room. It is a little early, but you are tired," so, putting his arm over my shoulders he quietly pulled me out of my chair and led me away, Timothy now quite himself again, gleefully trotting at his side.

My bedroom, quaint, clean, and cosy, and lit by a small brass lamp, looked all that I could desire, and bidding "goodnight" to my dear old brother and his faithful pal, I locked my door and was quickly in bed and almost as quickly asleep, my last waking impression being of a faint, soft, indescribably-sweet scent wafting over my face. "Lavender!" I murmured, drowsily, "how nice!" And I knew no more, until I was awakened by a thump at any door, and I heard my brother sing out:

"Time you were awake, lazy bones. Tim and I have been out for an hour."

"Shan't be long," I called, and I bathed and dressed in record time.

Our day was spent in prowling round and exploring the quaint sleepy little town, with its old-world people most of whom, stared at us with interest, but seemed too busy with their own little lives to trouble much over the doings of the strangers in their midst. We wandered back to the inn for lunch, which was excellent in a plain, simple way, and beautifully cooked and served. About an hour later we went out again, and this time went further afield where the country grew more hilly and rough, and was chiefly wild uncultivated land with very few trees.

"I don't think much of it," I ventured to remark, as we stood to rest a minute.

"Nor I," answered Dick, "except that it is quiet, the air ripping, and Timothy is having a great time."

"It may be," I said, "but I want my tea. Shall we try and get some here in a cottage? There is a light over there," pointing, as I spoke, to what appeared to be a cottage window.

"Very well, let's try," said Dick. So together we descended the hill and approached the cottage.

Our knock at the door was answered by a gruff voice bidding us enter.

"Doesn't sound promising," whispered Dick, but we obeyed the voice and entered a tiny kitchen, spotlessly clean, but evidently poverty-stricken. Two people sat before the fire, a grey-haired man in rough clothes, smoking a long clay pipe, and a pretty fair-haired girl of about eighteen.

"We wondered," began my brother, "if we might ask you to make us a cup of tea, my sister is tired, and we are a long way I think, from the inn.

"Welcome, Mister. Put the kettle on, Isobel, and come you near the fire, Miss," said the man, as the pretty girl rose and did as she was told without speaking, then he looked at us.

"At the inn, be you?" he said.

"Yes," I replied, "it is very comfortable." He grunted, and mumbled some words, of which I only caught a few about "rather be here than there," and went on smoking. The girl, meanwhile, filled a brown tea-pot, put a loaf and some butter on the table and curtsied, saying:

"That is all we can give you, Miss."

"It is splendid," I said. "I am very grateful to you." And there was no doubt we most thoroughly enjoyed our tea, but it was getting darker each minute now, and we had some way to go, so did not linger by the cosy fire loth as we were to leave it.

Dick offered the old man some silver, but he refused it with much dignity, saying:

"No, mister, you're very welcome. I wish ye a 'goodnight,' and if ye're any ways troubled, maybe I can help yer, if yer ask, but I'll not say ought until ye do."

This somewhat vague speech conveyed nothing to us as we smilingly nodded and took our departure.

It was quite dark now as we stumbled along the unfamiliar roads. Even Timothy lagged a little, as if he realised that his mileage was nearly double ours after all the hunting he had done. We were all glad I think, to see the glimmer of the red limps from the inn door come in sight, and our steps were a bit quicker as we covered the last few yards. The old oak door was closed when we reached it, the big white cat was sitting on the mat, as before.

"Puss! Puss!" I called, bending down, but the sight of Tim, with bristling hair, must have startled the cat; for, as I bent to pat it, it was no longer there.

"Which way did the beast go, Dicky?" I asked.

"Blessed if I know," he answered, with a laugh, "but Tim is evidently tired, or he'd have been after it, instead of standing growling about it. But come, let's go in," opening the old door as he spoke, putting an arm through mine as we tramped up the stairs together.

Our meal was ready for us, and the fire burning gaily, but there was no other light in the room. I left Dick, and went off to get tidy; and for the first time really inspected my room, as the previous night I was too tired, and this morning I was hurried out so quickly. It was a much larger room than I had thought, and there were two other doors into it: one, being hidden by a chintz curtain had missed my eye altogether; the other I had noticed vaguely, was studded with heavy nails, and both locked and barred. Well! that was safe, anyway, and the curtained one did not trouble me, since obviously, it was not for use. I moved my lamp and began to do my hair. How quiet it was, I thought, there might be no one else alive in the place; though, as this thought crossed my mind, I heard a murmur of voices close to me.

"Someone else coming to stay," I thought, and went on placidly doing my hair. Again I heard the voices, and a soft, tinkling laugh reached my ears. I paused, with my hair-brush in the air, to listen, and heard a man's voice speaking. I could nearly hear the words, the tone at any rate, was clear; a deep domineering note seemed to run through the whole sentence, almost a commanding sound, and then the silvery tinkling laugh. Pretty, I thought, but mocking; then there was silence, and I finished my dressing humming a snatch of a song, and left my room to join my brother. I found him asleep in the depths of his big chair, Tim at his feet, one eye steadily fixed on his master. Evidently the rest of our meal had been placed on the table unheard by Dick, for our coffee-pot was there also, covered with a gigantic scarlet cosy. Softly I bent over my dear lad, and planted a kiss on his forehead. He woke with a start.

"Hello, old girl, that you? I must have dropped off, I suppose, it's the strong air. I remember hearing you talking to someone, and then I dozed."

"I wasn't talking," I answered, "though someone was in a room next to mine; newcomers I suppose. Come and have supper, but not by firelight only, we'll light—er—the lamp."

"I really would like to light the candles," said Dick, "if they *will* light, but I'm going to put them over here out of any chance of draught," saying which, he lifted the heavy candelabra from the table and put it gently on the top of an old oak chest at the end of the room furthest from the fireplace, and striking a match, held it high above his head triumphantly.

"There!" he said. "I knew it was a draught."

"You are six feet tall," I laughed, "and are holding it quite two feet above your head, so the chances are it is out of a draught." Laughingly he brought the lighted match down, and suddenly gave a startled exclamation, as, with a quick flicker, the match went out.

"You touched my hand," he said, "and blew, I felt it."

I shook my head.

"Don't bother," I said, "the lamp will do"; and, reluctantly, Dick moved away, deep in thought, giving his hand a furtive rub as he went.

We did not try again, but had our meal by the light of the lamp, then drew our chairs close to the fire, making a place for Tim between us; but the old dog was uneasily moving about the room, hair on end.

"What's the matter, boy," called Dick, "come here." But Tim only roamed about restlessly.

"I thought I saw the white cat come in," I said.

"So also did Tim, I should think—look at him!" said. Dick, pointing to the dog standing rigidly glaring at the oak chest.

"He gives me the jumps," I said. "Make him lie down, Dick."

But Tim was deaf alike to entreaties or commands; and finally, Dick went to him and picked him up bodily, depositing him in the big chair beside him, where the old dog snuggled down with a deep sigh of satisfaction.

Presently the door opened, and old Martha entered, to clear the table.

"Have other visitors come, Martha?" I asked.

"Yes, Miss—no—I don't know," she answered, confusedly. "I only have to look after you, Miss. Goodnight," and she passed out more swiftly than I had seen her move.

"I know there are people—I heard them," I went on.

"Well, and if there are, said my brother, "do you wish for other company?"

"Never, while I have you, dear," was my reply. "I was only curious, it seems such an out-of-the world corner for anyone to come to. There I hear people speaking again; listen!" I said, and as we listened, we distinctly heard voices.

"We are not alone that's sure," said Dick, "our solitude is invaded."

"But this room is our own anyway," I answered, "and we will be comfy, but I must just run and get my knitting; don't go to sleep till I come back." And I went off to my room. It was in darkness, and I had to grope round for my knitting which I knew I had left on the bed. I was just about to put my hand where I thought I had left my work, when I heard again the silvery tinkling laugh, but so close to me, I thought someone had mistaken the room.

"Is anyone there?" I asked.

There was no reply, though I heard the soft swish of a silken dress, the quick tap of high-heeled shoes, and a door softly shut.

"Stupids!" I thought, "they might have answered whoever they were." And then, having discovered my matches, I lit one, and glanced round. I had just time to see the chintz curtain over the hidden door softly swaying, when my match went out.

"Um," I remarked, "I'll settle that door before I sleep." And forgetting my knitting, I groped my way to the door, bent on reaching Dick and the light without further delay.

As I closed my bedroom door, I felt someone brush past me in the darkness; I felt really annoyed at the stupidity of country people and their very sparing illumination.

I opened our sitting-room door softly, and went in. I was half-way across the room, when Tim suddenly sat up, and gave vent to a long moan, and then a series of short, sharp barks, and fixing his eyes beyond me, glared, snarling and growling.

I turned quickly to see why all this fuss, but there was nothing, no one, and I told the dog to lie down, and not to be foolish. I might have spared my breath, for Tim continued to snarl and growl, glaring always beyond me.

"He must hear these new people about, I think," I said, in answer to Dick's questioning look, "there was someone in my room, evidently mistaking the room, for they must have gone out by another door I have, for I saw the curtain which covers it, moving when I struck a match."

"Oh! but that won't do, old girl, I can't have mistakes of that sort happening. Come, and I'll fasten it," said Dick, rising from his chair, shaking himself free from Tim's too loving embrace.

So together we returned to my room carrying the lamp, followed by Tim, who came as if under protest, growling all the way.

Setting the lamp on the dressing-table, Dick glanced round.

"Where's the door?" he asked. "I'll jolly soon settle mistakes."

"There it is," was my response, "there under that chintz curtain."

"Why, you small cuckoo!" he said, laughing, "you must have had forty winks, for I dare bet it's many moons since that door opened, it's fairly rusted up; look at the lock and bolts, they are fast shut, and the key turned too.

I looked, but unconvinced, shook my head, saying:

"That door *was* opened, dear boy, and I intend to open it again, so help me."

"You are foolish," he said, "it isn't meant to open."

"Open it, there's a dear," I pleaded, "I must see through it."

It took us working together, a good half-hour to wriggle those bolts back and turn that rusty key, and though I was now ready to admit I was mistaken, I was quite determined to see that door opened. At last the key turned and Dick, exerting his whole strength, leant on the door. It creaked, moved, and finally, after one more terrific push, yielded slowly moving back on its rusty hinges. A rush of damp, musty air greeted us, and the sound of scurrying mice, or even rats, made us draw back, to grab the lamp, holding it aloft as we peered into the room beyond us. Amazed, speechless, we gazed.

The room was empty! carpetless! cold! grim! reeking of damp mould. Only one chair stood there, an old black carved oak chair, with a high back, faded blue velvet cushion moth eaten and hanging in rags. Long blue velvet curtains in the same condition hung across the windows, and from the torn fringes cobwebs cluttered, hanging in festoons.

Suddenly I stared, clutching Dick's arm, and as we looked, there came the sound of a silvery, tinkling laugh, and the tap of high-heeled shoes crossing the floor.

It was only the fact of my brother's arm suddenly catching me round the waist, that kept me from what he would have called "making a fool of myself," as it was, I felt as if turned to ice, even the scream that terror brought to my lips, seemed to freeze there, and as the tap of the little heels died away, my brother's voice sounded in my ears—

"Come, girl, pull yourself together," and half-carrying me, he took me back to the sitting-room, depositing me in the chair by the fire, looking at me in silence for some minutes, before he spoke.

"It is not explainable, Pat dear, is it?"

I shook my head, not daring to trust my voice yet; then he looked at his watch.

"Too late to move, dear; no trains."

This in answer, I think, to the appeal I knew he must see in my face.

Suddenly I missed Tim.

"The dog!" I managed to whisper.

"Ratting, most likely," answered Dick, in what he attempted to make a nonchalant voice, "but I'd better see. You will be quite all right for a moment. Sit where you are, I'll be quick." And he vanished, leaving me sitting trembling, in my big chair, feeling too done up to even think.

True to his promise, he soon returned, carrying Tim, whom he laid down gently and began to rub his limbs.

"What?" I asked.

"I don't know," he answered, gravely; "but he wasn't ratting, he was lying on the floor gasping and trembling."

"Did you see anything?" I managed to ask.

"No," he replied, hesitatingly, "except the white cat. I saw that. It was standing close to him. They have had a scrap."

"But Tim isn't scratched," I said.

"No—no—he's not," answered Dick. "Oh, don't let's talk of it, dear. Here, have a cig., and forget it. We will pile up the fire and I'll bring our coats, and we will sit here until it is daylight enough to move, then we'll scoot."

We did our best to cheer up; and after awhile, Tim revived, and became more like himself. We tried to keep away from the subject uppermost in both our minds, but the long silences were not like our usual happy silences, there was a disturbing element, and I fancy both of us, indeed all three, would have been thankful if it had been 8 a.m. and not 8 p.m.

Our meal was brought in and put ready, old Martha glancing at us more than once as she laid the cloth, but neither of us spoke Until she had departed; or, at least, Tim was the only one who spoke, and he glared at her and growled, as she moved nearer to us.

195

"What is it, old man?" asked Dick, soothingly; and, under the touch of his master's hand the old dog quietened down once more.

We made a poor pretence at a meal, and were thankful to ring the bell and get it cleared away.

As old Martha was finally leaving us, Dick said:

"Please don't disturb us again. We are both going to do some writing, and may be late going to bed, don't trouble to wait up, we shall not require anything further."

The old dame seemed on the point of speaking, but thought better of it, and moved away. Just as she got to the door, I heard a faint "Meow!" Tim sprang up, hair bristling and eyes aflame. I turned my head to look at the cat, and to my amazement, saw the old dame stoop down and stroke the empty air. Seeing me staring, she straightened herself and vanished.

"Don't leave me again, Dick," I implored. "I shall bolt if you do."

"All right, old lady; but just let me run for our big coats, sit tight for a minute, I will not leave you again—promise." And he was gone.

Am I more susceptible I wonder, to things unseen, than other people, for it seemed to me that the instant I was alone, the very atmosphere of the room altered. Shudderingly I endeavoured to "sit tight;" but, to my disordered nerves the room no longer seemed empty, and I sat grasping Tim's collar with one hand, and the side of my chair with the other, until I heard Dick's step returning; and with his entrance, some, at least, of the strain relaxed, and I breathed more easily. We heaped up the fire, drew the table with the lamp closer to us, put our chairs as close together as possible, and covered our knees and Tim with one of the coats.

"Try and sleep, Pat; I will guard," said Dick. But sleep was far from me, and I did not intend him to watch alone either, so we lit our smokes, and tried to read or chat.

A couple of hours had passed cosily and serenely, when a queer creaking sound arrested my attention, and I turned quickly. Dick looked up instantly, and our eyes turned instinctively to where stood the old-fashioned basket-work; and as we looked, we both heard the tumbling of a reel of cotton on the floor.

"Sounds as if the old cat had got loose among the work-basket," said my brother, trying to joke. "Oh! look at Tim."

I am certain the dog saw what we imagined, "the white cat," but he made no attempt to get to close quarters with it, only glared and bristled, hugging close and yet closer to his master.

"Can you go through it, dear?" Dick asked me, somewhat anxiously. "I fear we are in for something of a night."

"I'll try," I whispered. "I'll stick to it if I can, I've always hankered to see and hear ghosts, so I must be glad my wish seems about to be realised, but I prefer people to cats," I said, with a feeble attempt at a smile. As I spoke, the soft, tinkling laugh reached my ear. I grasped Dick's hand, as we sat, silent, intent on we knew not what.

It must have been somewhere about midnight when the door behind us opened suddenly, violently, letting in a rush of cold damp air; and through the wide-flung heavy door, we saw dimly the old, high-backed chair with its faded torn cushion, and a glimpse of the hangings in the distance.

"The same room," I managed to whisper, and Dick's whispered "Buck up!" and the calm pressure of his hand on mine, worked wonders in quietening the terrific throbs of my heart. We heard a heavy footfall, a tumbling, half-shuffling step, we heard the sound of something being kicked, we heard our furniture being knocked, we felt the presence of some other creature in the room, yet we saw nothing.

Somehow that other presence seemed to draw nearer, ever nearer to where we sat, and instinctively we rose and edged further and further from the fireplace, closer and closer to the door—the presence seemed to follow, and compel us to leave our refuge of safety, the door, and go nearer to the far end of the room beside the other door from whence "It" had entered, and then "It" seemed to relieve us of its following menace and go from us, and we heard as if a heavy body sank into one of the red leather chairs. I almost shrieked, but again the steady clasp of my brother's arm reassured me.

We did not speak, yet both were now certain we were not alone, and both waited as if there was—something we must wait for, then the tinkling laugh sounded close beside us, close enough to make me start and gasp. The heavy body seemed to lift from the chair and pass us, with a cold gust of air, and we heard the little tapping shoes in the room beyond. Together we crept closer to that open door, until we stood there against our wills, and yet powerless to fight the power that drove us there.

The room was no longer in darkness, nor yet in rags and tatters, it had every appearance of an exquisitely furnished and upholstered room. I was *beyond* horror now—I seemed to be the interested spectator of a wordless drama.

The room was no longer tenantless, for there, in the high oak chair, sat the figure of a girl, her small head with a wealth of red hair, was thrown back against the chair, and her blue eyes seemed to flash blue fire as she stared defiantly before her—one dainty foot in a silver embroidered shoe, with the highest of heels, was poised on an ebony or black oak stool, the other was impatiently tapping the floor. In her arms was the large white cat, looking at her and rubbing its head against her shoulder.

We saw a man go through the door by which we stood, as if he entered from our room—a big coarsely-made man, with the coarse bloated features of a hard drinker—we saw him go near to the chair where the dainty figure sat upright, defiant, we saw him raise a threatening hand, but the little figure only gazed at him with blazing, scornful eyes. We saw him bend swiftly and draw from his breast pocket something that gleamed, and, frozen to the spot as we were, we saw him plunge a keen knife into that lovely body, and withdraw it, to plunge it deep into the white cat There was a long moaning cry, and the mocking little lady lay a huddled heap on the floor, with the white cat clasped close in her arms. One shriek I gave, and fainted.

When I opened my eyes again, the grey light of dawn was stealing in at our windows, the fire was burning merrily, and a kettle hissing on the hob.

I was lying back in one of the big chairs, my brother was kneeling beside me, and a grey-haired, kindly-faced man was holding my hand. I came to myself, slowly, memory struggling to recall the "whys" and "wherefores."

Dick answered my unspoken question, saying quietly:

"Don't worry, dear, you are all safe." And then youth and health began to reassert themselves, and I tried to collect my scattered wits.

"She is all right, doctor, isn't she?" asked my faithful old brother.

A gruff, but kindly voice answered:

"Yes, but take your time, and then get her home."

"I—I—oh! what was it all?" I asked, consciousness and memory coming suddenly into their own. "Did I dream it? Where is the pretty girl? Oh! tell me what did it all mean?"

"Better tell her, doctor," said Dick, "there will be no peace otherwise."

Then the gruff voice bade me "get up and look into the room beyond."

"Must I?" I asked, shuddering.

"Come, girl," said my brother, and with his arm round me, he led me to the still open door. I looked—and saw an empty, dirty room—with cushions and hangings of faded blue velvet festooned with cobwebs—peopled only with scurrying rats and mice.

"Well! But—what—" I began.

"Ah! my dear lady," answered the old doctor, "I cannot tell you why, but from the accounts of your brother here, I can only say, that you appear to have witnessed the tragedy which happened long years ago in this old inn, and which gave it the unenviable reputation it possesses of being haunted by a pair of lovers and a white cat. I cannot tell you the story, but old Seth Manners, who lives with his grand-daughter a mile away, could, if you care to hear it, tell the story. I only know that once every year the whole scene takes place, but, except old Martha, who's

199

nursling the girl was, I know of no one else who has seen it. But then," he went on, "no one comes here. Did no one warn you?"

"Well, vaguely," I answered, as my mind flew back to veiled hints on the part of fellow travellers, the station master, the old man where we had tea, and last, but by no means least, if we had been intelligent enough to understand Timothy's warnings without end, from the moment we reached the door of the Star Inn, and met the white cat on its doorstep.

"If you feel like remaining on," said the doctor, "you may rest in peace, nothing more will happen until twelve months has gone by, and if you decide to stay, I shall be delighted to see you both any time—my house lies beyond the village, close to that belt of pines against the hill."

"Pine Side," I murmured.

"Exactly," said Dr. Moss, "Pine Side—it is also the name of my house, come and see it"

"Are you game, Pat?" asked my dauntless brother.

"Yes," I said, "I am. I want to call on Seth Manners, and hear the story of the lovers and the white cat."

And so we stayed, and were greatly bowed down to in the village, on account of what they called Lancashire grit; and maybe there is something in that same grit which enabled two unsuspecting, sensitive beings to witness, without losing their reason, a tragedy of other days, enacted as clearly as we witnessed this one. If I must be quite truthful, there is no other being in this world with whom I should have had the nerve to see it through with, but that one beloved brother, with his calm and steady courage and ever tender care.

We spent the remainder of our holiday there, where we began it, and not the least enjoyable part of it were the happy hours of talk and mutual interest we spent with our kindly friend Dr. Moss. We found under that gruff exterior one of the kindliest natures that ever lived; and our talk, in those quiet evenings beside his study fire, often led us into channels deeper than we could navigate. For, scientist as he was, he never succeeded in explaining away those things which we saw with our own unclouded eyes and heard with our keen ears, in our quaint sitting-room at the Star Inn. And one day, when I had recovered from the shock to my nerves, we called on our old friend Seth Manners; and, over a cup of tea and a crust from his big loaf, we told him our experiences at the inn, and begged him to tell us the story.

He took a great deal of persuading, but more, I think, because he liked to feel his was the important position of being the only person besides old Martha, who knew the story, and could faithfully recount it.

"It is no' a long tale," he began. "So sit you here, Miss; and when I gets me pipe a-goin' yer shall 'ave it."

"It's like this," he began, between the puffs of his pipe, "Sir Dan Barnes owned all this place, and thought he oughter own the souls and bodies of the people as well, and Miss Maudie, the rector's pretty girl, said always as 'ed not brow-beat 'er—she'd see to that. 'Appen 'er ole father knuckled under a goodish bit to Sir Dan, and w'en Sir Dan sets eye on pretty Miss Maudie, just when she come 'ome from school in London, the poor old rector was in a bad way for money. 'Is youngest lad was a wrong 'un and 'e got bettin' and drinkin', an' old Sir Dan got the lad in 'is clutches and led 'im on, till the lad forged 'is employer's name to a big pot o' money, and then begged of Sir Dan 'is-self, and Sir Dan said 'ed pay the cash, if Maudie would marry 'im. The girl was driven to it, though 'er 'eart, poor lass, was guv elsewhere.

"Sir Dan gave 'er a week to make up 'er mind, and she gave in, but must take 'er big white cat, Benbow, with 'er.

"Sir Dan 'ated that cat, it alus spitted at 'im, but the girl said 'Me and Benbow, or neither,' so 'e took them both, and w'ile the 'all was being done up, they lived at the Star. Sir Dan 'e was blind drunk every night, and he treated the girl shameful, but whenever 'e raised 'is hand to 'it 'er, Benbow spit at 'im and often clawed 'im, an' the girl just laughed and mocked 'im. 'E used to chase the pair of 'em round the room, and threaten to kill 'em both when 'e got 'em, but Lady Maudie used to laugh that little mocking laugh of 'ers, an' blow out all the candles and laugh again when 'e fell into the furniture in 'is drunk efforts to catch them.

"One night he ordered 'er to put the beastly cat down or 'ed kill it, and she chucked up 'er dainty 'ed and laughed in 'is drunken face and 'e whips out an old Italian knife 'e 'ad and stabbed 'er to the 'eart and then the cat; and some say as threw them both in the old chest in the room and then shot 'imself, and they didn't find Lady Maud for some days after, and then she was found in the chest with the body of the white cat still clasped in 'er arms.

"Old Martha nursed Lady Maudie as a babby, and watched over 'er when she could, and sez as she often sees 'er, and that Benbow follows 'er always. P'raps the old woman's dotty—she's near eighty, anyhow; she swears that her darlin' Maud still lives in the inn, and that those who have eyes to see, know that she is speakin' the truth when she says that Lady Maudie and her white cat still live in the Star Inn at Pine Side."

The old man stopped speaking, and seemed oblivious of our presence; so, laying some silver on the table, we slipped away, and next day our holiday ended.

We often speak of it, and it is always a vivid memory. The "whys and wherefores" remain—as they ever will—unsolved, until they and all else are made clear to our limited understandings. The fact remains—we saw what took place long before our time, and the sight of a white cat always has power to make me shudder and remember:

"PINE SIDE."